QUEST FOR FREEDOM

Cedric Saldanha

Publisher: Inspiring Publishers,
P.O. Box 159, Calwell, ACT Australia 2905
Email: publishaspg@gmail.com
http://www.inspiringpublishers.com

A catalogue record for this
book is available from the
National Library of Australia

National Library of Australia The Prepublication Data Service

Author: Cedric Saldanha
Title: Quest for Freedom
Genre: Fiction

Paperback ISBN: 978-1-923087-62-0
ePub2 ISBN: 978-1-923087-61-3

CHAPTER 1

Smita slid back in her seat and closed her eyes. The flight was overnight. The dimmed lights and quiet hum should have been soothing, but she couldn't sleep. Images flashed in quick succession, accompanied by waves of emotion. It had been six months of see sawing demands, arguments, pleas, tears and finally, submission. Her life now would never be the same again.

She was on her way to Melbourne, following a hectic arranged marriage in Mumbai.

She was joining her new husband to start life in Australia.

She had no desire to leave India. To be married at twenty-four, or to be a housewife, which was the expectation of her traditional Indian husband.

For the umpteenth time, she wondered why she'd not put her foot down. In this day and age, wasn't it time to surrender dated practices like arranged marriages and dowry giving? Should parents usurp the right to make what was probably the most important decision in one's life—choosing a life partner? In years gone by, families used marriage to link each other for mutual gain and a host of other reasons. But today?

She bit her lip in frustration.

Culture demanded she be respectful of parental wishes. Refusing would have resulted in an unbridgeable rift with her parents. She did not have the heart to do that. Her father had been given six months to live. She was his youngest child. It was his last wish to see her "appropriately" married before he departed this life.

The fact was she had failed herself; now she'd have to bear the consequences.

She was flying into a world of question marks. How was she going to live with this man whom she hardly knew? Would she get the opportunity to become the professional woman she aspired to be? How would she fit into this new country, to which she wasn't even keen to migrate to? She had lost all her friends. Would she find new ones?

* * *

She shuddered as she recollected the last six months. The crass bargaining over the dowry price. The prospective parents-in-law examining her like a piece of furniture for sale. Putting her on facetime with her husband in Australia to seek his views, as if she were some chattel. It was cringe worthy.

Then there was the tussle over who would pay for which wedding expenses, who would be invited, and where the ceremonies would be held? All this between the respective parents, treating her as if she were simply a spectator.

Her siblings and girlfriends were ecstatic for her, some even envious of her upcoming move to Australia, an opportunity she hadn't actively sought. She was beginning to resent them for their attitudes. For the first time, she realised how deeply her family and friends were entrenched in their cultural norms. She wondered how her values and life perspectives had diverged so much from theirs.

The wedding celebrations were even more depressing. Stilted, without a trace of spontaneity. Her two meetings with her prospective husband who had flown in just prior to the wedding were shy, nervous, and awkward, particularly since they were always in the presence of the parents. It was all revolting, outrageous. Her culture had squeezed out the spontaneous romance, love and joy that ought to belong to such a momentous occasion, one which should have belonged primarily to the two people concerned. She laughed bitterly at how far reality was for many Indian brides from the romanticised movie depictions.

Her first night in bed with her new husband was probably the worst experience of the whole process. It seemed that all he wanted was to manhandle her, feel her all over and get his orgasm done with as quickly as possible. Then, given the copious amounts of alcohol he had consumed at the wedding celebrations, he had fallen into a drunken slumber without comment.

She resented being married off in an arranged marriage and despised herself for conforming to her culture and family's expectations. It seemed the family's honour and the accomplishment of marrying off their last child was all that mattered; not her own happiness or consent. The truth was she had been bartered off as the price for her parents' happiness.

Snapping back to the present, she realized the gravity of her situation. She had made this choice for the sake of her parents. Now she had to face the consequences. The pressing question was whether she would continue to let her husband control her life, as her family had. In Australia, she was at a disadvantage with no job, income, friends, or understanding of the local lifestyle.

She gritted her teeth. She was leaving a stilted life behind. She was not going to allow herself to be drawn into a second one. It would be an enormous challenge, given her circumstances. But this was the last time she would allow 'elders' and others to bully her into doing what she did not want to do. She would become the master of her own destiny.

* * *

His name was Pravin, a junior partner in a small Indian-owned capital management and investment firm. He believed he had a bright future, especially with the increasing migration of Indians to Australia who preferred Indian professionals for investment advice.

Smita observed him from the corner of her eye as he drove her from Melbourne airport to his house in the suburb of Glen Waverley. A well-built man, as tall as her, with typical Indian features, slicky combed back hair, and shifty eyes. His welcome at the airport was surprisingly brusque. He claimed he had an urgent issue to deal with at the office, and had to rush back to work after dropping her home.

As he drove, she tried to make polite conversation. But he seemed preoccupied. So she spent the time taking in the views of her new city.

She was quite taken with the surrounds. Australia, and Melbourne in particular, was turning out to be rather beautiful, she reflected. The roads were well maintained, the landscapes green and immaculate, the houses neat and set back with attractive lawns. All very unlike her home town, Mumbai. But, where were the people? She missed the crowds, the noise, and the bustle of a typical Mumbai street. This place was rather too antiseptic for her tastes.

Still, she'd like to make a happy life here with her new husband despite her initial misgivings. But it hadn't started well. He seemed more preoccupied with his work than welcoming her.

She made an effort to be nice. She asked politely about his work. He replied in monosyllables or short, curt answers. She was nonplussed. She finally asked, "Are you not happy to see me here in Melbourne?"

He laughed bitterly. "What is there to be happy about?" he asked. "Your parents have fucked me. Royally."

"I beg your pardon? What did you just say?" she asked, genuinely mystified; taken aback by his language.

"Yes. They've robbed me of my dowry. And you expect me to be happy? The money they've remitted is thirty thousand dollars short, and the car and sofa set promised to my parents haven't arrived. What kind of people are you?" he demanded, his voice now laced with anger.

She remained silent. What could she say? This was a completely unexpected development.

"It's now your fucking job to make them pay up. I'm in a financial mess at my firm, and I need that money urgently. That was the bargain; I marry you and give you a home here in Australia, and your parents pay the agreed dowry. They have now reneged on the deal, while you have arrived here. You will now take responsibility. Do I make myself clear?"

His face was now contorted with rage; his hands gripped the steering wheel tightly.

Her heart raced. What had she gotten herself into? She hadn't been involved in the dowry negotiations, having opposed the entire concept. She was told it was a matter between the parents and that the bride shouldn't interfere.

"What do you mean by 'financial trouble'?" she inquired.

"That's none of your fucking business. Just get me the money I'm owed," he snapped.

This was a disaster, possibly the worst start to a marriage. But she was firm in her resolve. She was not be part of any dowry extraction from her parents.

An idea struck her. "Perhaps I could work and earn some money to ease the financial pressure."

He scoffed. "You know fucking nothing," he said contemptuously. "Do you think it's easy to find a job here? Your job is to cook and look after the house. That's why I married you. Now, start working on your parents and get me my money, fast."

They lapsed into silence. Finally, they arrived at his house. She observed it from outside as they drove in. Her new home. It seemed as unwelcoming as her new husband, with its unkempt garden and messy driveway. It was typical of the neighbourhood though smaller. One storied, brick lined, almost non-descript. The street was utterly quiet, not a car or pedestrian in sight.

He hurriedly grabbed her suitcase and carried it to the front door. "Welcome to your new home," he said, as he opened the door, managing a reluctant smile, and seemingly calmer. She smiled back and entered, wondering what awaited her within.

The stale smell of unwashed clothes and forgotten food hit her on entering. The stifling muskiness felt oppressive. She wrinkled her nose but steeled herself not to show distaste.

The house was larger than her Mumbai apartment but sparsely furnished. Inside the front door, a short corridor led to an open living area adjacent to the dining room and kitchen. On the left were two bedrooms. In the living area, the furniture consisted of a three piece sofa set, the TV, and a small bar with whisky bottles displayed prominently on top. The dining room had a four seater table, still littered with what was probably last night's dinner. A bachelor's home and direly in need of a woman's touch.

He showed her the kitchen and small pantry. "I have to rush off. There's urgent work at the office. I will be back by six this evening. There are condiments in the fridge, and spices and rice in the pantry. See if you can make some curry and rice for dinner," he instructed before leaving.

Silence descended. A quiet she had never experienced before. Broken by the call of a bird. Depression was quietly, surreptitiously creeping over. She shook herself out of it. I must not give in. I will somehow make this work.

Her first port of call was to open all the windows and air the house. Then, after cleaning the dining table, she sat to assess her situation. It seemed she would have to navigate life in Australia alone, unguided. Undeterred, she refused to let anything unsettle her her further.

She spent the next few hours exploring the house, checking the food supplies, planning dinner, showering, and freshening up, still battling jetlag from the long journey.

As she unpacked her suitcase, the hopelessness of her situation gradually descended on her. She stopped abruptly and sat on the bed. Tears welled up, uncontrollable, rivers of grief. She bent over, hands over face, and sobbed until her insides cramped. A darkness enclosed. Deep loneliness shrouded her. All meaning and purpose to life seemed to have disappeared. She had lost all - family, friends, career, even her beloved Mumbai with its familiar streets, sounds and smells.

She lost count of time as she cried. The sobs slowly diminished. She eventually got control of her emotions and wiped her tears. She had a choice, she realized. Play poor me, or get going and somehow make a life here.

The silence though was something she was going to have to adjust to, along with the lack of human interaction. Approaching the window, she noticed dark clouds gathering, symbolic of her mood. Tree branches swayed in the whistling wind, and the shrill call of an unfamiliar bird punctuated the silence, deepening her depression. She yearned for the bustle of Mumbai—the cooing pigeons, cackling crows, and hooting traffic. This silence was daunting.

As she continued to unpack, she resolved not to approach her parents for more dowry, regardless of Pravin's threats. Merely being a housewife in this quiet house wasn't an option either. Her only way out, she decided, was to find a job.

She reflected on the nature of Indian men, spoiled by their doting mothers and then passed on to their wives for care. Her brothers weren't much different. She had intended to take her time finding a partner, confident that some decent, emancipated Indian men existed. It was not to be. Her dream of becoming a chartered accountant had also been shattered.

Well, she had done her filial duty and sacrificed her happiness and dreams for her parents' wellbeing. Now, it was going to be just her, and how she made the best of a bad bargain. She would come out winning, she decided. She would find a job and in the process help relieve Pravin's financial woes.

CHAPTER 2

On her first morning, as Pravin left for work, she asked for money for groceries. He asked how much she needed. "You'd know the prices here better than I do," she replied.

He handed her a hundred dollars and directions to the nearest IGA grocer as he departed.

Determined to educate herself about Melbourne and her suburb, she turned to her laptop and friend Google. After a couple of hours, she had a better understanding of her locality, various grocery store locations, the shopping areas, and bus routes. According to Google Maps, there was a large mall nearby and a bus stop within walking distance from her house.

Thus began her solitary life in a new country. Pravin would return home late each evening, turn on the TV, start drinking, and talk about his work. He expressed frustration over recent investment decisions, unfair client and senior partner expectations, and their criticisms of his investment choices. But his alcohol fueled diatribes were mostly focused on the absence of the dowry money he had counted on to ease the cash crunch, and the lack of any urgency on her part to address the issue with her parents.

One evening at the end of the first week, while still cooking dinner, she glanced at him slouched on the couch, whisky glass in hand.

"You complain about money every day, yet you oppose my working to bring in some income," she pointed out.

"What job will you do? Stack some fucking shelves in one of those shitty supermarkets?"

"I can work as an accountant. I have an accounting degree. There must be jobs where my skills are needed."

He laughed mockingly. "You have no fucking idea, do you? Just shut the fuck up and get dinner ready."

Dinner was always late, served after he was nearly drunk. Initially, she waited to dine with him, but he showed no interest in sharing a meal or conversation. He would serve himself and return to the TV. After a week, she resolved to lead her own life if her role was merely to be a housewife.

On weekends he would sleep in late and then take her to attend lunch gatherings of his Indian friends at one of their houses. This was an occasion for the men to drink, chat, and gradually get intoxicated. The women stayed in the kitchen, preparing food, and being inquisitive about her life and family.

A few women were kind, but their conversations centred on children and schools, whereas she was interested in Australian culture and politics. She found conversation in these gatherings hard going.

* * *

It was the third week after Smita's arrival. Pravin was on his way home from work, later than usual, past 8:00 pm. He was tired and frustrated. Things at work were not going well.

Clients had become fussy, especially after some delayed fund distributions. He had promised to capitalize them, but most clients, particularly the Indian investors, wanted cash. He found this trait in Indian clients exasperating compared to the more easy-going Australian investors.

As he drove, his phone rang. Another complaining client, he assumed. Glancing at the phone in his car's coffee cup holder, he saw it was his mother. He pressed the answer button.

"Yes, Ma. How are you?"

"Beta, are you home?"

"Not yet; delayed by work issues. I'm on my way now."

"Good. I don't want to talk in front of that terrible girl. Is she treating you well, beta?"

This situation was another mess. His parents had promised him a submissive, caring wife, who would look after his home and make him happy. Instead, he felt burdened by her. She was stubborn, uncompromising, and recently been giving him the silent treatment. She was unmoving in her resolve not to call her parents for the remaining dowry money, despite all his complaints and appeals.

"Ma, the girl you and Pa chose is a disaster."

"Why, beta? Isn't she taking care of you?"

"She can't cook a decent meal, spends all her time on her laptop, and won't follow up with her parents for the remaining dowry. I shouldn't have accepted this marriage proposal."

"What can we do, beta. Everything seemed right – same caste, perfectly matching horoscopes, supposedly from a good family, educated, and a promising dowry."

"Yes, but it was not fully delivered. I should not have married until the entire dowry was given."

"They refused. The agreement was to give part before and part after the wedding."

"And now they're not keeping their end of the deal, right? And I'm stuck with her."

"Yes. We're also struggling to receive our portion of the dowry. The double bed they sent is of terrible quality, and the sofa hasn't arrived. They're claiming the car's delay is due to the company, but I don't believe them. They're asking for time, citing the father's hospitalisation and financial difficulties."

"Why the fuck…sorry, Ma, why the hell did we ever agree to this proposal?"

"Pravin, beta, just give her a slap or two, and insist she calls her parents about the dowry.

You have to learn to manage your wife. If she can't be controlled, then maybe consider divorce and we'll find a new match?"

"I need to get what's mine first, Ma. Leave it to me. I'll make sure she does her part."

"Yes. Please do. We're tired of waiting. I also want to …"

"Sorry, Ma, a client's calling. I'll call you back."

Pravin switched calls.

"Is this Pravin?"

"Yes, sir."

"This is Sundar Rajan. You manage my investment account, right?"

"Yes, sir. How can I help you?"

"You've missed my distributions again. Last month, you promised the distributions would resume this month. Where are they?"

"Sir, there have been temporary cash flow issues; but your capital is safe. Believe me. This is a completely temporary situation. I promise the distributions will resume next quarter."

"You don't seem to understand, Pravin. I am a retiree. I need a monthly distribution. That is what you people had agreed to. It was fine for a while. Now – nothing. I want to terminate my account and get my capital back."

"Just one more month, sir. The distributions will resume, I promise."

"I am not sure I can trust you anymore, Pravin. You said the same thing last month."

"Next month, sir, for sure."

"They better be, or I'll be contacting the Financial Ombudsman about your company." He called off.

Pravin cursed loudly. He punched the steering wheel with a free hand. The situation was becoming impossible. Problems were mounting. He was already in the senior partners' bad books due to some bad calls. The cash flow situation for his accounts did not look good. Now yet another client wanted to opt out. With threats to bring in the Financial Ombudsman. He needed to get that remaining dowry money to tide him over.

* * *

Smita realized the moment he stepped into the house, that there would be trouble that evening. His face was sour and tight. He did not respond as she welcomed him home. He went straight to his whisky bottle and poured himself a larger than usual drink. Then flopped on his sofa.

She decided to ignore his mood. She moved to the kitchen to prepare his meal while he gulped down his drink. The tension built as he sat silent, taking large sips of his whisky, waiting for her to bring his dinner plate to him as usual. The TV played in the background.

When she finally approached with his plate, he looked up, eyes cold and hard, making no effort to take it.

'My Ma called this evening," he announced.

So that was it, she now understood. She stood silent, waiting for him to take his plate. She decided she was not going to play his game.

"Don't you want to know what she was calling about?" he demanded.

She shrugged, determined to give him the silent treatment. She waited patiently for him to accept his plate of food.

He stood suddenly, staring at her, eyes bright with anger.

"My Ma was complaining your parents have not yet sent the dowry gifts owed to them. What kind of people are you?"

She looked back at him, in the eye. "I have repeatedly told you, I will find work and get you the money you need. Please don't bring my parents into this."

In a swift move, he shoved the plate of food aside sending it flying across the floor. Then he grabbed his phone, dialled her parents' number and shoved it into her face.

"Why the fuck can't you get on your own bloody phone and ask them to honour their commitment? Is that so difficult?"

Startled by his aggression, she instinctively pushed his hand away, and stepped back. Her resistance further infuriated him.

He grabbed her hair, pulling her face close to his, and screamed, "Phone your fucking parents, bitch!" Then he shoved her hard away from him, crashing her to the floor.

She lay there, stunned. This was the first time in her life she had encountered violence. She had always been the cherished youngest child in her family. She rose slowly from the floor, wondering if this was going to become a pattern.

Silently she cleaned the floor of the food, while he stomped around the room, muttering to himself, even more infuriated with her silence.

"There is more food in the dishes on the stove," she informed him. "I am going to bed."

She took her things and fled to the guest bedroom leaving him to his own devices.

* * *

As the days wore on, she learned to maintain her silence. Conversation only led to more violence as anger got the better of him.

The tension in the house grew taut. She tread carefully, feeling increasingly trapped in the lonely Australian suburb, a stark contrast to bustling Mumbai. With virtually no friends, her life was confined to the insular weekend gatherings with Pravin's Indian friends. He made no effort to introduce her to new places or people, and without a car, she relied on public transport.

She attempted to interact with neighbours during walks, receiving friendly but distant responses. Everyone seemed busy, leading lives vastly different from hers.

She kept doggedly at her job applications. She found useful information on job availability on LinkedIn, and on the local job advertising websites. She submitted multiple applications a day. Weeks went by, but there was no response to her applications. She tried phone calls; invariably if she did get through, they'd direct her to their websites or say they had no vacancies. She suspected the local market had little faith in degrees obtained in India.

In the meantime, she made a habit of visiting the mall just to be among people, as Pravin tightly controlled the household budget, leaving her with little money.

She began feeling trapped and depressed, a slave at the beck and call of her husband, with no recognition of her own personal needs.

It was now well into her third month in Melbourne. Life had moved into a dull routine. She realised she had to break away from the monotonous tedium. She was bright. She needed to put her mind and talents to work. The only way out, she decided, was to at least do some public service, volunteer. So she approached the local social service agency, the Melbourne Volunteers near the Glen Waverley station. She had found them on Google.

*　*　*

One evening, as he sat with his dinner and drink in front of the TV, she broached the subject. "I've spoken to the Melbourne Volunteers Group in Glen Waverley about helping out.

They've agreed to let me volunteer three times a week, assisting with their accounts, and they'll pay me a stipend."

He looked up, surprised and disbelieving. He stopped eating and stared at her intensely. Anger seemed to be building. She suddenly felt afraid.

"When did you arrange this? And why do you need a job?"

"I have decided to find a professional job, one way or another," she declared firmly. His anger was not going to deter her. Volunteering was another step towards that.

"Come on, Smita. If you think it's easy to land a job in Australia, think again. Unless you want to stack shelves in Coles or Woolies," he scoffed.

"Why not," she retorted. "In Australia, there's dignity in whatever work one does."

"No wife of mine will be a shelf stacker," he insisted, his eyes now flashing with anger.

"Why not?" she challenged.

"Imagine the embarrassment in my social circle. You'll do nothing like this without my permission. Understand?"

"Then help me get a professional job," she countered. "You've done nothing despite my requests. Your firm is in finance; surely, there's a place for an accountant like me?"

"Why can't you be a traditional Indian wife?" he exclaimed, exasperated. "You agreed to this when we married. Your parents were eager to marry you off to an 'attractive catch'. I'm surprised you're now reneging on your agreement to be a housewife and look after our home and future family."

"I'm done with all of that," countered Smita. "Pravin, you've lived for ten years in Australia. Are you blind to your surroundings? Look around. Women here define their own lives. You're living in the past, in traditional India. Wake up."

"Don't talk to me like that," he demanded, his eyes ablaze. He stood up, dinner plate in hand, looking threatening. She also stood, meeting his gaze. Suddenly, he pushed her hard, causing her to fall onto the sofa.

"You will do as told in this household, understand?" he yelled.

She decided this was not the time to fight this battle. She would go on with her efforts to find a job, despite his protestations. In the meantime she intended to keep her commitment to work with the Melbourne Volunteers. Discussion and arguments were not going to change either his or her mind.

She would get her job and deal with the consequences later.

CHAPTER 3

After two months at Melbourne Volunteers, Smita had embraced her new role. The organisation offered a range of services including child minding, transport for the elderly and handicapped, counselling, training, and helping the needy access government services.

She earned a stipend of $100 a week for three days of work in the accounts division. Though the pay was minimal, it brought her a sense of independence in her new country. More importantly, it triggered significant changes in her life.

The opportunity at Melbourne Volunteers provided Smita with a much-needed escape from her stifling domestic routine. It allowed her to leave the house regularly, offered her a sense of purpose and an opportunity to utilise her educational background. The work boosted her self-esteem, and she gradually earned the respect of her colleagues.

The staff at Melbourne Volunteers were kind, though sometimes patronizing. Smita faced a steep learning curve, adapting to Australian dress codes, social mannerisms, and local accents. While most colleagues were understanding and helpful, a few displayed overt racism.

Over time, Smita integrated into the team, making genuine friends and gaining recognition for her intelligence, accounting skills, and work commitment. She worked closely with Melody, the person in charge of accounts at the Glen Waverley branch. Melody was a single mother of two young children, and could only work part-time.

The accounts were often behind schedule, and Smita's assistance was invaluable. Soon, the accounts were up to date, and Smita found herself involved in various other organisational activities.

Smita and Melody formed a close bond. Melody's bright smile, twinkling blue eyes, and warm, motherly demeanour was just what Smita needed emotionally. Smita's well-being and adjustment to Australia and to the work at Melbourne Volunteers soon became Melody's primary concern. Smita though, remained reluctant to share her difficult domestic situation. She had noted that while Melody often spoke affectionately of her two little kids, she similarly never mentioned a husband.

During a coffee break one day, Melody shared her story. She had been married to an abusive alcoholic and eventually left him, finding refuge with Melbourne Volunteers. They provided her with accommodation and a part-time job. Despite this, she struggled financially with her children's growing needs.

"He was a very charming, sexy man. We dated for a year. Believe me, I could find nothing that would indicate he would later turn abusive and violent. He was kind, considerate, and seemed genuinely interested in me. At that time, I was an administrative assistant at a solicitor's office. He was a real estate salesman and we had come in contact as part of his job when solicitors get involved in the sale-purchase arrangements.

Soon, we were really serious about our relationship. We married and within a year, we had our first child. It was then that the trouble started. He could not cope with our child. It seemed beyond him to understand the needs and moods of a little one. And of course, I could not give him the attention he craved. I gradually realised how needy he was. He took to drinking every night and soon the temper tantrums began. One thing led to another and the violence got out of hand. I began to seriously fear for our child.

Eventually, I had to report him to the police and leave home. Melbourne Volunteers arranged for me to stay in a women's shelter. I took our child with me and was pregnant with our second at the time. It was an incredibly tough period. I had to quit my job due to the pregnancy and because he was still connected to that solicitor's office."

Melody sighed, "Here I am, four years later, with two little kids, managing on my own. Welfare payments, including allowances for victims of domestic abuse and financial hardship, have been a lifeline. People have been kind, but it's been a hard journey. I have a restraining order against him now, so he leaves me alone."

Smita listened, fascinated by Melody's story, feeling for her and identifying with her given her own situation.

Suddenly, Melody asked, "Smita, you never talk about your husband? How's your married life here in Australia?"

Smita laughed bitterly. After some coaxing, shared her story.

"My god, Smita, what you describe is essentially domestic violence."

"Well, Pravin's violence has mostly been pushing, shoving, and the occasional slap," Smita admitted, trying to downplay her husband's actions.

"Still, that's abusive behaviour," Melody insisted. "And he seems to control every aspect of your life. You mean you don't have any personal money apart from your stipend here?"

Smita confirmed that Pravin tightly controlled the budget, leaving her with little after covering groceries, transport, and phone bills from the hundred dollars he gave her weekly.

Melody opened the government's website on her computer to check whether Smita would be eligible for welfare benefits. Unfortunately, new migrants were ineligible for at least four years after residency. Frustrated, Melody banged the table. Smita was touched by her efforts to help.

"Let's visit the Centrelink office. It's near the station, and I know some people there.

Maybe they'll consider your situation and offer support," Melody suggested.

At the Centrelink office, as they waited in line, Smita observed the organized system for accessing benefits. Thinking back to India, she realised how different the situation for the poor was here in a developed country. The staff were respectful. The people standing in line, waiting, were of all ages but mainly women. She was not sure if the staff would actually help her, but her first experience of bureaucracy in Australia was generally positive.

The lady at the desk was empathetic and attentive to Smita's situation. She explained that while Smita wasn't eligible for regular welfare payments, she could qualify for assistance if she could prove she was a victim of family violence. Smita was given the eligibility criteria and information about potential support, and advised to return if her circumstances met the criteria.

They left the Centrelink office disappointed. But there were other issues to be addressed, Melody insisted. She took Smita to the bank and helped her set up her own bank account. Then back in office, they worked online to apply for her Medicare card. "I can't believe that Pravin hasn't helped you with the basic essentials to life in Australia."

At work, Smita dedicated herself fully, finding solace in her tasks. The work not only provided a distraction from her troubles but also a chance to make friends.

* * *

It was five months since she had left India. She called her parents every few days, worried for her dad in particular. His health continued to deteriorate.

One day she got the call she dreaded. It was from her eldest brother, Viraj. "Smita dear, Papa passed away last night. He did so quietly and peacefully. He was on heavy medication. So at least we're confident he wasn't in much pain. We're all in mourning. I don't think Ma is in any position to talk. But I thought I should let you know. We're sad you're not here to join in the ceremonies and say your goodbyes to him."

That was it. No query about her own situation, which was understandable in the context of the call. But Smita felt truly alone. Her father had been her closest confidant and champion, always encouraging her in her studies and ambitions. Now he was gone and a deep chasm remained in his place.

In the following days, Smita's depression deepened. She also realized that her decision to marry Pravin and move to Australia had been largely to please her father. With his passing, she felt no obligation to stay in an unfulfilling marriage. She had tried for five months, but the relationship was not improving, and she saw no potential for change in Pravin, who lacked the introspection and self-awareness necessary for transformation.

* * *

They were at a usual weekend get together at a house of one of Pravin's friends. It was a large sitting cum dining and kitchen room. The men sat sprawled on the couches, legs wide apart, the inevitable beer or whisky glass in hand, and shared banal stories.

The women stood around the kitchen top, some helping with the preparation of snacks and lunch, some making small talk. Smita stood with them, water glass in hand.

Smita had increasingly become a spectator rather than participant in these gatherings. She looked around reflectively. The scene was of a community of friends, primarily of men accompanied by their wives, locked within the prison of their habits and culture. Outside it was beautiful weather for the weekend. Yet here, the men were stuck in their routine drinking catch up, with women in tow to attend to their culinary needs.

She wished she could somehow escape these situations. They were not just boring. They stripped her of joy and spontaneity; they triggered the worst judgemental aspects of her character. She felt contempt and pity for the women, so subservient to their husbands. She despised the men for their selfishness, their insularity, their chauvinism. And yet, she asked, why did she complain? Did this not reflect Indian male society in general?

It was such a pity, she reflected. The Indian culture was actually rich and varied, though sadly still patriarchal in emphasis. Though, for that matter, were most societies. Many however, were making valiant effort to rectify this emphasis.

Pravin thoroughly enjoyed this company. He was a different person here. There was camaraderie written all over him. She had tried hard to engender the same amity into their own relationship at home. To no avail. It somehow did not work. He seemed most comfortable with her in the role of serving wife. She wondered if this was to do with the typical chauvinism engendered in Indian males via fawning mothers. She recollected the entitled behaviours of her older brothers.

Pravin was in deep conversation with one of his close friends, Ramesh; she saw him suddenly direct his gaze to her, intense and cross. Now what? The friend had obviously told him something about her that had upset him. There would now be a royal row either on their way home, or when they arrived.

* * *

Ramesh had indeed whispered to Pravin, "Mate, I did not want to raise this issue in front of the others. But what was your wife doing standing in the welfare line at the Centrelink office at Glen Waverley? You need to look after her better, buddy. Or is she trying to supplement your income by making some pocket money on the side?" he had asked snidely.

The comment left Pravin speechless. The news came as a shock. He tried to remain calm. Like most migrant Indians in Australia, he too looked down on welfare recipients. There was a self-belief in the community, that poverty was shameful, and that even if one is poor, they should work to increase their income and not beg for the state's generosity.

"Must have been some Medicare issue," Pravin defended weakly.

"No, mate. This was definitely the Centrelink welfare queue. I know one when I see one," he sniggered.

"Okay, okay. Just leave it. I will inquire about it." But he was mad.

* * *

As they drove home, Pravin's rage was palpable, his grip on the steering wheel trembled with anger.

"What the fuck were you doing at the Centrelink office?" he demanded.

She shrugged, refusing to be drawn into an argument. So this was what had upset him.

"Do you know, someone in the community saw you? This will get out inevitably. You are humiliating me."

She decided to wait until they were home to discuss it more rationally.

He opened the front door with an aggression she had not seen before, and confronted her in the corridor. Before she knew it, he struck her across the face; a hard slap without any warning.

She felt the sharp sting. It came as the shock. Then before she knew it, the slap turned into a barrage of blows. Hard, aimed at her face and then her body. She cowered into a corner, stunned. Tears streamed down her cheeks, more out of humiliation than physical pain.

"Now you know why I need to work," she said through her tears. "I need my own money. You treat me here as a slave. You control the budget. All you're interested in is having me cook for you, clean the house and provide sexual services. Who do you think I am?"

"You are my wife, and you better get that through your silly head," he shouted. Another series of slaps to her face.

She turned wordlessly into the bedroom, collected her night things and fled to the spare bedroom locking herself in.

The next day she appeared at work with large bruises on both sides of her face. Her office colleagues were concerned. Melody in particular wanted to know if she could help. But Smita shrugged. What could they do? She somehow had to work this out for herself.

But she promised herself, the next time he resorted to violence, she would leave, whatever the consequence.

CHAPTER 4

Smita waited at the bus stop near Glen Waverley train station, adjacent to the mall and not far from her office. The absence of other people at the bus stop made her wonder if she had missed the bus.

After a long, confined day in the small, windowless office, the open air and blue sky felt liberating.

The late evening cool breeze played with her hair. It reminded her of her balcony in Mumbai, not far from the sea. She would often stand there to enjoy the fresh evening monsoon wind, allowing it to caress her face. Oh, how she missed her home city, the noise, the bustle, the colour.

All this around here was so very different, she thought, as she surveyed the scene. It was now almost eight months since her arrival in Australia. But she still missed Mumbai.

Everything here was clean. Too clean. In the carpark, the cars were parked neat as sardines in a can. People observed rules such as pedestrian crossings. The cars did not hoot. Yes, all was so orderly but rather too sleepy and boring. It made her nostalgic for the chaos and confusion of Mumbai.

The hoot of a train leaving the station brought her to the present. Where was that damn bus? She looked at her watch. It was well past five thirty now. This was uncharacteristic. She always admired their punctuality. Now she worried. If she got home late, after Pravin, there would be hell to pay.

She approached the shop nearby, a convenience store. The old Chinese man looked up. He often hailed her, like he did other regular bus commuters.

"No bus today," he called as he saw her approaching. "Strike." She stopped mid-stride and took stock.

"You walk?" he asked.

She shrugged, smiled and started on her long walk home. She had no other option.

She tried not to worry. If Lakshmi, the goddess of luck, was on her side, she'd be back before Pravin. He was often late from work. But luck was in short supply these days. The gods seemed to have deserted her. Life at home had become increasingly difficult, unpredictable, verging on unbearable.

Perhaps the walk would help after all. She wasn't much of an exercise person but she had read about its positive effects on depression. In her current state, any relief was welcome.

The walk turned out meditative and refreshing. She observed the houses as she passed, their architecture, gardens, their residents sometimes chatting outside. Apparently Aussies moved houses on average every five years. That was unimaginable back in India, she reflected. You considered yourself lucky if you had an apartment; then held on to it for dear life. She enjoyed trying to figure out the character of each owner by the looks of each house.

As she approached her home, apprehension set in. The darkening sky mirrored her growing unease. What if Pravin had returned from work early?

Then, her heart skipped a beat. His car was in the driveway.

Fumbling with her keys in nervousness, she opened the door to the sound of a blaring TV. Pravin appeared in the corridor, whisky glass in hand, his eyes burning with anger. He stood astride, looking menacing. His face wore a tight expression, a prelude to an imminent outburst. Smita felt a deep sense of foreboding.

"Where the fuck have you been?" he barked as she took off her shoes at the front door.

"The buses were on strike, so I had to walk home," she replied, attempting to head to the kitchen while giving him a wide berth.

Pravin quickly blocked her path, his face contorted with rage. He had put down his whisky glass on the side table, and now had hands on his hips. It was obvious anger had been building. Smita braced herself for the confrontation. She had been hoping to defuse the situation by quickly preparing something to eat.

"This is why I don't want you to work," he screamed as he approached her. "You should be at home when I arrive, preparing evening tea and snacks for my drinks, getting dinner ready." In fairness, she had been doing this every evening. It was the expected practise among Indian wives.

"It's not the end of the world, Pravin. I'm just an hour late. Let me change and I will be in the kitchen in a few minutes," she said, trying to maintain a calm.

Without warning, Pravin struck her with a venomous backhand slap, sending her reeling against the corridor wall. His aggression had escalated recently.

Cradling her face, tears streaming, Smita pleaded, "Please, Pravin. Can we at least talk about this?"

His response was to launch into a brutal assault, striking her repeatedly with both hands. The intensity of his fury was bewildering and terrifying, as she struggled to comprehend the source of his rage amidst her pain and confusion.

She somehow managed to slip under his slashing arms and past him, her face and body stinging from the blows, and made straight to the refrigerator to get some ice. She did not want to show up at work again the next day with a new set of bruises on her face.

In a rage, he followed her, grabbed her by the shoulders and swung her around to face him, then shook her violently.

"Get this into your silly fucking head, you idiot. You will not go to work anymore.

That's it. I've had enough. Do you understand? Answer me."

She had never in her life experienced such rage, nor such physical ill-treatment. She wondered where it emanated from. But she had learnt not to fight back. She hoped being silent would calm him down.

However, her silence seemed to infuriate him further. He threw her violently to the ground and followed through with a vicious attempt to kick her. She rolled away, narrowly avoiding his foot. Seizing the moment, she ran to the guest bedroom and locked herself in. It had become her sanctuary.

Curled up by the bed, she sobbed from the pain, helplessness, and anguish.

Pravin ranted outside the door, kicking and banging, but she stayed put, fearing for her safety. Eventually, the noises ceased as he left the house, likely in search of food.

She opened the door cautiously, and checked to confirm he had indeed gone. Then, she got some food, water and ice for her bruises from the refrigerator, a set of clothes, and again retreated to the guest bedroom, locking herself in. It was then she realized it was the end of the road for her with Pravin. But she could not flee tonight. The evening was getting on and it was dark already.

She ate a little, just to keep her energy up. Then lay down, nursing her face. She heard him return, again attempt to open the bedroom door. He finally gave up.

* * *

Lying in bed, she sobbed quietly, engulfed by a feeling of deep hopelessness and abandonment. She reflected on the plight of many newlywed brides in India, facing dowry issues and domestic pressures, and wondered how they coped. She recalled stories she had read about newlywed immigrant women in Australia suffering severe abuse, sometimes leading to suicide or murder. She was determined to avoid this fate.

She had accepted this arranged marriage only because her father, on his dying bed, had begged her, so he could pass away in peace. Now that he was gone, it was time to leave this monster.

She had endured Pravin's domination, anger, and violence for months. Her refusal to pressure her parents for more dowry money had only worsened his wrath. This latest episode of brutality, however, had surpassed her limits of endurance.

Smita applied ice to her bruises, eventually crying herself to sleep. In the morning, she waited for Pravin to leave before preparing to seek Melody's help at Melbourne Volunteers, hoping for a referral to a refuge.

Despite her efforts with makeup, the bruises from the previous night's assault were still visible. Upon seeing Melody, Smita broke down in tears, overwhelmed by the tension, humiliation, and physical hurt. Melody comforted her, then listened intently to the account of the previous evening's events.

"Time to leave him," Melody stated firmly.

Smita sighed. "Yes, I also think so. But where will I go, Melody? Outside of some Indian families he has introduced me to, I have no friends except you people at Melbourne Volunteers. Can MV help me get a hospice refuge somewhere?" she pleaded.

Melody sighed. "I've been trying, Smita, without your knowledge. Unfortunately, there are no bed spaces currently. Why don't you go back to Mumbai? Go back and resume the chartered accountancy course you had interrupted. Start a new career there."

* * *

Melody brought her a coffee, then persuaded her to call her family in Mumbai.

Her mother thought Smita was calling to inquire how she and the family were faring after her father's death. Smita listened patiently as her mother recounted the last days of her father. Finally, she broke the news.

"I'm sorry to have to share this with you, Ma, but I'm leaving Pravin." She was on FaceTime and tried to shield the side of her face, which had the worst bruises.

There was shocked silence as her mother stared at her, unbelieving, from across the miles.

Then her mother asked abruptly, "What do you mean leaving? Am I hearing this correctly?"

"Yes, Ma. You heard correctly. I'm leaving him. I've tried very hard for eight months. It's been the most difficult time of my life. I've decided if I don't leave now, the situation will only get worse for me as time moves on."

"Why, beti, why?" she demanded.

"It's too long to explain, Ma. Just know that my life has become unbearable."

"But child, your father and I worked so hard to get you a good proposal. You are now in a beautiful country, in Australia. You have a husband who is well to do. You have a lovely house. What more can you ask for?" demanded her mum.

Smita broke into a bitter smile. "You both did well. You have done your duty. But now I need to make my own decisions. Pravin has indeed provided me all that you have said. But he can't provide me what I want the most."

"What is that, beti?" she asked, searchingly.

"Love, respect, freedom." She then turned her face so her mother could see her bruises.

"Oh, my!"

Then after a pause, "But maybe this is only a phase, child. He will pass over it. Men are like that," she counselled. "Please don't be selfish. You know how difficult it will be for your family here to face our relatives and friends if you break up your marriage. Do you know what outcasts we will become in our own social circle? And stop this silly talk about love, respect, and freedom. Most Indian brides have to cope with what you are enduring. We learn on the way. Believe me, it turns out fine."

"I do not expect you to understand, Ma. And I don't blame you for not doing so. But I felt it my responsibility to share this news with you before I leave Pravin. You now also know the reasons. He is and will always be a self-centred, dominating man. He is now becoming violent. He does not know what love is, what partnership in marriage is. And I'm not willing to wait around to change him."

Her mother disconnected the call abruptly. It was obvious Smita would not be returning to Mumbai.

* * *

Smita returned home with Melody in her car. Melody helped her to pack her things. Then she called Pravin at his office.

"I need you to come home immediately. There is an urgent issue which needs your immediate attention." She hung up before he could respond.

He arrived in a huff, anticipating another confrontation. She heard him open the front door aggressively, and stride in. Then he came to an abrupt, startled stop. He looked in disbelief. She stood beside her packed bags in the living room, Melody standing behind her. The bruises were now starkly visible.

Smita took control of the conversation. "I'm leaving," she informed him, in monotone. "Melody is here with me as a witness that I'm not taking any of your belongings."

He looked stunned for a moment. "What do you mean you're leaving me? We are married. You have responsibilities here. You can't just walk out like this. And where do you think you will go? You have no income, no real job, no house. Are you going to live on the streets?"

He was now shaking with anger. If Melody was not present, he would have slapped her.

He stepped forward and tried to lean over her. She did not move, determined to stand up to his bullying.

"You will not leave. Is that clear? You've called me from my office, saying it's an emergency. Is this the emergency? And bringing this stranger into my house? You," he turned to Melody, "get out of my house," he shouted, showing her the front door.

Melony stared at him and made no move.

He realized he was getting nowhere. He suddenly calmed down, took a step back, and asked in a conciliatory, exasperated tone, "Okay. What is it you want? I've given you a comfortable home. You have enough of food. I know I objected to you going to work for the Melbourne Volunteers. But your responsibility is to be here, looking after the house and both our needs."

"Our needs?" she asked bitterly. "Have you ever, in the last eight months, even asked what my needs were?"

"Come on. Don't act like a spoilt child. What more do you want. I'm providing you with more than many in Australia have."

"You can never provide me what I want, Pravin. That's why I am calling it off."

"What do you want?" he demanded.

"Love, respect, freedom. All of which I have been begging for the last eight months. I am done with begging. Now, I'm taking my life and destiny into my own hands. Good bye and I hope I never see you again except in the divorce court."

*   *   *

Melody insisted they immediately go to the police station. Smita was reluctant. She would never have dreamt of doing this in India, where the police always took the side of the man.

"I don't want to go to the police, Melody, please," she pleaded.

Melody looked at her sternly. "Smita, trust me. This is a situation I've been through, and I know how traumatic it is. You need to register your case with the police immediately because you do not know how far Pravin will take this. The police may not take any action just now, but registering your case at this juncture is critical in case it takes a more dangerous, life threatening turn."

Smita finally agreed. At the police station in Glen Waverley, she told her story. Melody provided a witness account of Smita's departure and the threats from Pravin. The bruises were evidence of the violence. Photographs were taken of Smita's swollen face. They made their respective statements.

As Melody had predicted, the police registered her and Melody's statements, but would only take it up with Pravin if Smita wished to pursue it further. At this stage she preferred to just leave it all behind. The last eight months had been traumatic enough. Pravin had turned out to be a horror story. She wanted to have nothing more to do with him.

Melody welcomed Smita to her house, as a temporary measure. The Melbourne Volunteers organization was in the process of trying to find her more permanent accommodation. Melody also took her to the Centrelink office, and helped her apply for financial assistance on the basis that she was now homeless and in financial distress.

CHAPTER 5

It was a small house, a unit in a row of bungalows, but full of warmth. For the first time since arriving in Australia, Smita felt at peace, loved and cared for.

Melody was a warm, kind hearted, cheerful woman. She was also physically big, with a hearty hug and a sometimes boisterous laugh. She brought cheer wherever she went. Judy and Jaime, her little kids, had inherited her love of laughter and cheer. They were the cutest kids Smita had come across.

Smita was deeply touched how all three welcomed her into their little home. She slept on the couch. She had little privacy with the kids regularly invading her space. But it was still the first time since her arrival, she began feeling she lived in a home. Soon, she had become part of the family. On her days off she looked after the little kids, took them to the mall to see the shops and treated them to the lollies they loved. But she knew it was not sustainable.

Pravin remained a constant, haunting presence. He phoned every second day. When she blocked his number, he phoned her from another number. His troubling presence in the background ensured she could not quite settle into a normal life. She was always looking over a shoulder, half expecting to find him there, waiting to grab her and take her back to enslavement.

There were times when she was sure she had seen him stalking her, in the distance, when she walked to and from work.

She had reconciled that she was now a resident of Australia. In any case, she did not have the money to buy a ticket home, and would not for a while. And even if she did raise the money, she was not sure she was welcome back in Mumbai. For now, she needed to find a job which gave her a living wage and a more permanent home.

Melody had helped enormously. But Smita feared for her as well. Pravin would remember how Melody had helped her leave him. He would not have forgiven her. He knew she worked at Melbourne Volunteers. He was a vindictive man. So staying with Melody was not a long term solution.

* * *

Smita was at her desk at Melbourne Volunteers, alone in the Accounts room at the back end of the office. It was Melody's day off. She was deep into entering and paying the latest invoices, when she heard loud voices in the front office.

She recognized his voice. Pravin was demanding to see her. He had finally plucked up courage to come to the office. She expected this would happen, sometime. She emerged cautiously from the Accounts room, and braced herself for confrontation.

"Hi my dear." Pravin greeted her in an uncharacteristic persuasive tone.

Smita looked at him from across the room, silent, blank faced and unflinching. Anger and hate surged within. The very sight of him was repulsive. She wondered how she had managed to live with him as long as she had.

The others in the office knew of her situation. They stood by and watched on, silently assuring her support was at hand if she needed it.

Pravin's discomfort was evident. "Can I speak with you privately?" he asked.

She simply shook her head and moved to return to her room.

"Hold on," he pleaded as he moved closer to her. "I've had a long conversation with your mother last night. She's been trying to call you but she says you're not picking up. She's asked you to come back home to me. I promise you, things will be different."

He looked hugely uncomfortable having to say this in front of her colleagues. It was admitting fault and eating humble pie; she knew this did not sit comfortably with him.

Smita again said nothing and simply turned to her office.

This got under his skin.

"Smita," he shouted, this time striding forward to take hold of her hand before she re-entered her office. She pulled it away determinedly.

"Do not touch me," she demanded as she pulled further away.

"Do you realize what a disgrace you are to yourself and my family? Do you know the emotional upheaval you are creating for your ageing mother? Have you no heart? What is your duty as a wife and a daughter?"

She had been prepared for this. She and Melody had visualized various alternative scenarios, based on Melody's own experience with her abusive husband. The strategy was to offer no concession. At all costs, avoid playing the other party's game.

She said firmly and loudly, "If you do not leave now, I will call the police. I have witnesses here. I've already lodged a case against you with the police."

This was not wholly true, but it stopped him in his tracks. Frustration mingled with puzzlement on his face. He seemed to be querying - where had this new Smita emerged from? She was thwarting him repeatedly. It was increasingly clear she was not returning to him. He turned away seething and stomped out, promising to return.

* * *

A couple of days later, when in office, a call came through. It was from another brother of hers, Rohan. He had always had a soft corner for her.

"Hi Simmy." She knew immediately who was calling; he was the only one who used that nickname. "How you doing?" he asked.

"I'm fine," she answered warily. She was pleased to hear his voice, but after her conversation with her mother about leaving

Pravin, she had become cautious about family reactions to her recent separation. Pravin's visit to her office and saying he was in touch with her mother put her even more on guard.

"Look Simmy, I'm really worried about you," he began.

But Smita quickly interjected, "Rohan, thank you for calling. It's nice to hear your voice, but if you're calling to convince me to return to Pravin, you're wasting your time and we should end this call." She was tired of this. She simply wanted to move on with her life.

"Hold on dear. I did not tell you as yet why I'm calling. Can I simply ask – what exactly has happened? I'm getting rather confused info from Ma. All I want to know is what exactly is the situation and if I can help? You know you are very dear to all of us."

She hadn't anticipated this reaction. Her resolve broke. She wept, holding the phone, struggling to speak coherently. On the other end, Rohan's concern grew.

"Look Simmy. I'm not calling to upset you or make any demands. Just take a deep breath and try to relax. I'll stay on the line. Don't worry. But I do need to hear the story from your point of view, please? If that's alright?" he urged gently.

She gradually calmed down, and recounted everything - Pravin's behaviour, his dowry demands, his verbal, physical, financial and emotional abuse, and how she had had no option but to run away.

"The bastard," Rohan concluded. "If he were here I'd wring his bloody neck. The coward, treating his wife like this. Where are you now and how are you surviving?"

She told him about the Melbourne Volunteers, her job with its meagre stipend, and Melody's kindness and generosity.

"That's a relief to hear, Simmy. But this is obviously not sustainable."

He paused a while, seeming to consider options. Then he continued, "I can send you money for a return ticket back to Mumbai. I think that may be the best option for you. This thing with Pravin will probably not work out. The problem will be where you will stay when you return. Ma is very angry with you and I wouldn't recommend you live with her even if she allowed it. She'll give you hell every day. There's no place at my home since I have my in-laws living with us. The rest of the family seemed to be quite upset with your decision to break from Pravin, though they've not heard your side of the story. I will need to check with ...."

Smita interrupted him, "I'm not sure, Rohan, that I want to return, given how Ma and the family feel about this. But I'll give it some thought after your generous offer for a return ticket."

"But if you don't, how are you going to manage Simmy? You're completely on your own there, in a new country."

"Paradoxically, Rohan, the people who have helped me here are not of the Indian community, but regular Aussies. As I said, let me think about it."

They agreed to leave it at that.

* * *

The head of the Melbourne Volunteers, Glen Waverley Branch, Shirley Lumley, came to Smita's desk the next day.

"I need to have a quick chat, Smita. Do you have time?"

Smita smiled uncertainly. She hoped Shirley was not going to raise the embarrassing issue of Pravin's invasion of the office.

"You're the boss, Shirley. I have to make time for you, don't I?" They laughed. Smita loved this place, the warmth of the people working here, the respect they showed each other and their clients, most from the lower economic strata of society.

"I know you've been staying with Melody, kind and generous as she is. But eventually, you'll need to find some permanent accommodation. I've been in touch with Seva which is a Melbourne city-based NGO providing housing assistance for migrant women in need. You remember we'd talked about this a while ago?"

"Yes, I do remember," said Smita. "I really can't keep staying at Melody's. It's unrealistic."

"The good news is, Seva does have a bedspace for you, but it's in the Richmond suburb, a few kilometres from the city. This will mean that you'll have to leave Glen Waverley and the Melbourne Volunteers. It will be too expensive for you to commute up and down from there. On the other hand, there will probably be more job opportunities available to you – more than you'll find in our suburb of Glen Waverley. It's a choice for you to make. If you do decide to take up their offer, let me know, and I'll be in touch with them."

She left Smita in a reflective mood.

* * *

Melody and she debated the two options on the table. Melody was in favour of her going back to Mumbai, and to her family. Smita shook her head.

"Melody, you have no idea the extent of social sanction that awaits me in Mumbai. My mother will not want to have anything to do with me. The rest of my family, except my brother Rohan, will also shun me. I doubt I will be welcome in my circle of friends anymore. My own experience here in Australia, now for almost a year, has changed me dramatically. I have come to realise how narrow-minded and insular many people in India are. On the other hand, I have encountered here in Australia, people who are much more egalitarian and liberal. I find this freeing. I'm not sure I want to go back."

She continued, "The other option is I move to the city and accept Seva's offer of a bedspace. I'm not sure for how long it'll be. I don't know where I'll find a job in the city. Apparently, the bedspace is in Richmond. Will I be able to find a job there? My mind's pretty mixed up at this stage, Melody. I really don't know what I should do."

"Sleep on it, Smita. There's no hurry to take a decision."

"Thanks. But I can't stay here at your place either, indefinitely."

* * *

The next evening, Smita was walking back from work to Melody's house. It wasn't far, about a fifteen minute walk. But she was deeply apprehensive. It was getting dark. She was alone since it was Melody's day off. Pravin's hostile visit to the Melbourne Volunteers office last week was still uppermost in her mind. His persistence in trying to get her back made her tense and nervous. She was also afraid he would harass Melody. And the last thing she wanted was to bring more strife into Melody's already difficult life.

Suddenly, there was a screech of tires nearby; she recognised Pravin's car coming to a sudden stop just ahead of her. She stopped, startled, fearful. She realised, deep down, she had expected this ambush. He was not one to give up easily. He was a proud, self-centred narcissist who had to have his way, particularly in his domination over her. She was determined, however, never to return to him and his house again.

He jumped out of the car and strode up in front of her. She looked around for help. No one on the road at this time of the evening. She knew she was physically no match for him. He reached out, grabbed her hair and pulled her violently towards the car.

No. She was not going to give up so easily. The pain was unbearable. With all the energy she could summon, she let off an almighty scream. Then the struggle began. Her strength and determination appeared to take him by surprise. She continued to scream.

"Shut up, bitch," he yelled, "or I will hit you."

She did not stop. He hit her. Hard and repeatedly. But her screams seemed to have attracted attention. Footsteps were now running towards them. They gave her strength. She resisted being pushed into the car, and tried to elbow him in the stomach. By then help arrived.

"Stay away," Pravin shouted. "This is my wife."

"Mate, she maybe your wife, but she doesn't want to come with you. So lay off or I'll fuck with your face."

Startled by the suggested aggression, Pravin turned to eye his adversary, still holding Smita by the hair. Smita turned too, to check out her potential saviour. He was shabbily dressed, heavily bearded, probably a homeless man, but well-built, much larger than Pravin. Pravin reluctantly let Smita free; she stepped away sobbing.

"Go on, dearie," the stranger encouraged. "Make your way. I'll look after this bastard."

Pravin was about to argue, then decided it was wiser to back off. He would deal with Smita another day. As the stranger moved towards him, he jumped in his car and took off in a hurry.

The stranger's parting words to her were, "Dearie, if you take my advice, get as far as you can from that bastard."

"Thank you," Smita called out gratefully, wiping the tears from her eyes and holding her sore jaw. "I don't know what I would have done without you. You're very kind."

"No worries, little one. Now go on. And if you do move away, as I think you should, make sure that bastard does not know where you're going."

* * *

She opened the door to Melody's home, sobbing bitterly. It was a shock to be assaulted again. She thought she had left the abuse and violence behind when she had left Pravin almost a month ago.

Today, he had finally caught up with her. It was the ambush she had long dreaded. As Melody calmed her down and Judy and Jaime sat with her, consoling her, she realised she would have to leave.

The stranger's words kept ringing in her ear – "*…you need to get as far away as you can from that bastard…*"

Melody insisted she have a hot shower and feel refreshed. The assault had obviously unsettled her badly. Melody was hoping a shower would have a calming influence.

"Take your time. I need to put the kids to bed and I will get dinner ready. Then we can talk leisurely," she said.

Over a hot plate of sausages, potatoes and carrots, the typical Aussie dinner which Smita had got used to and found comforting, she recounted the incident again. They talked quietly, as the kids were now in bed. The cosiness of the dining room and Melody's soft voice were soothing after the evening's dramatic events.

Smita realised she had indeed come to a crossroad. She could not stay on in Glen Waverley. Pravin had given every indication he would make life difficult if not dangerous for her. She was consumed with anger against him. But there was nothing she could do.

She could not endanger Melody and her family. They had already suffered enough at the hands of Melody's husband. She could not repay Melody with another misfortune.

She also realised she needed to get out of the modest comfort zone she had created with the help of Melbourne Volunteers and Melody in Glen Waverley. The situation was not viable in the longer term. She was young and still ambitious. She wanted to explore her talents. She was sure there were opportunities awaiting her. She needed an opening. Perhaps it was time to use this incident to move on to something else.

She slept a restless night, but by morning had come to a decision. She informed Melody she was leaving. She shared that besides needing to get away from Pravin, she also needed to protect Melody.

CHAPTER 6

Where could she go from here? No home, no job, no shelter. Was she homeless, like the man who saved her yesterday from Pravin? How would she survive now? Where would she live? She couldn't stay with Melody, not with Pravin being able to find her so easily. Never in her wildest dreams had she thought this could happen to her.

She thought back to before it all began, when she was home in Mumbai. All she'd wanted was to pursue a career as a chartered accountant, perhaps become a partner in a firm. Why not? Organisations in India were now more accepting of women in their executive ranks. She had a future then. Now, it was all in ashes. All because culture demanded she respected the wishes of her father and marry. To what end? This?

She was stuck in a foreign country where she had no friends other than Melody and her work colleagues at Melbourne Volunteers. She was a foreigner in a land where the culture was still alien to her. And now she had to leave the only friends she had and go where? To Melbourne city? Would Pravin find her there? Could she just lose herself in the city?

"You okay, Smita?"

She shook herself out of her reverie and nodded silently as she trudged alongside Melody, a backpack with all her belongings hitched on her shoulders.

"Don't worry dear. Please understand this visit to the police station is really important. You never know what Pravin will do next and it's important to get the facts from your point of view registered."

She had agreed reluctantly. But she saw no purpose. In truth, she had given up hope. She just wanted to lie down and die. If he was to find her again she would fight him, hard, but in the hope that he'd beat her to death. There was no purpose to life anymore. Her future had been shattered. No light on the horizon. Returning to Mumbai would plunge her into unimaginable misery. While here, the prospects of getting a decent job, and making a living were virtually zero. She had tried, but they had rejected her.

They arrived at the police station. The female officer recognised Melody and Smita from their previous visit. Smita went through the motions, describing Pravin's attack last evening and being saved by the homeless man. The police listened and recorded her statement. This time, it was her word against Pravin's. The only witness was the stranger who had saved her, and Smita could offer no guidance as to who he was or where he could be found. She described him as best she could. Finally they left, with Melody satisfied that at least the attack and kidnap attempt were put on record.

They next visited the Centrelink office, again at Melody's insistence. Smita informed them she was leaving Glen Waverley and Melody's home and explained why. With her being homeless now, she requested them to expedite her application for emergency financial assistance. The Centrelink staff were sympathetic and promised to do so. They asked where she was going. She had no idea, but probably the city. She planned to get on a train that morning and get out of Glen Waverly. Currently, that was the only objective. They asked her to keep in touch via her phone.

Finally, a teary goodbye at the Melbourne Volunteers office. She hugged Melody tightly. She would never forget her kindness, her selfless generosity, her motherly protection. Were it not for Melody, she dreaded to think what would have been her fate. She wished she had the same courage that Melody had to rise above her own misfortune. She bade goodbye to her other work colleagues and left for the station.

Her head was in a whirl. Her emotions in turmoil. She was not thinking straight. Though one objective was clear - she needed to put as much distance between her and Pravin as she realistically could. Fate would decide what came thereafter.

As she boarded the train to Flinders Street station, the terminus in Melbourne City, she spied the homeless man who had saved her from Pravin the previous evening, sitting quietly in a corner on the train. She caught his eye, acknowledged him with a nod of thanks, and sat not far away. His eyes twinkled. He raised a thumbs up. She smiled, wanly, and gave him back a thumbs up.

The train started, and she watched with relief as Glen Waverley gradually slipped away. She knew she would never be back, despite saying to Melody she would visit again.

* * *

The last time she arrived in Melbourne it was by plane. She had arrived in hope though tinged with uncertainty. This time, she was arriving in the city by train again assailed by doubts. Should she have simply taken the easy way out and called her brother in Mumbai for his help to repatriate to India? It would have been simple. But she shuddered at having to cope with all that awaited her in Mumbai.

No, she thought, this was the right decision – to go to Melbourne city and seek her fortune there. But what if Seva no longer had a bedspace for her? What if she couldn't land a job? Without a stipend from Melbourne Volunteers, would she be forced to beg? She shook her head reassuring herself – I will somehow find a job, whatever it takes. Yet, she would miss Melody. There would be no friends to talk to, to confide in.

She shook off her doubts. They weren't helping. She needed more self-belief if she was going to survive.

Suddenly her gaze met that of homeless man across the seats. He was watching her, seemingly reading her self-doubt from across the seats and encouraging her not to worry. She also noticed that as passengers boarded the train, they avoided sitting next to him. This saddened her. Here was a man who, though poor and rough shod, probably homeless, was essentially a kind human being. He deserved better. Impulsively, she rose from her seat and sat opposite him. He looked as surprised as the other passengers.

"Thank you for what you did for me yesterday," she said.

"No worries, little lady. It was the least I could do. Fortunately I was on the scene."

She was curious now. She wondered if he lived around there. If he slept on the street, did he stick to one area? She had no idea if it was polite to ask but she decided she had nothing to lose.

"Do you live in Glen Waverley?" she asked.

He laughed. He was big in the face, as in body. His generous beard and long hair, and his shy smile with twinkling blue eyes reminded her of Hagrid, the gentle giant in Harry Potter.

"My home, lady, are the trains and the streets. By the way, may I ask your name?"

"Smita. And you?"

"Bernie," he replied. "Nice to meet you, Smita. I'm really happy you've left Glen Waverley. That husband of yours is a good for nothing."

He spoke gently, in a sing song manner. His eyes were the most expressive part of him. They were kind, deep and seemed to invite confidences. She wondered how he had found himself in the situation he was.

"I too am happy I'm leaving Bernie. But I have nowhere to go," she confided. "Though I have a contact with Seva, a charity organization in the city, which may have a bedspace for me. "

"Good for you. I hope it works out, Smita. But if it doesn't, and you have no place to go, I have friends who sleep quite comfortably under the bridge near Flinders Street station. It's at the junction of Flinders Street and Queensbridge Street. Under the rail line bridge. Just ask for Meg or John and say you're a friend of Bernie's. You'll be welcome."

"That's very kind of you. May I ask why you are homeless? Is it a choice?"

"It's a long story and I won't bore you with it. But I do have a message for you."

He leaned forward as if to confide in her. "You must have confidence in yourself," he insisted, looking intently into her eyes. "You're still a young lady. There's a bright future waiting and maybe some man out there who will treat you better than that bastard. Keep yourself open and take the opportunities when they come. I did not, when I was your age. Now, it's too late."

"That's sad," said Smita.

"Oh don't be sorry for me, Smita dear. I am happy, believe me. I've got used to this life. And I do have many friends. They may not be well to do. But they are dear to me and I to them. That's what's important in life – friends. If you do meet Meg or John, you'll see what I mean."

They sat quietly for a while, enjoying the passing greenery. As if on reflection, he added, "There's another friend I'd like to introduce you to in Melbourne city – the Yarra River."

"A river?" Smita was intrigued momentarily forgetting her worries.

He nodded enthusiastically. "The river flows literally through the middle of Melbourne. Take time to sit by its banks, and enjoy what it offers you. It's a comfort for those in trouble. You'll find as you watch its gentle waters flow by, your troubles will gradually diminish. It'll soothe your soul if you allow it."

Smita smiled. Such an interesting character. This man was so unlike anyone she had come across. "I do hope I'll meet you again, Bernie. I owe you and I won't forget."

"No worries, Smita. Take care; and best of luck. Believe in yourself."

They arrived at Flinders Street Station.

* * *

Flinders Street, in the Melbourne CBD, was the train's terminus. It seemed as good a destination as any. She checked Google Maps and realised it was in the centre of Melbourne, part of the central business district. It seemed the logical place to go to at this time. She could easily lose herself in the city.

Shirley of Melbourne Volunteers had given her the contact of Seva. She would find their office hoping they'd still have a bedspace for her. She had about a hundred dollars in her pocket to see her through for a few days. The welfare office had promised they'd expedite her case for financial assistance. Melody advised her to inform Seva of this. They would help to track her application and see it though successfully.

Approaching Flinders Street, Smita marvelled at the huge skyscrapers reaching up to the sky in every direction. Unlike Mumbai, the city centre did not appear as bustling, crowded or dirty. She spied the river that Bernie had mentioned. She decided it would be nice to sit by the water and think about her next steps.

The river, though modest by Indian standards, was picturesque flanked by towering silvery buildings on each side and a tree lined promenade. It was an attractive, eye catching sight. She found a bench along the north bank, and sat to enjoy the views. A soft cool breeze wafted along the river. She closed her eyes and let her spirit become one with the water. She wished it could wash away her troubles and usher in a new and happier phase in her life – as Bernie had suggested. Wishful thinking, she realised. It had been a bitter and dejecting nine months since her arrival in this, her adopted country. There was no going back.

This city was where she would make her life. And make it successful, she decided. Never again would she allow men to dominate her, to violate her, to emotionally or physically abuse her. The river rejuvenated her spirit, giving her courage and determination to set up a new course for her life.

She sat back, deciding to give herself time to enjoy her surrounds before she took on the reality of finding a life in the city. Here she hoped she was well and truly rid of Pravin.

She was fascinated by life on the riverbanks. Cyclists of all ages whizzed by, dressed in the latest cycling gear and helmets. Lovers held hands and strolled by. Tourist boats plied up and down, the kids waving to the people on the banks. It was all peaceful and beautiful – like out of a tourist magazine. She was soon lost in her thoughts.

She shook herself out of her reverie and checked her watch. It said 4 pm already. She realized she was hungry, but more importantly, she needed to get to the Seva office before it closed. Her Google Maps indicated it was close to the station, on Flinders Lane, less than a block from the station.

She made her way there, absorbing the sights of the city as she walked. The footpath cafes fascinated her. The sight of so many young people, stylishly dressed, enjoying themselves, talking animatedly, gave the city a vibrancy and liveliness which was absent in Glen Waverley. She liked it. She realised she was more at home here than in the suburbs.

She arrived at the Seva office at 4.15pm to find it closed. Dismayed, she realised this presented a difficult issue. She had hoped that Seva would still have that bedspace for her. She regretted lingering by the river. Yet, the little time she had spent there had somehow given her new courage and hope.

But where to now? She had no other contact in the city. Reality then hit. She was indeed homeless and would probably have to sleep the night on the streets. There did not seem to be any other option. But now she had to get some food. Hunger was gnawing. She also had to be mindful of her limited money. Probably the easiest option was a cheap burger at McDonald's.

In an hour, she was back to the riverbank. Her bench was still available. There was a familiar comfort about the river. She looked around for toilet facilities. Yes, there was one across on the south bank. So she made her way there.

All evening, the south bank was agog with people and revellers. It was lined with bars and restaurants; and every one of them was packed, with people chattering like flocks of birds. She was amazed at how many people were out, enjoying the evening, and this was not yet the weekend. But this was no place to get a night's rest before what promised to be a challenging next day. It was becoming windy as the evening fell. A drizzle had begun. The air had chilled.

She made her way back across the river along Queensbridge Street, looking for shelter. As she crossed the river again, she found the street went beneath the rail lines. The broad footpath alongside and under the rail bridge seemed to provide protection from the elements. There was a group of people already squatting under the bridge. They appeared to be homeless like her. She remembered Bernie's suggestion that should she need a place to sleep, she could join the homeless group who slept under the rail bridge. This must be the group, she thought. She had found them quite fortuitously. She approached cautiously.

They were about ten, three women among them. That gave Smita some comfort. One of the women noticed Smita looking at them curiously.

"What's it, love? You a researcher who wants to know how we homeless live or one of those do-gooders who wants to lock us up in some home?" she called out.

Smita smiled uncertainly and approached closer. Compared to them she was well dressed. She also lugged a heavy backpack, with her belongings.

"I am like you," she ventured, "homeless. I am looking for a place to sleep the night."

"Really," said the woman who had spoken. The others looked up, curious.

"You don't look homeless to me. But if that's so, sit. We can have a chat," invited the woman. "I don't think it is a night to be out without a shelter over your head. The rain is coming. This bridge is pretty good with keeping us away from it. It's broad and wide. And if you can cope with the trains passing over every few minutes, it's as good a place as any in the city."

Like most homeless, they appeared scrubby, bleary eyed, slouching on their sleeping gear. Smita was grateful for the invitation to join them. She had few other options.

"Who the fuck is this nigger, Meg, that you just asked to join us?" demanded an aggressive male voice at the outer edge of the group. Smita looked up in concern. It was a tall, thin man, scraggy beard, narrow piercing eyes, sour face.

The aggressiveness reminded her of Pravin. She ignored his comment. She had decided never to back down from male bullying.

"My name is Smita," she ventured, addressing the woman. "Are you by any chance Meg who is friends with Bernie? He told me about you."

"Good to meet you love. I am indeed Meg, a friend of that silly bugger, Bernie. Glad you met him. He is a sweetheart. This is Joan and Annabel. As for that grumpy guy, his name is Mark; just ignore him. He's always complaining. And the rest of the guys – it's just not worth knowing their names."

There were guffaws and complaints from the men, mostly in a good-natured way. Mark continued to grumble and complain about Meg inviting every Tom, Dick and Mary into the group.

Further introductions ensued. It was a pretty disparate group of people. But there was an air of camaraderie among them that appealed to Smita. She sat next to Meg and put her backpack on the ground.

"Do you always sleep here," Smita inquired?

One of the men chuckled. His name was John. "No honey. We'd like to. It's a great place for the night. But the bastard police come off and on and move us. Or try to ship us to God knows which godforsaken suburb."

"Yes, we do sleep here on most nights," confirmed Meg. "We have no choice. But of late, they have left us in peace. You know, we don't harm anyone. We mind our business."

"But if they are offering you a roof over your heads, why don't you take it?" she asked.

John explained. "Love, they separate us, and you never know where they will dump you. The last time I allowed them to take me, it was to a place in Springvale. I had no friends. I had druggies as my companions. I could not find the closest post office to claim my welfare payment. It was terrible. You have no choice of where you will live. You go where they put you. You have no idea who will be your neighbour in the next bed. Man, I need the support of a family. These are my family," he said gesturing to those around.

They began asking how Smita had found herself homeless. She shared her story with them. They in turn shared their stories; each was touching in its own right. Smita was struck by how this disparate group of people had banded together to make themselves a family, supporting each other.

It must have been past 8 pm when Meg opened up a bundle next to her. "Time for dinner she announced." John, on the other side, also opened a bag, and out came from both bags an assortment of food - bread, cans of cooked sausages, some bananas and some bottles of water.

"Welcome to the Banana Alley community dinner," announced John, who seemed to be the informal leader of the group. He and Meg made shares including one for Smita.

"Is this place called Banana Alley? It's a funny name," suggested Smita.

"Yes, love," explained John. "Behind us are the so-called Banana Alley vaults, built under the rail lines. They are over a hundred years old and were originally used to store goods, particularly bananas that came by ship from Queensland up the river. Later they converted the vaults into shelters for us the homeless. But now, they've gone up market. They are leased to different businesses particularly gyms."

"By the way, if you don't mind me asking, where do you get your money for food?" asked Smita.

"Most of us are on welfare, love. But we also pass by the Salvation Army outlet on Bourke Street, which helps us with canned food."

Smita ate gratefully.

They helped make her comfortable for the night. She shared the bedspread with Meg. It was large enough to accommodate both. As she lay reflecting on her day, she wondered what her family and friends in India would be thinking if they knew she was now homeless, sleeping on the streets of Melbourne. The Smita from a middle-class family in Mumbai, who wanted to be a chartered accountant and become a partner of a firm, was now virtually destitute in a foreign country.

Surprisingly, she was not depressed. She was enjoying the company of this group. The women in particular were protective and helpful. She enjoyed their stories. And that river next door, yes, there must be something to what Bernie had shared about it. It had a spirit which it imparted to those who opened themselves to it.

It was a cold and uncomfortable night. Meg had warned her that sleeping on hard ground would take a while getting used to. The chill wind did not help. Despite three sets of clothing, Smita shivered through the night.

The next morning, Meg took her to the public facilities close by. There was running water as well. The only thing missing was a nice shower and a hot coffee.

Meg reassured her that if she stayed on with them, she would take her to the mobile shower facility which moved from place to place each day in the Melbourne CBD. It came to Flinders Street occasionally. Though sometimes, they had to go to other locations in the city to access it.

CHAPTER 7

Back at Glen Waverley Pravin's financial pressures were escalating. The number of clients demanding their capital be returned was growing. His partners were getting impatient. He was also tiring of the repeated phone calls from his mother, berating him for not ensuring Smita got her parents to pay up before she left him.

For the umpteenth time he wondered why fate had played him this hand. There were probably hundreds more financially well off young women in India whose parents would have gladly married them to an attractive prospect like him with a permanent visa in Australia. He now monitored the office of Melbourne Volunteers every evening he could, swallowing his pride and hoping to entice Smita back. He would promise her whatever kind of life she wanted, even a job, as long as she got that damn dowry money, and soon. But he dared not enter the office to check if Smita was there, after his previous encounter.

One evening he plucked up courage and approached Melody as she left her office on her way back home. He came up cautiously, with his hands up indicating he had no ill intentions. She continued walking, ignoring him. He shouted after her asking where Smita was. She stopped, turned and replied – "Nowhere where you will ever find her; and if you approach me again, I will call the police."

Pravin backed off, frustrated. He now had to consider his options.

* * *

The living room was a mess. The coffee table had two half-eaten pizzas lying in their open boxes, looking rather sad. The whisky bottle seemed better looked after, with more than three quarters emptied. The two men sat sprawled on the couches, talking in slurred tones.

"You don't know how to treat a woman, Pravin. That's why she left you," claimed Ramesh.

"What the fuck do you know about treating women, yar?"

"Look how cooperative my Asha is. It's always – yes Ramu, no Ramu, what can I get you Ramu? It's the art of female management."

"Come on, fucker. It's just that you've been lucky with Asha. You should have got that chuthiya Smita. I would have loved to see how you managed her."

"Never mind Smita, now. All you have to do is simply divorce the ungrateful bitch. Then ask your parents to set up another marriage proposal and bargain more vigorously for a bigger dowry. It can all be done in six months and your financial troubles will be behind you. Fucker, this is an opportunity, can't you see?"

"It's not so easy, Ramu, in this fucking country. It would be easy in India. But here, if I file for divorce, I will have to fork up spouse maintenance. Why the fuck should I pay out good money to that bitch when she has denied me my rightful dowry payment?"

"But think of that attractive new dowry waiting for you, yar. That will more than make up for these payments. Free capital, ready for immediate investment."

"The other thing is that my parents will hit the roof when they realise I will have to pay alimony to Smita. They're already mad they did not get their part of the dowry payment from Smita's parents."

"Okay, then, if you're so determined to stay married to that bitch, find her and get her back in your service."

"That's exactly what I intend to do, fucker. But we are in Australia. So I have to go about this carefully. There are no authorities I can bribe. She claims she has filed a case against me with the police. Bitch. But I'm not sure. If she had, they'd probably have been at my doorstep with questions."

"So how you going to find her?"

"I'm going to hire a detective to find where the fuck she's disappeared."

Ramesh hit his head in exasperation. "Why the fuck would you want to throw more good money after this bitch and then land up with an uncooperative cunt? Believe me, you are well rid of her."

"I need to teach her a lesson. And I am going to, believe me. She also owes me a lot of money from that dowry. Let's have another drink."

* * *

Pravin subsequently contacted a number of detective agencies. He was stunned by the costs involved. Retainer fees, expenses, travel costs, with no guaranteed results. He wondered if Ramesh was right. This course of action could be a fool's errand.

What then was the solution? Take Ramesh's advice and seek a divorce? He struggled to accept what he saw as defeat. He was also worried how his parents would react to such a decision. He decided he'd try a detective first, but invest only a limited sum in the venture and for a defined period of time. If that did not work, maybe he'd undertake finding her himself. Melbourne was not as big as Mumbai. If he put his mind to it, he'd find her.

CHAPTER 8

At Flinders Street the next morning, Smita left the homeless group with her bag on her back, making her way to Seva's office. She promised she'd drop by later and update her newfound friends about her situation. Meg, in particular, insisted that if she could not find a place to stay she was welcome to join their family. She left, grateful there were such beautiful and generous people in Australia.

The morning felt fresh and clean. A cool wind blew through the city's road corridors bringing with it a sense of exhilaration that did not seem justified. But then she was still alive, and free from Pravin. Through the night she had grown increasingly convinced she could lose herself here in the city. The traffic, the office goers, the general bustle, all seemed familiar and brought back reassuring memories. Yes – she would make Melbourne city her new home.

As she left the group under the bridge, and walked along the Banana Alley vaults towards the office of Seva, she saw a notice pinned to the door of the third vault. It said –

"Admin Assistant needed. If interested, please apply inside"

She looked up at the sign above. It said – **"J & J's Power Zone - for Fitness, Strength and Power"**.

A gym. With a job available. She stopped. Maybe she could…. no; she was trained to be an accountant! And what did she know about gyms? She'd never been near one in her life. Aside from advertisements in newspapers and magazines, she didn't even know what the inside looked like

Except, whether she liked it or not, she needed a job and an income, urgently. This was an opportunity. Seva may be able to offer her a bedspace, but she did not hold much hope for any stipend-work like that which MV had provided her in Glen Waverley.

She needed to think. There was a bus stop a few steps away. She took a seat and considered her options. She was homeless, almost penniless. It was irrelevant what she was trained for. Earning an income was the priority. This was an opportunity worth considering. At MV's, besides helping Melody with the accounts, she did all sorts of odd jobs to help out, and did them all efficiently. Surely she'd be up to the job of an admin assistant. An inquiry wouldn't hurt.

Plucking up courage, she returned to the doorway and stepped inside the vault. She found an interesting structure within. Concaved, with intermittent arches, the vault stretched over fifty metres from the Flinders Street footpath entrance to the river bank on the other side. It appeared to have been built below the railway lines. Thus, the temperature within the vault was at least a couple of degrees cooler to the outside.

The lady at the front desk was in her mid-thirties and obviously more than an administrator. She had the sculpted body of a gym instructor, rippling muscles, and yet quite feminine in her own way with long blond hair pulled into a messy bun. Behind her, the interior cavernous rooms were well lit, one leading to the other, all equipped with shining gym equipment. It all smelt clean and looked spotless. Smita saw both men and women deep into their routines, oblivious to anything around them, even the trains which rumbled above every few minutes. An interesting place to house a gym, she thought.

The lady looked up at Smita. "Yes, can I help? Are you looking for a membership or just a day pass?"

Smita smiled. If only she could afford a gym membership.

"I saw the notice on the door for an Admin Assistant. May I know what salary you are offering and what are the hours?"

The lady looked a bit surprised, eyeing Smita with her backpack. Smita was unsure what first impression she made on the lady. She did not seem particularly friendly or welcoming.

"Its 20 bucks an hour, from 7 am to 10 am, which are peak hours, and then from 5 pm to 8 pm, again peak hours. That's six hours each day for six days a week."

Smita nodded, mentally calculating the pay.

The lady's brow knitted into a frown. "I know it's not great money, and the shift times are awkward. But that's all I can afford. By the way, I'm Jill."

Jill seemed to be the owner. A hundred and twenty dollars a day, thought Smita. That sounded great. More money than she could have dreamed of earning at this juncture. The timings were indeed awkward. But then she had little else to do.

"What does the work entail?" she asked.

Jill now appraised Smita with renewed interest. "I need someone to manage this reception desk while I'm conducting training sessions. The duties involve greeting clients, checking them in, handling payments, and updating the accounts. I also have sale items here, as you can see." She waved her arm at the merchandise that sat on shelves behind her - water bottles, sportswear, protein powders and lollies. "The person at the reception keeps an eye on these and takes payment for sales. When I'm back at the reception desk, the assistant has to clean the equipment inside, mop all the floors, and ensure the toilets are clean. We have five rooms like the one behind me. I like to keep my gym in top condition. Cleanliness is critical. It's hard work and the person has to be on the ball. I am a demanding boss. So if you're not up to hard work, don't apply," she concluded bluntly.

Smita was still trying to read the lady. She was brusque, perhaps verging on intimidating. But perhaps that was because she seemed to be under some degree of pressure. She tried to imagine working for her.

"I've had two others in recent months who could not cope. So I'm giving you fair warning," she added, lifting an eyebrow.

Yes, definitely overworked; a woman who needed help. Her help. Jill was probably just a typical straight talking Australian, not meaning to be unkind.

"So, do you still want to apply?"

Smita appreciated the directness. She found such candour common among Australians. An attitude that said – this is who I am, take it or leave it. It did not matter. She could cope with matter-of-factness. Without hesitation, she replied – "Yes. I'd like to apply."

The impromptu interview followed with Smita still standing. Jill probed about the work Smita had done, did she have identification, any referrals, her residential address. In the process, Smita's story emerged, how she was a recent immigrant, she had permanent residency, a Medicare card, no Australian driver's license as yet, but an Indian one. She suggested Jill may wish to call Melbourne Volunteers in Glen Waverley to check her short work history there. She had no current address, as she was couch surfing.

Jill remained silent for a moment, leaving Smita still standing and fidgeting nervously across the desk. Finally, Jill asked for her identification papers. Smita offered her recently acquired Medicare card and her Indian driver's license. Jill suggested she take a seat while she called Melbourne Volunteers. This surprised Smita. She thought Jill would have asked her to come back later while she followed up with the referral contact. Was this a good sign?

Smita was not sure who came on the line at Melbourne Volunteers, but a long conversation ensued. It was strange being in the room while this went on; but Jill had not told her to leave. So she sat and looked down at her hands, examined the ceiling, noted her rumbling stomach and remembered she had had nothing to eat since last night's meal. She needed this job. The next few minutes would decide if she got it.

Jill's questions were probing and indicated thoroughness and professionalism. Smita felt a sense of relief as Jill appeared satisfied with the answers from the call.

"Sorry to keep you waiting while I did that. I just got interested in your details."

Then she stopped to consider a moment. Smita waited, her mouth dry, her hands clasped. Could she dare to be positive?

Suddenly the lady looked up and asked, "When would you be willing to start?

Smita was taken aback; speechless for a moment. Her heart leaped. She could not believe she had a job offer on her second day in the city. Without further thought she replied, "Immediately, if I can."

* * *

Smita began work that day. She learned that Jill Haynes was the owner of the gym. She had run it with her husband until he had met with an accident a couple of years ago and passed away. She was now managing it alone.

It was good work; and easy for Smita. She soon got the hang of the reception desk routine; when Jill went off to take a one-on-one training session, she found herself managing quite easily. Once Jill was back, she got to the cleaning work. She found it invigorating. It gave her some direly needed exercise, while allowing her mind to wander over the issues she was still grappling with. Where would she stay if Seva said they did not have place for her? What were Pravin's next steps going to be? She knew he would not give up so easily. Her departure was a major blight on his reputation particularly within the Indian migrant community.

Time seemed to fly. At one pm that afternoon, Jill suggested she had finished her morning three hours, and she could leave to return at 5 pm for the evening peak hours.

This was fine with Smita. She still had to visit Seva and find a place to sleep. She left Jill and made her way to the Seva office.

* * *

"You were supposed to come in yesterday," the lady at the Seva office reception desk said, frowning as she referred to her computer screen.

"I'm sorry," Smita offered, apologetically. "I was delayed leaving Glen Waverley. And I arrived at your office after it had closed yesterday."

She waited anxiously, hoping her late arrival hadn't cost her the promised bedspace. The lady continued to frown, rechecking her computer, scrolling pages and files. Then she abruptly turned around, and went into the office behind. Smita was now mentally chastising herself for being late the previous day.

The lady returned. Her face said it all. "Look. I'm really sorry. We've had three other pending requests and bed spaces are limited. The one we had for you was booked out this morning, since you hadn't shown up yesterday. I can put you back on the waiting list again, if you wish. But I'm sorry we aren't able to help you immediately."

Smita's felt her world crumbling. She could not forgive herself for being late the day before. Now she was well and truly homeless. Her shoulders dropped. She let out a long sigh.

"Look," the lady offered, now looking sorry for Smita after seeing her disappointment. "Vincent de Paul's isn't far from here, on Bourke Street. You can try them. They often have places falling vacant."

There was some hope then. Smita took her directions to the office of Vincent de Paul's and set off. Though deep down, her pessimism had returned after hearing such bed spaces were in demand.

Her intuition was correct. Vincent de Paul's also had no place for her but kindly offered to put her on their waiting list as well.

Smita left the office, deeply dejected. On the footpath, she found a quiet corner and leaned against the wall, watching people pass by, coffee in hand, chatting animatedly, looking happy, going about their daily routines. It made her think of her life back in Mumbai, carefree, and filled with hope for an exciting future.

She sighed. It looked like her home was now going to be the footpath under the bridge. Never in her wildest dreams had she thought she'd end up homeless. In India, millions slept on footpaths, too poor to afford a rental. They were pitied by society. Often, looked down on. She remembered how she'd observe them from her first floor window while she worked at her desk in her apartment room in Mumbai. She had often wondered about their lives and how they coped without a stable roof over their heads, constantly battling the vagaries of the weather. Now, she was one of them. She wondered what her family and friends would have to say if they heard of her plight.

Then she remembered Bernie's sage advice, one of the many he had offered her on the train yesterday. Always look on the bright side, dearie. There never fails to be a silver lining to every difficult situation. The good news was that Meg and John were kind people. Except for Mark, she liked the others in the homeless group. They were kind and welcoming. So why not? In time she'd find a more permanent place. In the interim, if people like Meg and John had been able to adjust to life on a footpath, why couldn't she? She was still young. She had a job and a decent income now. A step at a time, dearie, she said to herself, echoing Bernie.

Her spirits lifted.

She decided to get some lunch and then perhaps use the gym facilities to freshen up. It was a good job, she thought as she made her way to the nearest fast food outlet. If she could get on with Jill, and work to her expectations, it seemed she could continue working there for a while. She would deal with the issue of housing down the road.

* * *

It was just 4 o'clock when she returned to the J & J's Power Zone gym. She had left her backpack behind, with Jill's permission.

Jill was surprised to see her back early. Smita explained that she had nowhere else to go; so if it was okay she'd use the gym's facilities to freshen up and then she'd be back at the reception desk again. Jill need not pay her for the extra time put in. Jill simply shrugged and agreed.

As she walked to the showers, she reflected on her funds. They were pretty much running out. She wondered if she could ask Jill at the end of the day for her wage for that day. She knew it was unusual in Australia. Wages were typically paid bi-weekly. But perhaps, if she worked really hard and impressed Jill, she may be amenable.

The freshening up cleared her head and she felt invigorated again. She went to work with renewed focus.

At 8 pm Jill came to the reception desk and suggested she could call it a day. This was her moment. As she rose from the desk and computer and Jill took her place, she cleared her throat and asked timidly, "Would I be able to talk to you about something?"

Jill was now seated, looking at the computer screen. She looked up cautiously.

Oh God, thought Smita, hoping this was not going to be an issue. But she did need the money badly. In a quiet voice she asked if Jill could pay her for the day. "I'm um… a little short of money."

Jill appeared a bit put off. She frowned and crossed her arms across her chest.

"Look. I usually pay on a weekly basis," she said. "It's standard practise here. Many companies pay fortnightly."

Smita lowered her head, not wanting to meet Jill's eyes. She bit her lip. It was probably a mistake to have asked.

"But I'll make an exception for you for the first two days."

"You will?" Smita's head shot up. A broad smile spread across her face. Jill's expression softened. She probably recognised Smita's situation.

"Do you have a place to sleep tonight?" she asked, with some concern.

Smita grinned, gratefully. Jill did have a soft side to her after all, under that severe exterior.

"Thank you, yes. I do." She left it at that with no further explanation.

As soon as Smita received her pay, she made a beeline to the closest MacDonald's and stood in the long dinner queue. A sense of relief and hope swept over her. She could now afford her meals. Not just for herself. She got a bag full of burgers and fries. Armed with her large dinner packet, she marched back triumphantly to Banana Alley and Meg's group.

Her heart felt lighter as she saw Meg's smile and John's welcoming wave. They seemed happy to see her. Even more delighted when she told them she had brought dinner.

A whoopee went around. Meg in particular was keen to know how her day went. But for Smita, offering the burger dinner around was more important. The food was welcomed. Even Mark grudgingly accepted a burger and murmured a thanks. With this food offering, Smita seemed to seal her membership of the little homeless community. She still lacked a bedspread. But Meg insisted she share hers again. She promised to take Smita to the Vincent de Paul's opportunity shop the next day and get her some bedding and clothes.

* * *

Work at the gym proved more interesting than Smita had initially anticipated. She was fascinated by the diverse range of patrons. There were young attractive women, who appeared consumed with their looks and body. They worked at their exercise regimens as if the world depended on it. She was amused as they stopped mid routine, checked their butts in the mirror, then took a break to give each other workout tips. There were the male jocks who'd strut in with sleeveless tops and tight shorts, flaunting their muscle. And there were the oldies, struggling to beat their aging bodies into the shapes they had lost.

There were the regulars, who were there morning and evening, sometimes up to four hours a day. And there were the casual drop ins, self-conscious about their unfamiliarity with some equipment and the exercise moves.

The whole spectrum of humanity, in terms of physique, personality, looks and fitness level seemed represented. Smita had never before realised how consumed some people could be with exercise. With some it seemed an addiction.

Smita found the vaults intriguing. Their entrances ran along both the Flinders Street on one side, and the Banana Alley on the other side facing the river. On the Flinders Street side, the vaults stretched for over 100 metres, with some 15 doors opening into different vaults. The width of each vault was about 60 metres. There were well over 40 vaults.

The vaults housed various enterprises including gyms, hairdressers and small retail. Each occupied between three and eight vaults. Jill's gym leased five. It was the interior of these vaults that took Smita's fascination. They resembled old medieval prisons or tombs, with arched domes and corridors, limited natural lighting and poor external ventilation. Smita could visualize how these rooms would have been ideal for their original purpose, storing bulk fruits and vegetables, in cool conditions with limited light, thus ensuring better preservation.

Despite their austere structure, the gym owners including Jill, had done their gyms up tastefully. Most were equipped with special ventilation systems to ensure fresh air intake and circulation; they were all well-lit; the floors were lined with gym rubber to ensure soft landings and to minimise injury. The tomb-like atmosphere ensured one was literally shut out from the outside world and completely focused on the immediate goals of the exercise regimen. The regular rumbling of the trains above soon acquired a rhythm that seemed to fit right into the atmosphere.

Jill gradually warmed to Smita as she saw how hard she worked at her job, and how conscientious she was. Smita was always there punctually, at 7 am to begin work, and would regularly return early from her afternoon break, never expecting extra payment.

Under her tough exterior, Jill was a warm, kind hearted person. Her own personal story was tragic. Smita learnt that she and her now deceased husband, James, had been childhood sweethearts and gym fanatics. They had worked hard to save money to lease a gym in Collingwood. The business rode the wave of the rising popularity of fitness. Their income rose proportionally till they had enough money to buy out a long term lease on a set of Banana Alley vaults. They took loans to outfit it to the best standards and now it had the reputation of being one of the best around town.

Then tragedy hit. James had been on a fishing trip down at the coast. The area was notorious for its windy conditions and sudden changes in weather. Despite all their precautions, James and his friends were caught unaware by a sudden and severe storm. The boat sank and all three occupants disappeared. Their bodies were never recovered.

Though the incident happened two years ago, the lines of grief were still written on Jill's face. Despite her huge heartbreak, she carried on courageously. Ever since James' death, she had to take on an assistant to help with the gym. She was determined to keep it alive and make it work. She retained the name "J & J" as a testimony to their love, partnership and hard work.

*   *   *

Smita gradually became an integral part of the homeless community. She often bought food with her salary for the whole group. They were always grateful, never asking for more than she brought. Meg had taken Smita, as she promised, to the local Vincent De Paul Op shop and helped her purchase some cheap but sturdy bedding and clothes. She was now fairly comfortable with sleeping on the pavement. The concern was always how and where to store her things which had grown bulkier. She had no option but to bring a heavy bag together with her backpack each day to work. She could not leave it around in the sleeping place area for fear someone would pick it up. Jill often wondered about this but refrained from asking what the bag contained.

Smita also grew used to the routine. She ensured Jill remained unaware that she slept just around the corner under the bridge. Similarly, her homeless community did not know she worked literally a hundred metres away. At work, Jill kept giving her increased responsibilities which Smita happily took on. The work was therapeutic. She hardly thought of Pravin these days. And she enjoyed the gym. She began making friends with some of the clients. And she was learning – about exercise, body fitness, the importance of strength for health and safety, particularly for women.

Weeks passed and Smita felt settled at last. Kind of happy. She often thought of Melody and still called her every other week, just to see how she was, and how the kids were faring. Her secret agenda was to know if Pravin was pestering her. But it seemed that Pravin had left her alone on coming to know that Smita had left the suburb.

CHAPTER 9

She was a month into her gym job when Jill asked Smita, quite out of the blue, "What were you doing sleeping rough on the footpath under the bridge last night?"

The question caught Smita by surprise. She had avoided directly answering Jill's regular queries as to where she was sleeping at night. It now appeared that Jill had seen her last night. There was no avoiding the question anymore and she hoped it would not endanger her job.

She replied hesitantly. "It's where I sleep each night. I have nowhere else to go," she shrugged helplessly.

Jill was quiet. Then she asked, "Do you know those people, who regularly sleep there?"

Smita nodded. "They were the only ones who welcomed me when I turned up in the city, fleeing from my husband. They are good people, Jill. It's just that fate has dealt them a difficult hand. They do no one any harm. They, and I, are simply after a peaceful night under a shelter from the rain. They do not beg. They do not take drugs or peddle them. I can assure you Jill, my association with them poses absolutely no risk to you and your business – reputationally or security wise. They do not know where I work. And when I leave from here each night, none of your clients who are still in the gym know where I'm going."

Jill stayed silent and Smita went about her work, perhaps with greater zeal, hoping this would dissuade Jill from throwing her out because she mixed with questionable people.

Later that day, just as Smita was going on her afternoon break, Jill asked if she could have a word with her. Expecting the worst, Smita braced herself. At least it was good while it lasted.

"Smita, would you be willing to introduce me to your friends under the bridge?" she asked.

Smita was taken aback. She had least expected such a request. She grew suspicious.

Jill saw the suspicion in her eyes. "Let me assure you, Smita, upon my word, I have no ill intentions. It's just that I have often seen them and wondered about them. They are my neighbours. I just want to get to know them and perhaps later, help if I can. But for the present I would prefer they remain ignorant of the fact you work next door, and that I own the gym here."

Smita reluctantly agreed. "It will probably have to be tonight after the gym closes at 10 pm because during the day they go about their business in various parts of the city." Jill agreed; she would come with Smita that night.

Smita kept wondering through the day how her homeless family would react to her introduction of Jill. She felt sure suspicion would be aroused, given their vulnerable circumstances. But she had no option.

That evening Smita stayed on till 10 pm, locked up with Jill, and walked around the corner to the bridge. Some of the group had fallen asleep. But most were still chatting, some having a good laugh. The conversation stopped abruptly when Smita rounded the corner with Jill.

"Hi," greeted Smita. "Just wanted to introduce my friend, Jill."

The group eyed Jill cautiously, wondering where Smita had met up with her. She did not look like a homeless person. As usual it was Meg, the openhearted one, who broke the ice. "Well Jill what brings you here? Sit down if you wish. Any friend of Smita is welcome."

Jill smiled and promptly sat down next to Meg.

"So tell us, what can we do for you, Jill?"

Jill shook her head. "Nothing, Meg. I just wanted to meet Smita's friends. Smita works in my gym in town, and I was wondering who her friends were and where she sleeps."

Jill took her time, chatting mostly with the women, but also with John who talked about how the group got together, and the difficulties they coped with. He patiently answered the inevitable questions as to why they did not accept the shelters that were offered by the government and charitable organizations. After a half hour chat Jill stood up, thanked them for allowing her to join in for a chat, and walked off.

* * *

The following day, Jill waited until the evening to bring up her visit to the group. After completing her one-on-one sessions, she sat next to Smita at the reception and said, "Smita, would you like to sleep here in the gym at nights? I have given it some thought. There is a small room at the back. You can lay down your bedding there if you wish every night after all the clients have left."

Smita was moved to tears by this generous proposal. It was such an unexpected offer. "Thank you so much, Jill. You are so kind and understanding. But till I get some kind of permanent place, I think I will continue sleeping the nights with my friends. I don't think I can bear the thought of sleeping here inside, so close to them, while they are still out there in the cold."

Jill nodded. "Just keep in mind, Smita. The city is a dangerous place at night. Don't be too lulled into feeling you are safe. You do need to be on your guard."

With that, Jill seemed to close the issue. Smita was grateful that she did not see her association with the homeless as a problem.

* * *

It was late in the night, exactly two weeks later. Smita and the others had fallen asleep despite the noisy trains above and the boisterous night revellers. It was the weekend, and raucous young people regularly passed by after visiting the Crown Casino across the river for a drinking night out. The homeless group had gotten used to these noises. It was worse on weekends; but they coped.

Smita was in deep sleep when she felt a sharp shooting pain in her chest. She awakened startled and in fear, hoping this was not a drunken attack the group was always wary about. Every night, John never forgot to provide his counsel – "Keep your belongings ready; we never know when we will need to pick up and run, whether it's the police or the drunks."

Through groggy eyes she saw it was a group of young men, well dressed, but obviously very drunk. They had invaded the group for what looked like a sport, kicking out wildly at the helpless, sleeping figures, shouting repulsive insults. Smita raised her arms in instinctive defence as she thought of Meg. She hoped Meg had escaped this initial assault. She was getting on in years and rather frail.

The men in the homeless group were more agile. Most had jumped up, hurriedly collected their respective belongings and tried to make a quick getaway.

But the attacking group were in no mind to show mercy. It was now progressing beyond a sport. It was becoming a fierce game. Smita was shocked at the aggression.

"Get off your fat butts, you fuckers. Can't you get a decent place to sleep in? Why the fuck are you cluttering up our city?"

"Welfare spongers! Living off our hard-earned taxes. Bastards!"

Cruel laughter and abuse continued, accompanied with repeated kicks and blows. Smita managed to get to her feet to defend herself better. When they saw she was young and the prettiest of the lot, the young men lost interest in the others and focused on her. There seemed to be three in the lead, perhaps more in the background watching on.

"Ha ha! We actually have a rather decent looking one here. Come on sweetheart. Why don't you come with us for some fun?"

The leader laughed and grabbed her around her shoulders, and tried to kiss her.

She bit him hard on his cheek. He howled, pushed her away, and then enraged, kicked out viciously. The others laughed at how she had countered him. The leader was now truly incensed. He charged and grappled her to the ground. His two colleagues joined in. They knelt on her and began to tear off her clothes. She screamed, and kicked, and bit, then screamed again. But no one seemed to come to her aid. Her homeless friends appeared to have made their escape, except for Meg who was lying prone and quiet beside her.

As they kept clawing at her, she realized she was on her own. Some primal force unleashed within her. She kicked out wildly in every direction with all the strength she could muster. She broke her hands free and scratched the faces of those attacking. She seemed to be making contact as one or the other backed off in turn, perhaps to lick his wounds and gather a second wind. Then, a third party tore into the group of three and tried to pull them off her. A glance told her it was John. The young men were momentarily distracted, warding off John. Smita took the opportunity to get up again and have a good look at all three of them. Then she pitched into the melee, to help John. She aimed for the eyes of the two nearest. She made contact and this time there were more painful howls.

"You fucking bitch. I will kill you."

The attackers overpowered John with ease, stunning him with a series of blows that floored him. Now they focused their energies on making her yield. The three once again grappled her to the ground and pinned her down. She could see two of them were bleeding in the face. It was obvious they intended to rape her, there in public on the street. If they thought they had bent her will, they needed to think again. Despite the intense pain from the blows to her chest and her face, she fought back with a grit they had not expected.

Finally she heard the sirens. Someone must have called the police. The attackers fled. Exhausted, Smita sat up, sobbing bitterly, her clothes in tatters, blood streaming from her mouth and face. She looked around dazed. Meg stayed prone and still. She forgot her own pain for a moment and leaned over Meg. John joined her in tending to Meg, battered though he was; together they tried to revive Meg who seemed to be unconscious.

Two police officers finally arrived and took over. By then, Smita had given in to her trauma. Seeing Meg lifeless on the ground was just too much for her. Later, she would not remember how they had administered to her, and how they had transported her to the hospital. All she knew was she had sunk into a deep hole, into the depths of darkness and agony. Convulsive sobs wracked her body; she felt intense pain and then anger in the core of her soul. The animals had violated not just her body, but her humanity.

She found herself on a bed, white sheets, bright lights, and a reassuring hand on her arm. She felt relief that it seemed to be over. Then she remembered Meg and John. She tried to ask, but no words emerged. The lady next to her was a nurse with kind eyes, reassuring her all was okay. She slipped into a blissful sleep. The sedative had taken over.

She had no idea how long she slept. When she awoke, she found she was in a cubicle, part of a larger hospital ward. She heard the nurse walking around, administering to other patients. She called out, weakly.

The nurse was a middle aged lady, motherly, with an air of authority.

"Hello dear. I am the head nurse in this ward. Please don't worry anymore. You are safe and you will recover."

Smita looked at her, then said, "I have just one question."

"What is it my dear," asked the nurse.

"I just need to know how Meg and John are?" she whispered.

The nurse looked at her. "Meg is here with us; we patched up John and he has gone. We're doing our best for Meg. Please do not worry your pretty head about her. Now do try to sleep. Your body and mind need it."

Smita did not like the news. It meant Meg was seriously injured. But at least she was in good hands.

The next two days she drifted in and out of sleep. She thought she saw Jill by her bedside from time to time, holding her hand, reassuring her. She found it difficult to move, pains shooting through her rib cage with even the smallest movement. Her jaw ached all the time. Eating was difficult; they kept her on a liquid diet. But it was the deep emotional pain that kept dragging her into a hole.

When conscious, her mind would not stop replaying the previous night's events. The aggression; the mindless violence; the attempted rape. Most of all, the sight of poor Meg lying motionless next to her. Her kind, gentle friend who had probably never hurt anyone in her life.

On the third day she felt strength gradually returning. The pain began to retreat.

The nurse brought in two police officers, a female and a male.

"Dear, these officers have been waiting to interview you. If you don't mind, they will now. Is that okay?" asked the nurse.

Smita nodded.

"We are truly sorry for what happened, Smita. Is that your name?" the female officer asked.

She nodded. John must have told them.

"My name is Senior Constable Emma Dickson. This here is Constable Andrew Gould. We were the ones who arrived at the scene of your attack that night. We need your statement, Smita. We need to find these people who attacked you folks. Take your time. But please tell us all."

"First I need to know how Meg is," Smita insisted.

They looked at each other. Then Dickson stepped out of the cubicle and called the nurse.

"What is it dear?" the nurse asked Smita.

"How is Meg?" asked Smita. "Please tell me truthfully."

The nurse fell silent. Smita guessed. Pain bit through her. She did not realize how attached she had become to Meg.

"I am sorry, my dear. Meg did not survive the attack. She had a very frail frame and ongoing health complications. The assault was too much for her."

Grief tore through Smita. But she bit down the tears. Then grief was replaced with a burning anger. An anger at all men, their violence, their selfishness, their domination and exploitation of women. *Bastards*, she thought. *Animals. They will pay for this.* She had the faces of those three attackers burned in her memory. She would not forget.

Poor Meg, so caring and so compassionate, with always a kind word for everyone. And this was what fate had dealt her. Smita decided, deep down, she would be avenged.

The police officers tried to restart their interrogation. Though she was fully conscious now and off her sedatives, Smita met their questions with silence.

"Smita, this is serious. We need your help to find these people and bring them to justice?"

Smita continued to look on in stoic silence. *Vengeance will be mine,* she thought to herself. *It is I who will bring them to justice. I have had enough of aggressive, predatory males. No court of justice will give them their just deserves.* Besides, she feared they would contact Pravin, or that her name would find itself in the local papers and Pravin would get wind of where she was.

"Look Smita," continued Dickson. "The assault case has now morphed into a murder investigation. You just heard from the nurse that poor Meg has passed away due to the injuries she received. This is now really serious. We need your testimony. You can give it to us here, or we can arrange for you to visit the police station after you are discharged to give us the statement. Which would you prefer?"

Smita finally said, "I know you both are doing your duty. But what can I say? It was dark. They were a group of animals. Obviously drunk. They attacked us just for the fun of it. And you've seen the results." She steeled herself and fought back tears as she thought of Meg, John and the others.

"Can you give us some description of the assailants?" pleaded Dickson.

Smita shrugged. "As I said, it was dark. And we were asleep when attacked. I know they were young men. But other than that fact, there is little I can tell you. Thank you for coming to our rescue. But I'm sorry, I have nothing to add."

Try as they might, they could get little more out of her. They finally and reluctantly departed, having taken a statement from her and recorded her injuries.

As they left, she heard Dickson say to Constable Gould, "I can't help but feel she's not telling us all she knows. And I have no idea why. We're going to have to keep an eye on her, I think."

* * *

That afternoon Jill visited Smita. It was off peak hours at the gym. She must have got a temp staff to fill in.

Smita gave her a weak smile. She hugged Smita carefully having been warned by the nurse that Smita had several broken ribs and severe bruises. It would be a while before she had fully recovered.

Jill said little. She sat by Smita, in comforting silence, holding her hand. Her presence spoke volumes more than words

After a while she said, "Smita dear. I have only one thing to tell you. When they release you, I will be taking you home with me. You can stay at my place and recover fully. Your job will still be there for you."

Smita's eyes filled with tears. What did she do to deserve such a friend? She had indeed been worrying what she was going to do when discharged. Where she would stay? She would not be able to work for a while. Did that mean she had lost her job?

Two days later Smita was discharged. She was given strict instructions not to move around too much, to let her ribs heal. They would fully recover, in about six weeks if she was careful. She was lucky. Meg was not.

As she walked slowly down the corridor to the visitor's room, where she was told Jill was waiting, she thought – *I have a mission now. Those bastards will pay for killing Meg and harming my friends. I am tired of violent and juvenile men. They will be taught not to violate women again.*

Jill was waiting for her. She hugged her. "Why so serious, Smita? Are you okay? Are you in pain? You have no worries now. I'm taking you home."

Smita hugged her friend back. "Thank you Jill. I will never be able to repay you for this kindness."

She reflected how these generous women in Australia had come so selflessly to her aid though she owed them nothing, and could give so little in return. The same could not be said of the men.

CHAPTER 10

Jill's heart went out to Smita as she drove her home from the hospital. Smita had hugged her gratefully as they emerged from the hospital, but then had fallen strangely silent. Jill thought she'd be happy to be out of hospital. She wanted to talk about how she'd help with her recovery using her physiotherapy skills. But Smita seemed withdrawn, lost in distant thought. All through the drive she sat quiet, pale and still, looking out of the window in silence.

The girl had come to her gym less than a year ago. Now, they were not just employer and employee. They had become friends. Smita had infused new energy into the business with her enthusiasm and enterprise. She had made friends with the clients and often took on extra hours at work without complaint. The gym had never looked so exceptionally clean and tidy. Jill had raised her salary, though Smita never asked or took advantage.

What had really impressed Jill, though, was Smita's dedication to her homeless group. She thought she understood it. It had been after all a tight knit group of disadvantaged individuals who provided each other with the crucial emotional and social support they each needed. Now, the group had been not just disbanded, but destroyed. Meg had been killed, and Smita had lost a vital social connection. She was still grieving; and Jill empathised. She had been through this herself not very long ago. Jill promised herself she would help Smita cope with this loss and recover quickly.

They arrived at the house. It was modest but cosy, located in a tiny lane in the Carlton suburb of Melbourne. It was the first Jill had ever owned, together with her late husband. She was still paying off the mortgage.

She led Smita in with a welcoming smile and took her to the second bedroom. It was small but comfortable. Jill had purchased a new set of clothes and toiletries for her; they were lying on the bed.

"I think they'll fit," said Jill, with a sheepish smile. "We are about the same stature. In any case I will take you to buy some more of your own choice when you are better."

Smita surveyed the room, the clothes, then suddenly turned and hugged Jill, her eyes streaming with tears. Jill was taken aback. Smita was usually reserved. She gave her a gentle hug back, aware that Smita was dealing with a fractured rib cage.

"Welcome, my dear" she repeated.

She took her to the kitchen, helped her sit and gave her the meal she had prepared. She sat to keep her company. But Smita seemed to have little interest in food.

"Tell me, Smita, do you want to be well again, back to your normal self?"

Smita looked up. She realised what Jill was getting at.

"I'm sorry, Jill, for being so ungrateful. You've been kind and generous. I promise I'll get better soon. And I'll eat to help me along. I intend to come to the gym tomorrow already."

Jill protested. But Smita convinced her that she would only sit at the reception desk initially. She could not bear the thought of sitting alone in the house with her thoughts.

The days settled into a quiet, steady routine. They now drove to work together and back in the evening. Smita spent all day at the gym, and seemed happy to do so. After a week she gradually began getting back to her cleaning work as well.

The two steadily grew closer, though Smita always seemed to feel she needed to do more to carry her weight in the relationship.

The change in Smita since the assault became ever more apparent as time wore on. Jill noticed she was quieter, more determined and intense in everything she did. Within five weeks, she had fully recovered, quicker than expected. Then she surprised Jill by expressing a desire to begin working out in the gym during her off-hours.

This was something new. To date Smita had never indicated any interest in exercise, in using the gym, or in fitness in general. Jill was thrilled with this development. She looked on it as a new project. She helped Smita plan a gradual fitness regime.

"Your first goal, dear, is overall fitness. I am not saying you are not fit. But your body has not been used to disciplined exercise. On the other hand, you're still young, lithe and flexible. And have a beautiful figure," she added with a smile.

"Fitness means regular work outs, to build stamina, and keeping a healthy diet. We will begin with using body weight." She taught Smita squats, mountain runners, burpees, kangaroo hops and duck walks. She encouraged her to start push ups and pull ups, though she could initially count the number of reps she could do on one hand.

Ever so gradually, Smita began building strength and stamina. Consistency, persistence and discipline were the secret, Jill repeated again and again.

Smita took to doing the grocery shopping for both of them. She learnt from Jill about correct food choices, especially for health and fitness. She began sharing in the preparation of their meals. She gradually became even more involved in the business of the gym. They now regularly debated issues on fitness trends, progress by clients, and the merits of the latest dieting fads.

A few weeks later, Jill suggested Smita was ready for her next step. "The next goal, Smita, is strength. This is important before moving to the third step of developing power. I like the way your fitness is improving. Your stamina has a way to go but it will improve as you push yourself each day to do more. It's strength, though, that needs even more discipline."

She introduced Smita to the weight machines, the dumbbells, bar bells, kettle bells and the cable machine. Jill taught her basic principles and moves, and how important it was to focus on posture, movement and reps in working with weights. They sat together and

Jill drew out a daily regime for her in two sessions a day. It was to be a controlled, systematic path to fitness and strength.

"Tell me, Smita," Jill asked one day, "why this sudden interest in getting yourself fit and strong? Don't get me wrong. I'm really happy you're going down this path. I'm just interested where this motivation is coming from."

Smita gave her an enigmatic smile. "I'll tell you in time, I promise."

Over the next six months the change in Smita was remarkable. She spent several hours a day, during her off hours, alternating between aerobic and strength training, building her body with determination and focus. Jill had never had a better student.

"You know Jill, you charge your clients for your instruction and guidance. I'm paying you nothing," she said one day.

Jill countered, "Smita, you're a friend, a dear companion. I enjoy training you. And I'm chuffed that you're doing so well. Besides, you do a lot more work at the gym than I pay you for."

* * *

"Has Pravin ever contacted you again?" Jill asked Smita one day as they drove home from work.

Smita was grateful for Jill raising the issue. "Thankfully, he has not found me yet. But I need to get a formal divorce from him. I can't escape that. The problem is I'm not sure how to go about it. I've been checking the internet. Lawyers are expensive."

"No problem, Smita. I have a cousin, Joan, who is a lawyer and does pro bono work. I'll ask if she can help. If she can, I'll get you an appointment."

They met with Joan not long after. After listening to Smita's situation, she felt there was a strong case for a divorce. "Leave it with me for a few days."

A few days later, she called Jill and Smita back. "Pravin says he'll agree to the divorce if you get your mother to pay the remainder of your dowry, Smita."

"I'd rather be homeless again than do that," was Smita's immediate reply. "But I have to somehow be free again, Joan. I hate being tied to that bastard."

Jill was surprised with Smita's intense reaction.

"I thought so, Smita," Joan replied. "I don't think you have to worry. The law will probably favour you since you've reported incidents of domestic abuse back in Glen Waverley. But it might take time."

They left the matter with Joan.

* * *

More than six months had passed since the assault. The J&J gym was thriving. Clientele had increased, particularly of young ethnic women. Word of mouth had spread that the Banana Alley gym was run by two women, both very competent and supportive.

Jill generously acknowledged Smita's role in the gym's growing popularity.

"You've been a timely tonic for my gym, you realise that I hope," she remarked one day.

Smita shrugged, embarrassed at the compliment.

"It's true. I've noticed. Clients like how you treat them. The proof is they're bringing in their friends. New clients. Membership has grown by at least twenty percent in the last few months."

"I doubt it's been just me, Jill. But you know what? I never dreamed I'd be working in a gym and enjoying it. But I do. It's given me new purpose. That and your friendship. Thank you." She gave Jill a grateful hug, tears welling up.

"I'm also glad you're stepping in to guide the new youngsters. The beginners. They seem to find it reassuring. We must start on getting you certified as a trainer."

"Thanks. I've been hoping I've not overstepped my role. Remember, I am the admin assistant," she replied, arching an eyebrow and giving Jill one of her rare grins.

'Soon, you're going to be co-trainer, if I have my way."

* * *

One evening at 10 pm, both women had their bags over their shoulders and were readying to depart for home. As they approached the gym's entrance door, it swung open with force. A young, well-built white male quickly stepped in and shut the door behind him. Of medium stature, arms tattooed, dressed in stretch pants and a baseball cap, he looked at them with drugged, shifty eyes.

"I need your hand bags, cunts," he announced gruffly

A knife appeared in one hand while the other stretched out for their bags.

Jill noticed that Smita stifled a cry, fear flashing across her face. She placed a reassuring hand on Smita's arm, while she silently maintained eye contact with the young man. She made no move to hand over her bag.

"Come on, hurry up," the man muttered impatiently, looking around to see if anyone else was still in the gym. "Hand over those fucking bags unless you want some ugly tattoos on those pretty arms?"

Smita's calm seemed to have returned. Jill was sure this incident must have triggered memories of the assault of six months ago.

Jill simply said to the young man, "You're getting nothing, mister. Why don't you just back off and leave us in peace."

The man taken aback by this composure, a bit nonplussed. Then, he made a sudden grab for Jill's bag.

Jill anticipated his move. She stepped back smoothly, moving to her side at the same time, and shoved a hard shoulder followed by her elbow into the young man's leaning face catching him completely off guard. He lost balance and toppled over to the ground. She turned to the counter, whipped out a baton which was kept there for such eventualities, and struck him on his head.

He lay stunned, his eyes out of focus. She hit him again, on the other side of the head, though not too hard this time. As he lay prone on the floor, holding his head in pain, she retrieved a twine bundle from behind the counter, kicked him over onto his stomach, and tied his hands behind his back. She instructed Smita to call the police and not to touch the knife on the floor. It was crucial evidence.

As they waited for the police, Jill kept watch over the man, baton ready in hand. Smita stood, looking on with wonder. She finally remarked, "Jill, I'm amazed. How did you manage that? I'm ashamed I was of no help at all."

Jill shrugged the praise off. "Gym fitness helps," she replied. "Remember – fitness, strength, power. It's our motto. We practice it as well."

"But Jill, those moves? Where did they come from?"

"I tell you later. It looks like the police are here."

The officers Senior Constable Dickson and Constable Gould commended Jill on her swift action.

"Well done, Jill," remarked Senior Constable Dickson as she took their statements, while Constable Gould took photographs of the scene.

Before departing with the handcuffed man, Dickson advised Jill to install a CCTV immediately within the gym, noting the rise in similar crimes within the city.

Later, as they drove home together, Smita again remarked, "Jill, I'm just astounded at your skills. Where and when did you pick those abilities of self-defence?"

Jill smiled. "You may have seen the fight-club signs on some of the gyms in our line on the Banana alley. One of them is dedicated to martial arts, and specifically offers Krav Maga lessons. This particular martial arts technique was developed by the Israelis. It teaches its students to function both mentally and physically when under duress. I believe Krav Maga can empower women to protect themselves against violent situations like sexual assaults. They learn how various parts of their bodies like elbows and knees can become weapons when necessary. So I visit them off and on and take lessons."

Smita's ears pricked up. A self-defence gym almost next door.

"So they're in the same row of gyms as ours?" she asked, trying to confirm what she had heard.

"Yes. Just a few doors away. I can see this has perked up your interest, Smita. Am I right that wheels are moving in your pretty head?"

Smita laughed. "Oh Jill, am I that transparent?"

* * *

Soon after the incident at the gym, Jill had the CCTV system installed in the gym. It seemed a good idea from a number of points of view. It also helped them monitor the different types of clients - regulars, casuals, visitors and the walk-ins.

CHAPTER 11

Smita, intrigued by Krav Maga, wasted no time in seeking out the gym. It was literally four doors down the alley. She enrolled for sessions during her off hours, keeping this a secret from Jill for the time being.

There was another issue upper most in her mind. She broached it with Jill soon after the intrusion incident.

"Jill, it's been many months now that I have been using your hospitality. I'm thinking of moving out and being on my own. I'm really grateful for how much you've helped me. But it's time I started living on my own."

"Smita, you're absolutely no burden, you know that. It's a pleasure having you as a house companion. I hope I've not given any indication that I want you to move?"

"No, not at all. But I think I need to get on with my life. And you need some privacy in your own home. I'm grateful enough you've given me a great job which I enjoy".

"You've been a huge plus for my gym, Smita. I'm hoping you'll continue on."

"Absolutely. I enjoy it."

Smita found a shared apartment in Brunswick, within an easy commute by the tram to Banana Alley. She liked the area. It had a youthful vibe which made her feel much more comfortable than a suburb like Glen Waverley. Its bustle and activity was reminiscent of parts of Mumbai.

Jill helped her move and made sure she was comfortable in her new home.

Another reason for Smita's move was that she had observed Jill's interest in William, a regular gym client. William was a lawyer, in his forties, who worked in a solicitor's office in the city. He came in regularly, twice a week. Slightly balding and trim, he wasn't great at his exercise routine. But he made an effort. He was shy and never tried to chat up the girls as most other men who came in did.

William was the only man, Smita noticed, who perked Jill's interest. She had observed Jill's eyes follow him from time to time. It would be nice for Jill to get into a relationship again, she thought. It was now almost four years since her husband had passed away. Jill was still young. Smita wondered if her staying at Jill's place was coming in the way of her establishing a relationship. Probably not. But it would be nice for Jill to have a little more freedom and privacy.

* * *

Smita's introduction to Krav Maga was a resounding success. She learnt that this Israeli "hand-to-hand" combat system dated back to 1891 and was still used by the Israeli Defence Forces. It was the perfect outlet for her pent up anger. She was still recovering from the abusiveness of Pravin, and the assault under the bridge. The rage against the violence and arrogance of men continued to burn intensely.

The Krav skills she was learning opened the opportunity to turn tables on predatory men. This prospect was liberating, empowering and therapeutic.

She appreciated Krav's no-nonsense approach and practical techniques. The moves did not require equipment, were adapted to different real-life scenarios and instilled confidence in coping with physical confrontations.

Smita had requested a female trainer and was paired with Esther.

Esther brought a sense of humour and light-heartedness to the training. "Smita dear, you're too serious, too intense. Lighten up. It's important for your mind and muscles."

Esther hailed from an Israeli family, a recent migrant like Smita, and was still getting used to Aussie accents. They bonded easily, laughing uproariously as they tried out different Aussie words with local accents on each other.

Despite their fun, the training was rigorous and focused. Esther taught her basic attacks, defences, timing, feints, tactics, movements, and vision.

"Goodness, Smita. I don't think I've ever encountered a client as focused as you. What's driving the intensity?'

Smita simply shrugged the comment away. She had a mission which she preferred to keep to herself.

She practised incessantly, mastering the basic moves Esther taught her within four weeks. As her physical confidence increased, she noticed psychological changes too. The world seemed safer while her self-confidence and social well-being grew. She eagerly anticipated testing her new skills. But she counselled herself to remain patient. Reason told her she had a long way to go. Bide your time. Prepare and then prepare some more, because failure would not be an option.

Into her third month of Krav training, Smita asked an intriguing question –

"What are the most painful and effective moves of Krav?"

Esther was not sure she heard right. "Do you mean painful for the one doing the moves, or for the one receiving them?

They both laughed. "Oh, Esther, for the one receiving, obviously."

"Okay, here we go. Krav Maga, as you already know, focuses on attacking the soft spots of the attacker's body. These are the eyes, nose, ears, throat, jaw, groin, knees, and Achilles tendon.

We'll begin with the easiest and yet most the useful; the Palm to the Nose technique. Here, show me your hand. Now, open your palm, and direct it to the nose of the opponent as straight as an arrow, with your elbow firm. Hitting the nose in this way, with the force of your body behind the move, can numb your opponent for several moments and make it difficult for him to focus on the fight. Let's try it out before we move to more deadly and difficult moves."

She took Smita to the row of punching dummies in the corner, shaped like persons. They looked weird, standing in a row, just waiting to be hammered. Smita wondered why they needed so many. Then she learnt the punching dummies were padded to different resistance consistencies, progressively getting harder as one went down the row. This allowed the one practising to test out their strength on varying body consistencies.

Esther demonstrated the move. "Stand with a wide stance, legs at shoulder distance. Bend your palm backward. Separate your fingers so they're not clenched. Then put all your weight into your arm and extend it like an arrow aimed at hitting your opponent just under the nostrils with the lower part of your open palm; continue the movement up into the attacker's head. Have a look."

Smita was impressed. It was a move of limited, crisp movements, relatively easy to learn.

"I'll teach you two more moves. Then you'll need to practise these until I am convinced you're ready to move on."

The second move was the Blow to the Throat. A powerful punch can hurt the windpipe, cause excruciating pain, and paralyse the opponent for a while. The hand was positioned to form a chisel fist, much the same as the standard fist formation. The only difference was at the knuckles. The bones that make up the knuckles were to be kept straight, the fingers closed and the thumb tucked in hard against the pointer finger.

After demonstrating the Blow to the Throat move on a dummy, Esther moved to what she described as the third move, the Knee or Foot to the Groin.

"This is the third and last move I'll teach you at this time. As someone approaches you, stabilize yourself as best you can, lift your dominant leg, which for you is the right one, and drive the knee upward. If you are flexible enough, and I think you are, you can also simply extend the kick so that your foot, rather than the knee, makes contact with the groin. Some women aim for the shins. I don't recommend this. Men's shins are pretty hardly, generally. The groin is the most vulnerable and will incapacitate the guy for at least a few minutes."

"All of these moves," concluded Esther, "assume the attacker is coming from the front. In the next round, we'll deal with attackers coming from the side and back."

Esther also advised Smita, "I often suggest to my clients that they read the book of Maxwell Maltz, written over fifty years ago but still relevant and enormously helpful when learning self-defence. It's titled *Psycho-cybernetics*. It's available on Amazon. It focuses on the power of visualisation to achieve what we want. All of us have this ability, to visualize. Use it to practise your Krav Maga moves; imagine in detail how you'd react in different situations. This is critical in self-defence. Literally, you need to sit back, close your eyes, and visualise the situations when you will use your self-defence moves, how your opponent will attack, how you will counter, how you will neutralise. The more you play out these scenes in your mind, the deeper the moves embed into your subconscious, and influence your muscle memory."

Esther stopped and smiled, amused at how enrapt Smita was during her explanations.

"Last piece of advice, Smita. Always keep your emotions under control. If you want to be effective, do not let anger, fear, or any kind of emotion interfere. You must at all times keep your mind absolutely in charge, acutely aware of what your opponent is doing, what you are doing, and how the opponent will react. It is as much a mind game as it is a physical contest. Remember this always."

Smita left the session with much to contemplate and practise.

* * *

That night, as Smita lay in bed in her new home, she reflected on her progress. Since her hospital discharge consequent to the assault under the bridge a year ago, she had formulated two clear goals, her mission. First, she wanted to confront Pravin and teach him a lesson before she filed for divorce. She believed this was vital for her own closure but also to prevent him from mistreating future partners. While a divorce would free her, she dreaded how he'd treat a future wife who would inevitably follow. She felt a responsibility to ensure that Pravin understood he could not just continue his bullying ways with women.

Her other goal was retribution against the three brutal bastards who attacked her homeless family under the bridge, tried to rape her and killed her friend Meg. She could not forgive them. The anger still seethed within her, fuelled by the conviction that they continued their arrogant and aggressive ways with complete disrespect for women and the helpless. She was determined to teach them a lesson they would not forget.

She was getting there; she felt it in her bones. Consistency, persistence and discipline, she reminded herself. Her skills were now almost on par with her sparring partners in the Krav gym.

Jill unexpectedly discovered her hard at training one day. "So this is where you go to in your off time. And you've kept it a secret," Jill chided.

Smita looked sheepish and ashamed.

"I've been watching you quietly from that corner the last few minutes. I'm amazed at how much you've progressed in your fitness, strength and now Krav skills. But I'm also worried where all this is leading to, Smita." There was genuine concern in her voice and on her face.

"Thanks Jill. But please don't worry. One day, I promise, I will have a chat with you on this."

Smita was sure Jill had guessed her intentions. Probably not the details, but the general focus. But she was not to be moved from her goal.

Perhaps a few more months, she thought. Pravin would be the easier one. He was a coward. But she needed to plan meticulously to ensure that he attacked her first and that the attack took place in public, before the eyes of others. That would be the evidence she needed for her divorce. Then she would teach him a lesson in his own language – physical domination.

As for the three murderers, that was more complicated. She was still not sure she could cope effectively with three at one time. She had to assume they were not as physically fit as her. And then she had to find them. But for now, one step at a time. Pravin. Her nerves tingled with anticipation.

CHAPTER 12

The next day at the gym, she found Jill looking at her curiously. "Smita, I find you very pensive these days. Are you okay?"

She laughed it off. She really must be transparent given how easily people read her. First, Esther telling her she was too serious; now, Jill.

"Sorry, Jill. Nothing to worry about. I'm fine. But I do worry about you from time to time."

"About me? Why, Smita?"

Smita realised her attempt to deflect was rather obvious, but she had been waiting for an opportunity to raise an issue.

"Can I ask a sister to sister question?"

"Yes, of course."

"Have you closed yourself off any relationships with men?"

Jill laughed. "That's impertinent, isn't it Smita?"

"Jill, we're like sisters now, right? And I'm worried about you, just as you are about me. That's where I'm coming from. Have I stepped out of line?"

"No worries, dear. I know you only have my best interest at heart. The short answer is no, Smita. I've not written off any serious relationships with men. It is true it's taken me a while to get over the passing of James. It is now coming on to four years. I'll always have a place for him in my heart. But I realise, I have to move on in life. As I get older, I get lonelier. It would be nice to meet someone who I respect and with whom I can develop a serious relationship. That's not happened as yet. But maybe it will."

"What about you, Smita?"

Smita stayed silent.

"Come on Smita. You asked me and I gave you a frank answer. You can at least reciprocate."

Smita sighed. "The truth is, Jill, I've become wary of men. My experiences have been largely negative. Perhaps disastrous. Most seem selfish and arrogant, treating women as a means to their own ends. They'll never accept us as their equals; we are there to make their lives happier, easier, to give them pleasure. But for you, my sincere wish is that you find a decent man you will love and who will love and respect you in return. I really do wish you well, Jill. As for me, I've had enough of them."

* * *

Smita balanced her work responsibilities at Jill's gym with her own Krav Maga practise. She used every opportunity in her spare time, even when in Jill's gym. She'd move to the furthest back corner of the gym, to remain out of sight of the visiting clients.

One day, she caught William watching her.

She stopped mid-routine, and walked up to him in a challenging demeanour. "What?" she asked. "You interested in learning as well?"

He was embarrassed at being caught out staring. He turned shyly away. "I'm sorry. That was impertinent of me. I really should have respected your privacy. But I was just blown away by your moves. You're so different to a year ago when you started working here. I never knew you had these skills."

Smita gave a grudging smile. "I did not. I've acquired them over the last year or so."

"You're joking, right?"

"Seriously. Once you put your mind to it with focus, there is a snowballing effect."

He still did not believe her, she thought. But she was quite surprised that he had apologised to her. This was a first from a man in her experience. Perhaps he was a decent guy.

"I've seen you come here regularly, doing your usual thing. Frankly, you don't seem to be improving. Would you like to take your fitness .to a next level?" she asked surprised at her own candour. Perhaps the Aussie bluntness was rubbing off on her.

He too, seemed surprised with the directness of the question. But in truth, he'd been asking himself whether he should indeed be trying something new. He was getting on in years. He was not improving whether in strength, flexibility, or general fitness.

"Would you have anything to suggest?" he asked.

"Try my boss," she replied.

"You mean Jill, who owns this place?"

"Oh, good, you know her name. That's a start. She's a fantastic trainer. I am where I am today in fitness thanks to her."

"But I've never seen her train anyone else besides women," he countered.

"That's because you men are too proud to ask for help from a woman, particularly in the physical arena." Again, blunt. Perhaps she should be more cautious. But she was keen to get William and Jill talking to each other. This seemed to be an opportunity.

"Look. If you're interested, let's walk over to her and have a chat. Wouldn't hurt. Let's try it."

She did not wait for his response, but began walking to Jill. He followed, behind, tentatively.

It appeared that Smita's subtle encouragement was all that was needed to spark a connection between Jill and William. William's gym visits became more frequent, and there was a noticeable improvement in his fitness and skills

One evening, three weeks later, they were closing up for the night, when Jill asked, "Smita, was that suggestion that William take lessons from me as innocent as you implied, or do I read something else in that move?"

Smita simply turned around, hugged Jill, and said, "Jill, my greatest wish is that you be happy."

* * *

Smita's plan to confront her past was finally set in motion. One evening, when all was quiet in the gym and she was at her desk, she got out a set of vinyl gloves typically used in clinics, which she had purchased from the local chemist. She put them on carefully and with gloved hands took out a clean sheet of paper from the printer. On it she wrote, in careful print, a note that said:

Smita works at J & J's Gym in Banana Alley, Flinders Street, Melbourne CBD

She carefully folded the note into an envelope, addressed it to Pravin in Glen Waverley, and stuck on a postal stamp. With gloves on, she inserted it carefully into her backpack.

That evening, on the way home, she used her handkerchief to remove the envelope from her backpack and slipped it into the local mail box opposite Flinders Street station.

* * *

A day later, Smita casually said to Jill, "By the way, if Pravin comes here at any time in the future, and gets into an interaction with me, can you just leave us be, please? I would prefer to deal with him myself."

"But how would he know you work here, Smita?"

She shrugged. "You never know, Jill. He's persistent. I'm convinced he will not give up. He's been trying to get in touch with me on phone even after I've had his number blocked, using other numbers. He still wants that dowry money as Joan indicated."

"Smita, I'm worried about you. Am I right in guessing you're trying to set up a confrontation with Pravin?"

"Aww, come on, Jill? You worry unnecessarily. It's just that I know him well. He will not let me go on with my life in peace. He has not forgiven me for leaving him. It's a humiliation for him within his community. So he'll come after me one day, inevitably."

"Smita, I'm increasingly concerned. Ever since I introduced you to Krav Maga, I've noticed how serious you've become about it. You're now practising Krav moves for hours a day here in every free moment you get outside your reception and the admin duties.

It's clear this isn't about fitness anymore. You've become obsessed with revenge. "

She continued, "Now, you're saying Pravin might come in to the gym any day, and you expect me not to intervene in whatever transpires between you two? I can't but help think you are on a vendetta. I've seen how your anger at Pravin and those who attacked you under the bridge is consuming you. It's not good for you, Smita."

"And if I am on a vendetta, so what, Jill?"

"This is not you, Smita. We've now known each other for almost two years. You're kind, warm, and caring. You always look after me though I am your boss, and reach out regularly to your homeless friends. Please rethink this, Smita."

"Jill, you remain my best friend, and someone I'd do anything for. But please let me handle this. It's a path I've chosen, and I need to see it through. I've spent years trying to appease men, giving in to their demands and domination. It never works, Jill. Standing up to them is the only way."

"Yes, I agree. But not with violence, Smita."

"I can assure you Jill, that I'll never ever be the one who starts the physical confrontation. I truly want to be left in peace and live my life as I wish. But in my experience, men always want it their way or no way. Just look at this news item in today's feed: one in three Australian women will experience physical abuse in their life time. On average, one woman is killed every week by a current or former partner. Every day eight women are hospitalised with critical injuries inflicted by an intimate partner. Would you like me to continue reading?"

"Smita. I understand. But there must be a more constructive way to encourage better behaviour from men rather than countering violence with violence."

"Jill, dear. I love you and admire you. But I also think you might be a bit naive. And yes, to tell you the truth, as of now, my obsession is to bring Pravin and the men who attacked me and killed Meg to justice."

"What?" Jill seemed taken aback, though she had suspected such intentions.

"Smita holding on to these vengeful thoughts and intentions is not healthy for you."

"Healthy or not, Jill, it's a mission I must address before I move on in life. I assure you, I will do nothing that will bring your gym into disrepute. The only thing I ask is that you let me handle this matter without intervention, please," she begged.

Reluctantly Jill let it go.

CHAPTER 13

Back at Glen Waverley, Pravin was at Ramesh's house immersed in a boozy weekend dinner. He was now a regular visitor to Ramesh's place, seeking solace consequent to Smita's desertion.

"You're looking pensive, Pravin. Still thinking about that bitch? I told you not to waste your money on detectives. Just go and find another bride and maybe with a bigger dowry, yar." Ramesh tried to lighten the mood.

"She's asked for a divorce now," Pravin replied grimly.

"What, she's been in contact?"

"No. Through her lawyer. Another bloody woman."

"So? What's your response?"

"Only if she agrees to get the rest of the dowry from her mother. I will have to pay alimony. The least I want is to recoup some back through the dowry still owed to me."

"Just give her the bloody divorce and cut your losses. Then make sure you get a better dowry from the next one," Ramesh advised, pouring another round of drinks.

Pravin remained silent, his mind racing. They both sipped their whisky quietly.

He finally replied, "I know where she is."

"You mean that fucking detective actually came through?" Ramesh leaned in, all attention now.

"Not the detective. You were right. I've wasted my money on that guy. I got this letter in the mail yesterday. I want your opinion."

He handed the letter over to Ramesh. Ramesh read carefully; then again.

"Sounds bloody suspicious, if you ask me," Ramesh finally said.

"Why?" asked Pravin.

"Why would someone tell you this anonymously, unless this is a trap?"

Pravin nodded, his suspicions confirmed. "That's exactly my concern. Why? And from whom?"

They both considered the situation in thoughtful silence.

Then Pravin ventured. "Were I to go to this address and confront her, then what? If she refuses to come back with me, can I force her?"

"Look Pravin, if you really want her back, the only option in my view is to persuade her. Play nice guy. Sweet talk her with promises that things have changed. Tell her that if she returns, you and she will talk and come to an agreement about any work she wants to do; and how she'll manage her household duties too."

Pravin remained silent, still considering.

He then came to a decision. "I need back up, mate. I need you to come along and vouch for me. To say that even the Indian community in Glen Waverley wants her to return and start anew. A new leaf. And, most importantly, to help me get the remainder of her dowry from her mother. Can you come with me?"

Ramesh thought a while.

"Come to think of it, I'm almost sure it's one from our community who has sent this anonymous letter, in the hope you'll get her back. It's not good for the reputation of our Indian community here and certainly not for some of our young colleagues whose parents are trying to arrange their marriages with a bride from India. Okay. I'll come."

* * *

Two weeks after Smita had posted her letter, Pravin and Ramesh arrived at the gym. She had waited, patient and ready, though the presence of his friend, Ramesh, startled her. Her ploy had worked.

He had walked into the trap. But now she also had to deal with the unexpected variable. She remembered Ramesh from those boring weekend afternoon lunches. The tension built within her.

Pravin entered the gym with a confident swagger, surveying the surroundings. Ramesh trailed behind. He spotted Smita at the reception desk and strutted over, leaning on the counter with a cynical smile. He looked down at her with insolent eyes, unaware of the storm brewing within her.

"So this is where my wife has been hanging out after deserting me," he sniggered. "In a fucking gym, can you believe that? Wait until I break the news to your mother in India."

She looked back at him coldly. "I've been meaning to contact you to follow up on my lawyer's request for a divorce. I will no longer tolerate your abuse, Pravin; I want nothing more to do with you. I need you out of my life."

"No my dear. You're not getting any fucking divorce, unless you get me my dowry money. Alternatively, you're coming home with me to look after house as we agreed at our marriage. This is your duty. I've brought Ramesh here to tell you that the Indian community disapproves of how you've left me. It's inappropriate and in fact scandalous. Instead of being grateful that I helped you migrate from India to Australia, you've shamelessly deserted me and brought a bad name to NREs back in India."

"Pravin, please leave me alone. I'll be sending you my divorce papers soon. After that, I want nothing to do with you."

"You silly little girl. Who do you think you're ordering around? Don't you know you're here in Australia on a dependent visa? I can have you deported any time. So don't mess with me. Come on. I've come here to take you home."

"You're taking me nowhere, Pravin. Please leave."

Their voices had been rising, and now those in the gym turned to see what was going on. Ramesh began looking distinctly uncomfortable. Their agreed strategy had been one of persuasion. But Pravin seemed unable to restrain himself. He couldn't cope with his wife talking back at him. He was getting visibly impatient. Ramesh looked like he wanted to calm the situation, but unsure what to do. He too was not used to women talking back so aggressively.

Smita remained seated, making no move to rise. Pravin finally came around the reception desk, grabbed her arm and tried to pull her up. "Come on. I don't want to cause a scene here."

"You're not taking me anywhere, you scum. Leave me alone." She pulled her arm free and returned to her seat.

Rage seemed to consume Pravin now. He had planned to play it cool after the discussion with Ramesh. But Smita's aggressive responses were too much for him to handle.

Smita could see his anger bubbling beneath his intense stare. She wondered how she had lived eight months with this monster. He found it impossible not to resort to violence when his wishes were frustrated, especially by someone he considered his dutiful wife.

The dam finally burst. He slapped her hard with his right hand, grabbed her arm again and violently pulled her to the door, shouting to the gathering crowd, "This is my wife. All's fine. I'm just taking her home."

Ramesh followed, on the other side of Smita, trying to guide her to the door. The situation was unfolding very differently from what he had envisaged. He had never encountered female resistance such as this.

Two male clients moved to come to Smita's rescue. But Jill held out a firm hand, indicating they should not interfere. They backed off, faces puzzled and worried.

With her face still stinging from the slap, Smita once again shrugged off Pravin's hold and Ramesh's guiding arm, making her way back to the desk. This time, Pravin seemed to lose control. He grabbed her by the shoulders, shoved her toward the door, and tried to push her out.

She had been patient until now, waiting for a justified reason to do what she intended. She wasn't sure she had it yet. Perhaps just one more provocation. She hoped the CCTV was recording, although there were now several witnesses.

She turned to him at the door and mocked, "You call yourself a husband. You don't know what love and respect are. You can't even make love to a woman properly."

This seemed to push him over the edge. His patience exhausted, he launched into a frenzy of hard slaps to each side of her face. Madness enveloped his face. The aggression was more than she had anticipated, his pent up anger erupting uncontrollably.

Under the volley of blows she momentarily panicked, struggling to shift from the mindset of a fearful victim to that of a composed, Krav Maga defender. For a moment, she felt she had lost it. When she needed those skills and that mindset she had worked so hard for, they seemed to be deserting her.

Then, suddenly, she felt in charge again.

Before Pravin knew it, she stepped back, then launched fiercely into him hand forward, palm into his face, under his nostrils. A sharp intense pain seemed to run through his face. He reeled back, clutching his nose, shocked by her unexpected attack. Ramesh stood by, aghast.

Pravin's rage now seemed to increase tenfold. This time he lashed out blindly, with both arms, seething in pain and anger. She copped another hard hit on the face, but this didn't stop her delivering a hard kick to his groin. She did it with more vehemence than she should have. Her emotion was now getting the upper hand. Esther would not have been pleased, she thought, in that split second.

The kick was effective. Pravin collapsed to the ground, holding his groin, writhing in pain, gasping for air. He had never experienced a beating like this before.

Jill quickly joined Smita's side, while the other gym goers surrounded the prone Pravin, ensuring his attacks had come to an end. They needn't have worried. Pravin was for all intents and purposes, paralysed by his pain. Ramesh looked on, stunned and helpless. Someone had called the police.

Smita turned to Jill. "Thank you, Jill. I think everything was caught on CCTV. I'm fine," she said despite her battered face, red bruises on both sides, her nose bleeding profusely, and one eye swollen shut. She looked like a wounded soldier.

She was painfully aware of the beating she had endured. "Jill, please use your phone and take some pics of my face, quickly."

Jill was visibly shocked by the request. She hesitated as if surprised by Smita's presence of mind despite her ordeal. But she complied.

Someone had helped Pravin to his feet. He was shaky, still reeling from the shock and pain. They made him sit on one of the reception's chairs. Ramesh stood around appearing out of place. The police soon arrived. Coincidently, it was Senior Constable Emma Dickson again with another officer. They began the meticulous process of taking statements from both parties and the witnesses. Jill informed them that there was a live CCTV on all the time and they could have the real-time video. They requested access to it.

After taking Smita's statement, Dickson remarked, "You seem to be attracting the aggression of men quite often, Smita."

Smita looked at her with hard eyes. "Perhaps you can explain what you mean by that remark, Officer?" she demanded.

Dickson realised she had overstepped with the remark. "Sorry. I did not mean anything inappropriate. I was just struck by the coincidence that I'm here again, within a year, taking a statement from you on another attack."

"Perhaps that question is better directed at my male attackers, don't you think?"

"As I said, that remark was inappropriate. I take it back. Let's move on."

She inquired if Smita wished to press charges against Pravin. Smita declined, requesting instead a restraining order to prevent him from entering her personal space

They departed with Pravin in handcuffs, and Ramesh tagging along. They said they would charge him with criminal assault. Smita could pursue a civil case against him if she chose to at a later date.

* * *

Jill was solicitous, providing ice for Smita's face, a drink, ensuring she was comfortable, and repeatedly asking if she was okay. She suggested they go to the hospital to check out her bruises. But Smita declined. She assured Jill she was fine, though her face was burning from the beating, one eyelid was closed, her face swollen.

Yet she smiled. A triumphant smile. Her spirits lifted. The training had paid off. The first milestone had been achieved, successfully.

Later that evening, when Jill and she were leaving for their respective homes, on the street away from the CCTV, Jill stopped Smita.

"Dear, that was impressive. But far too dangerous. You are indeed one determined woman. I can't help but admire your courage and skill despite your deviousness. But I truly hope this is the last."

Smita hugged Jill. "Jill, I could not have done this without your support and love. I'm fine. Thank you for everything."

As they departed their respective ways. Smita reflected on the day's event as she walked home. She analysed her performance, questioning if she had maintained control, if her emotions had interfered, the efficiency of her Krav moves, and how well she had adhered to her training. This was just a practice run, and an easy one compared to the next assignment which awaited her.

CHAPTER 14

Smita set up the dummies in a triangular formation, then began trying out her moves with them. She worked systematically, but it was soon obvious she needed guidance.

At her next training session with Esther, her request was specific – "How do I cope with three attackers?"

Esther looked at her, intrigued. "Why three?" she asked.

Smita shrugged. "Okay, two or four, whatever. But I want to learn to defend and attack multiple opponents."

Esther nodded. "Okay, here goes. Some fundamentals first. The most basic yet crucial principle is spatial awareness. You need to be constantly aware of the position of your opponents, their distance from you, the spacing between them. You must ensure, at all costs, you are not surrounded. This awareness must be maintained at all times."

"Okay, that's pretty basic."

"Yes, basic, I know, but fundamental," said Esther. "In the heat of battle, emotions come to the fore. As I've been drumming into your head, keep the mind always in charge. Control the emotions; don't let them get in the way. Keep scanning, look your opponents in the eye, keep analysing. This is as much a mental battle as it is a physical encounter.

Footwork is also critical. Your ability to outmanoeuvre your opponents and maintain balance at the same time depends on that footwork. I can't emphasise how critical this is. Keep moving. Learn to be agile; learn to fight on your toes, to swivel with the art of a dancer. Krav fighting is akin to a dance, though a deadly one and not for art's sake. Here, let's practise these principles with the dummies – spatial awareness, mental control, and footwork.

Finally, always remember, blows need to be powerful and decisive. If you're striking, make sure it counts. This isn't a game. Often, your life can depend on it. And be prepared for counterattacks. Inevitably, you will get hit. Don't wait to recover before striking back. Your opponent will usually not expect a sudden counterstrike. That's your opportunity."

The session lasted an hour. After Esther went off to attend to another client, Smita continued. Soon she was drenched in sweat; but she worked with intense concentration and focus.

* * *

Jab, cross, hook. Then again, jab, cross, hook.

Change stance. Kick, cross, swivel. Kick, cross, swivel. Repeat.

Step back, shoot arm, kick, swivel, duck.

The routine went on, and on, and on.

"Hey, you're pretty intense, aren't you?" It was a good looking guy, a regular at the martial arts sessions in this gym. She had seen him around. He was skilled, and seemed to be a loner.

"Excuse me asking, but aren't you of Indian descent?" he asked.

She wondered whether to just ignore him and continue her practise. But then, perhaps a break would help. She was feeling a bit fatigued.

"So what if I am?" she asked defensively.

"No offense, lady. I was just curious. It's pretty out of the ordinary to see a person like you, from your community, practising Krav. So I just wanted to get to know you better."

"What's wrong with me?" she challenged. "Or the community I come from?"

He now shook his head. "I am really sorry. I truly did not mean to offend you. If anything, I'm impressed. But I did notice that you are probably ethnically Indian, and it's rare to see a woman of Indian descent involved in martial arts. So I was curious. By the way, I'm part aboriginal, and proudly so."

She now noticed his slightly swarthy complexion.

"Yes, you're right. Women from my community rarely if ever get involved with this stuff. Perhaps they should more often."

"Why so?" he asked, curiously.

He seemed pretty inquisitive, she thought. But she answered.

"Women in my community are often too submissive. The men take us for granted. It's part of our culture. The men are raised to think they're the privileged ones in the family. The women are there to serve them. I think our women need to wake up, assert themselves."

"Ha. I like your spunk. My name is Ed. What's yours, if I may ask?"

"Smita"

"Nice. I like you Smita. Any time you need a partner to practice, and if I'm here, I'm available. And by the way, what you say about men in your community sometimes applies to mine as well. Maybe we have something to learn from each other."

His offer to partner her in practice was a generous one. She couldn't help but appreciate it. She gave him one of her rare smiles.

"Thank you Ed. Good to meet you. I might indeed take you up on your offer."

It wasn't long before Ed became Smita's regular sparring partner. Despite his forwardness in their introduction, he proved to be a decent guy, respectful and helpful. His passion seemed to be martial arts. He worked in the city in corporate finance, which according to him, was about the most boring job one could do. He would frequent the gym during his lunch breaks and some evenings, working out his frustrations, and refining his skills.

* * *

A month had passed since Pravin's assault at the gym. Things had progressed rapidly for Smita. With Jill's and Joan's assistance she had received pro bono legal help in preparing and filing her divorce papers. Joan assured her the divorce should now be straight forward. With Pravin's criminal charge and his public assault on her to back her case, it was almost a given.

Smita then, with the help of Jill to vouch for her, applied to the Department of Home Affairs to change her status from being a dependent on Pravin's visa to having her own independent visa. She included a copy of the criminal charge case against Pravin and her divorce papers in her application. According to the immigration lawyer she had hired, her case should be strong given Pravin's misconduct.

Things seemed to be going well. But Smita knew not to be overconfident. She felt she wasn't completely free of Pravin yet. In the meantime, she had incomplete business that needed to be dealt with.

*   *   *

When she felt ready, she made her move.

"Jill, I usually finish work at 8 pm but I think it's time I took over the late evening shift from you. I'm happy to work till late so you can leave earlier. It's about time you started enjoying some time off work."

Smita had noticed that Jill and William now regularly went out for lunch or coffee during the day. It would be nice if they also got an evening out. Besides, the late night shift fitted in with Smita's plans. Jill seemed pleased with the suggestion.

Soon thereafter, after she locked up and left the gym well past 10 pm, Smita began her weekend night vigil under the rail bridge. It seemed a remote possibility that the three scumbags, who'd tried to rape her and had killed her friend Meg more than a year ago, would be repeating their weekend night trawls. But then, she thought, tigers don't change stripes. It was a long time ago, but habits die hard. Drinking and partying around town on weekend nights was one. Something told her they were regulars.

She waited under the bridge each weekend night, starting at about 11 pm, trying to stay as inconspicuous as possible. She dressed provocatively, hoping to attract their attention as and when they arrived. On her second weekend night out she was approached.

"Hi honey, your date has arrived," a voice called out.

105

She turned to see a white male with a shaved head, wearing a leather jacket, likely making his way from the casino towards the CBD probably to meet up with friends on King Street. Not good she thought. He looked like a typical gang member, the kind usually to be avoided.

She did not respond, turned and walked away.

"Hey, hold on," he said, grabbing her by her shoulder, and spinning her around. "We made a date, and you can't just walk away."

"I think you've mistaken me for someone else. I was waiting for a different person," she replied, hoping someone would pass by.

But the street under the bridge was deserted, with only distant sounds of partying from the casino and restaurants across the river. No one came by.

He grabbed her shoulder again and pulling her to him this time.

She pushed back firmly. "Look, I don't want trouble. I just want to be left alone, please."

"What do you mean 'left alone'? You're out here, on a Friday night. If you wanted to be alone, you shouldn't have come the fuck out," he screamed.

"I have as much right to be here as you." She turned for the third time and tried to hurry away.

This time he came from behind, pulled her to him and tried to kiss her.

She hadn't anticipated this situation. She should have, in retrospect. Men somehow simply assumed a single woman on the street was there only for purposes of a sexual transaction.

This time she forcefully pushed him away with both hands and started to run.

He chased after her. As he approached she realized she had no option. She stopped abruptly, stepped aside to avoid his ongoing rush, and aimed a kick at his groin. It did not connect as intended and didn't appear to hurt.

Now he turned around, enraged, and charged at her like a bull.

This time Smita was fully prepared. She timed her blow to his nose perfectly, outstretched arm, palm open, driving its heel deep into his tender nostrils. He collapsed on his rump like a deflated balloon. His nose burst into a blood stream. He clutched his face and he screamed, perhaps more in shock than in pain.

She too was shocked at the results of her defence. Her move had worked. She had to resist her female instinct to rush to his aid. She reminded herself it wasn't a life threatening injury. He would be found by someone else. In any case, he deserved what he got. She ran, leaving him to his devices. On Elizabeth Street, not far away, she spied a public telephone booth. She called 000 and reported a man bleeding profusely from his nose under the Queensbridge Street bridge. Then she hung up.

She decided it was wise to wind up for the night. As she sat on her bed later, she reflected on the evening. It was a terrible start to her campaign to trap those three killers. Was this what she should expect as she sought them out on weekend nights? She needed to think this through. It all seemed to return to the issue of men and how they viewed women. The bastards. They needed to be taught a lesson, in their own language. A lesson to respect women.

* * *

On the following Monday, when Ed entered the Krav gym for practise, she was there, waiting, grim faced.

He seemed pleased to see her. "Hi Smiley, why so serious?"

"Smita, please," she insisted, though she was amused. "I need your help in practising defending against an aggressive person."

He was a bit taken aback by the request. "Why? Did something happen on the weekend?"

She brushed the question off. "No. I just want to be prepared. Now, I want you to come at me and try to grab me by the shoulders roughly."

Ed looked uncertain. He finally shrugged, and half-heartedly attempted what she requested.

"Ed, I'm serious about this. Can we make this realistic? I want you to be really rough."

"Jesus! You're serious about this stuff, right." He sighed. "Okay. I'll try, but I hate doing this to a woman."

"Just do it. You'll be doing me a favour. It's important for me to learn how to defend myself against aggressive men," she insisted.

He stood back for a moment. "Wait. I think I'm starting to understand what you want. Let's try to work this out conceptually first. When guys are aggressive, they can come at you with varying approaches. The gentlest type, come alongside, and put an arm around your shoulders. They're the amorous guys and will usually get the message when you tell them to buzz off. Then there are those who come up front and take hold of your shoulders, aggressively. They can push and shove, and try to dominate you. We'll try to work out how you deal with them. And then there are those, who, if you reject their advances, will try to whack you into submission before trying to sexually assault you. Let's work out the defences you'll use for each of these scenarios, and possibly other attacks. Okay?"

"Now we're getting somewhere. Let's go."

So he tried again, a bit more aggressively. She countered back as aggressively, which took him by surprise. He should not have been.

Slowly, they both got the hang of the move-counter move rhythm. He gradually increased his aggression and force. He then began mixing attack tactics. Smita responded with equal force, surprising Ed with her determination.

"Ed, you should be ashamed of yourself."

It was Esther, looking accusingly at Ed.

Both Ed and Smita froze, mid action. He looked at Esther awkwardly and shrugged, gesturing to Smita.

Smita laughed. It was the first time she had laughed in a long time. It was a laugh of triumph. She had suddenly discovered all her learning and skills coming together to the point where she was giving Ed a hard time. Ed, on his part, was consciously trying to moderate the force he used, while struggling to keep up with Smita's tactics and moves.

"You've come to my rescue, do you realise that, Esther?" asked Ed.

When she heard that Smita was the initiator, she joined in the laughter.

The sparring with Ed now took a serious turn.

"What is this, Smita? Are you on some kind of mission?"

"None of your business, mister. Just move on before I get the better of you."

Amidst all the jostling and action, they had come to enjoy a growing camaraderie in Smita's project to refine her fighting skills. Esther looked on proudly at the significant progress she was making.

CHAPTER 15

It was well past midnight, and the city had quietened down. Traffic was sparse, and the roads empty of pedestrians. The wind continued its whining journey down the city's corridors. Smita stood under the bridge, mere metres from where she and Meg had lain on the night of the attack over twelve months ago. She watched and waited.

She wasn't sure how many hours she'd been there, her feet numb and her legs aching from the icy wind. But she remained undeterred.

She recalled Meg's aging, gentle face, her wispy hair, her piercing blue eyes, and her motherly bosom as she hugged Smita upon hearing her story.

Just thinking about her friend brought fresh tears. She would never, could never, forget Meg's generosity.

Smita shook herself out of her reverie and refocused. There was no time for emotion now. She was here on a mission. If it took the rest of her life she would avenge Meg.

It had been weeks since she had taken up vigil under the bridge each Friday evening and weekend night. Was it unrealistic to expect those bastards to turn up here again, crossing from Southbank into the city? An objective observer might say she was being fanciful. The likelihood of all three coming together as they had done that night was slim? It had, after all, been more than a year.

Yet, something inside told her not to give up. To maintain the vigil. The bastards would come, eventually. As her father used to say, 'A leopard cannot change its spots'. They would come, seeking their violent entertainment. Except this time, they would be the prey.

Sure, there were risks involved. During her weekly watch she often had to deal with the inevitable advances of predatory men. While some were aggressive, she found ways to smoothly brush them off unless they became violent. Thankfully, no encounter had escalated to the level of aggression of that first encounter. And if – no, when – those men returned, it was possible she might not be able to take all three down if they attacked her together. But she had worked hard with Esther and then with Ed, to prepare for such an eventuality.

This was what she had been preparing for over the last twelve months. Now, she was ready, both mentally and physically.

Jill, now her closest friend, would be vehemently opposed if she knew Smita spent her Friday evenings and weekend nights after work on night watches. She'd already expressed strong disapproval when she guessed Smita's plan to entrap Pravin. Jill was also shocked at how Smita had allowed Pravin to assault her as part of her plan to entrap him on CCTV. Jill believed the vendetta was over after that incident. Smita preferred to keep it that way, hoping Jill would remain oblivious of her larger mission.

Reflecting on her journey in Australia, Smita marvelled at how different she was from the shy, unhappy newlywed who had landed at Melbourne airport almost three years ago. She sometimes wondered if she'd have been happier if she had just said no to her parents, refused the marriage proposal, and stayed in India. But, despite all the suffering, she felt she was a much stronger person now than she would have otherwise been. She also had an important mission, a social justice contribution to make – teaching men to better respect women.

Time ticked on and still no sign of the three. Other stragglers weaved their drunken paths into town from across the Southbank. She was about to close shop and go home when she spied a rowdy group of revellers, laughing and slapping each other's backs, as they walked across the river. They were three. Could they be the ones she was waiting for? She waited, a lioness hoping for her prey.

They reached across the river when they spied her. "Hey honey. You look just our type. We're looking for company," one shouted.

They jogged up to her - young, slim, of medium stature, stylishly dressed with white sneakers and tight pants.

She became present, aware, controlled, conscious of every move they made, and of her own stance. Anger bubbled to the surface. She pushed it down. Keep cool. That was the name of the game.

The one who had called out appeared to be the leader. French crop, ambitious pompadour, not unlike a strutting rooster. Hook nose, narrow bridge, long chin peppered with hairy stubble. She recognised him, and the others. She could never forget those faces. A thrill shot through her. The moment she had been waiting for had finally arrived.

"Nice piece of cake I see." He swaggered up to her and leaned forward to kiss her. The others behind shouted encouragement.

Too easy.

In a blink of an eye she stepped back deftly so his face met thin air; then, out of nowhere, she delivered a vicious kick to the groin. Disciplined, arched perfectly, toes pointed to the target, core muscles stable and controlled, hip flexor muscles engaged to ensure maximum power. She felt a deep satisfaction as she applied as much force as she could muster. She felt the crunch.

He screamed in pain, grabbed his crotch desperately, doubled up and fell to his knees. He kept shaking his head, unable to believe what had happened. Where did that kick come from? The prey had turned predator.

Before he or his friends could recover, she followed it with a second kick to his temple. It sent him sprawling flat to the ground. She was sure it would keep him there for a while.

Now for the others. It had happened with lightning speed, in a flash, while they stood rooted in shock, mouths open, probably trying to work out how this went so wrong. They'd been enjoying themselves, attracted to an easy target that would've made their night so much more fun. Instead, their leader was on the ground, holding his crotch, moaning in pain.

Then they sprang into action. Enraged and humiliated, they rushed her in parallel, looking to grapple her to the ground. She evaded them nimbly, leaping to her left while at the same time aiming a kick to the groin of the one nearest to her, mirroring her first move on the leader. She got him where it mattered and sent him also into a crunch, shuddering with pain.

However the third assailant had somehow adjusted his direction and before she could recover, he'd landed two successive blows to her face. Reeling from the impact, Smita struggled to keep her balance. Stars punctured her vision. The punches hurt. But she was used to pain. Pravin had made sure of that. The lessons from her sparring sessions with Ed kicked in.

She stepped back, and regained her balance. When he advanced, she stepped back again, feigning fear. But the retreat was helping her recover. As her focus returned, her face still smarting from the blows, she noted the second guy had risen and they both came at her again, this time from different directions.

She could see the hate and rage welling up in their faces. Mouths were twisted in anger, teeth gritted, jaws clammed down with determination. If they ever got her down, she knew she could expect no mercy.

She kept her cool, remembering Esther's constant counsel – fight with your head. Your strength and skill will follow. This time they approached cautiously, with more respect, she noted. They were working out the best strategy to take her down. As Smita continued to back, they approached, till suddenly she stopped, looked over their shoulders, and shouted, "Here please, help."

As both swivelled to see who the newcomer was, she leaped into a drop kick aimed directly at the jaw of the one on her left. It landed with explosive energy, perfectly, as planned. He dropped like a stone.

She landed back on ground, safely and in one smooth movement was ready for the third man. He seemed to have now abandoned all cautioned. He rushed her, fists clenched, adrenaline surging, eyes burning intensely, arms swinging wildly, determined to land a killer blow. Anger had now taken over his alcohol-doused brain. It would be his undoing. They never learn, she thought. Drink and rage made them sloppy.

The swinging blow is one of the slowest attacks to mount on a martial arts specialist. She easily leaned back and avoided his first blow, and while he was into his second arm's swing, her right arm shot out like an arrow, palm facing up, and caught him under his nostrils in a forceful blow that had him spinning, flailing, wondering what had hit him. His hands came up to his nose as he bent over in pain.

She had game played this scene. She was lucky she'd got the first one completely by surprise, and the other two were slow learners. That had helped.

The first two were still sprawled on the ground, rolling in pain. She was hoping her kicks to their heads had not been life threatening. That was drama she didn't need.

The third man was now shaking his head, trying to clear it, still holding his nose which was bleeding profusely. He looked unbelievingly at his colleagues still prone on the ground.

With his attention distracted, he encountered the trademark kick to his groin. "Owww," he howled. Yes, it had to be the groin. The bastards had tried to rape her. Here was a taste of their own medicine.

"Welcome," she said coolly. "I thought you'd enjoy that. Now tell me, do you still go around kicking homeless people, raping women, and murdering the elderly?"

All three were now on the ground, though the first one was rising to his knees. He seemed the most recovered. Shaking his head, he looked at his companions then spat out, "Fucking bitch!" But he was still not recovered enough to launch a counter attack. "Okay, bitch, you got us. Now leave us alone." He tried to rise to his feet.

"Bastard, you certainly don't like being treated the way you treat women, do you?"

Another forceful kick, this time to his solar plexus. In his haziness, he did not see it coming. He doubled up and fell to his knees again, gasping for air.

His two colleagues were getting their wits about them and also rising. Before they could stand, she aimed a kick at each of their solar plexuses as well. They screamed and doubled down in pain.

She now stood over them, dominant. Emotions controlled. Fully aware and ready.

"Do you remember, a year ago, when you scum attacked a group of homeless under this bridge. You killed a kind old lady and you tried to rape me. You are murderers and rapists. I'll show you how much fun that can be. Now rise slowly and kneel. The moment any of you tries to rise to his feet again, I will kick you where it matters, is that clear?"

No answer.

"I asked a question. If I don't get an answer, I will indeed kick you where you least enjoy it."

"Yes, Yes," they pleaded, all three, as they slowly moved into kneeling positions.

"Okay. Keep kneeling. Now take out your driver's license and hold it in your outstretched hand. I want no suspicious movement other than what I indicated. Go ahead."

They put their hands into their back pockets, fumbling for their wallets. She was surprised in a way; she had expected this to be harder.

The leader was on his feet in a second, a switchblade in hand ready to go.

He was quick, she thought, considering the beating he had taken. But she was prepared. Before his hand got in front, he encountered a kick straight at his throat throwing him back on his back and the knife spinning away. The kick was potentially life threatening, she knew. She hoped it would not be fatal.

The other two looked on stunned.

"Any more ideas, guys?" They shook their heads and held out their driver's license.

"Okay, you," she indicated to the man closest to his fallen comrade. "Still on your knees, crawl over to your brave companion, get his license out and hold it up with yours. Not a single movement out of place or you will get it worse than he did."

The leader remained prone and still.

She soon had all three licences in her hand.

"Okay. I have your identities. I know your addresses. I am going to report you to the police, that you are responsible for the murder of an old woman, under this bridge, a year ago. Also, how you attacked a young innocent woman, and how you do this regularly. If you ever try to do this again in future, I will come after you. And the next time I will show no mercy."

"Now, just so I have a safe goodbye…" She kicked the kneeling two in the throat in quick succession, though this time she held back their lethal potential. She then left them, lying prone on the ground, alongside the shimmering open switchblade waiting to be repossessed.

She made a beeline to the public telephone booth which she recollected was on Elizabeth Street and called triple zero. She explained to the operator that three men had attacked a young lady, and were attacked back in turn by a good Samaritan. They were lying under the Queensbridge Street bridge near the river. She hung up, providing no other information. As she walked home, she heard the sirens start up. There were police always on patrol in the CBD and on the Southbank, except they never seemed to be in the right place when women needed them most.

A decent night's work, she thought.

But there was still more work to be done. In her view, why was it that only men were able to walk the streets at night freely. Why did women have to regularly fear for their safety? Men did need to be taught a lesson. In a language they understood. She decided her mission was not done as yet. Her weekend night forays would now take her into the streets of the city.

CHAPTER 16

S enior Constable Emma Dickson looked up from her desk at the detective standing in front of her. They were in the Melbourne West Police Station at 313 Spencer Street.

"Hi. I am Detective Mal Simpson. Your report about the assault on the Queensbridge Street of four days ago was handed to me by the Assistant Superintendent. Can we have a chat in the meeting room?" he asked, indicating the room down the corridor.

"Sure," said Emma. "I'll also call Constable Andrew Cream. He was on duty with me that night."

They sat across each other in the small meeting room.

"I have gone through your report, Senior Constable…"

"Call me Emma. We'll skip the formalities, Mal, if it's okay with you?"

"Sure, Emma. As I was saying, I've gone through your report. Pretty thorough."

Emma nodded at the compliment.

"The case has some intriguing features. So I thought I'd have a chat with you guys."

Emma and Andrew both nodded.

"These three young men, according to your report, sustained pretty severe injuries, but are reluctant to offer any information about their assailants? Is that correct?"

"Yes. It's unusual, I agree," said Emma. "Victims typically are keen to share as much info as they can. Also, they did not call for the police. It was an anonymous woman from a phone booth on

Elizabeth Street. She claimed three men had assaulted a woman and a good Samaritan had taken them on. The victims' version however differs from the caller's. They denied attacking any woman."

"I had forgotten they still have these telephone booths around," remarked Simpson.

"Interestingly, some weeks ago we had another assault under the same bridge, and it was also called in by a female from the same booth. In that case as well, the guy injured was pretty vague on who attacked him."

"The other aspect about this case that struck me," Simpson continued, "is that all three appear to have lost their driver's license?"

"Yes. This was odd. We asked them for their driver's licences so we could verify their identities. None seemed to have their licences on them, though they were registered drivers. We asked where the licences had gone. They gave us evasive answers, saying they were probably lost. It seemed improbable that three men, on a weekend night out, had all lost their licenses at the same time. It then turned out that they had driven to Crown Casino in one car, and had parked in that car park. They had been heading across the river to a nightclub in the city, when this incident happened. If they came by car, logically, one of them at least should have had a licence."

Simpson nodded. "In regard to their injuries, you report they would not say anything about how they were injured or attacked?"

"Yes," said Andrew. "They did not want to file a complaint. They would not divulge any specific information on the assailants, saying they were a bunch of thugs. They just wanted to get away without answering further questions. Their injuries were not life-threatening, though one of them was nursing what appeared to be a rather badly injured throat. We did find a switchblade knife a couple of metres away from where we found them. But as far as we could see, they had no wounds. They must have suffered some pretty severe blows to the head and neck as evidenced by the marks and bruises. You will see this from the photographs we insisted on taking."

Simpson asked, "So, your conclusions? You don't offer any in the report, since no complaint was made. But you still felt it important to file this report."

Dickson answered. "We filed the report due to its similarity with a previous incident, in the same area, with similar severe injuries. We're monitoring emerging patterns. As for perpetrators, we did not speculate in the report without concrete evidence."

"Okay. I understand," said Simpson. "But at least across the table, would you be willing to share your theories?"

"Andrew and I disagree on this. Perhaps I'll let Andrew go first."

Andrew cleared his throat. "My guess is that it's a case of rival underworld gangs, and a fist fight. Though, I must admit, after having checked the background of the three victims, they have nothing on record to show they're involved in any underworld activity. All three come from the suburbs and are involved in small respectable business enterprises like car repairs and construction."

"And," asked Simpson, "why do you think they would not offer any information on their assailants?"

Andrew shrugged, "Possibly, because they've been threatened with severe repercussions if they do."

"And on why they did not have their driver licences?"

"That's a tough one," said Andrew. "The licences couldn't have been taken away to prevent them from driving, because they still can, on temporary ones. I simply can't figure that one out."

Simpson turned to Emma. "You obviously think differently."

"Yes and no" Emma offered. "What Andrew has suggested is a possibility. But another possibility, which I think Andrew believes isn't realistic, is that these men have initially attacked a group of women. The women turned out more than capable of taking them on. Hence their reluctance to admit they've been bested by women."

Simpson smiled. "And the absence of their licences?"

"That is what clinches my theory, I think. I suspect the women took the licences so they have possession of the identities of these men. As a threat for them not to attack women again."

Simpson nodded. "Hmmm, interesting theory; though, like Andrew, and looking at the photographs of the victims and their injuries, I find it hard to believe that they would've been beaten up by women."

Emma smiled. "Not an unexpected comment from a male, may I say."

Simpson departed, taking the file. He wanted to study it further. Though, with no complaint, it was of a limited interest to the police.

* * *

She was engrossed in her Krav practice in the gym next door to J & J's, when Ed came by, during his usual afternoon break time from the office. Their sparring practise each afternoon had become a routine. They both seemed to enjoy each other's company. He had long been a practitioner and she had learned a lot from him.

"Hi Smiley," he greeted her chirpily.

"Will you stop calling me that?" she reprimanded, though quietly pleased with the teasing. It was nice to have a male friend who respected her while also playfully teasing her.

"You know why I call you that, don't you? I'm going to continue till I see more smiles on your pretty face."

They had reached an easy camaraderie. He was still trying to figure her out though.

"It's easy for you to smile, Ed. There's not much for me to smile about in my life."

"Careful about making assumptions about anyone, Smiley. Everyone has their story. But now, I really want to know about yours?"

"Are we going to practise or gossip?" she asked.

"Okay, let's compromise. I'll teach you some new moves. After an hour, we go out for a coffee; I really want to hear your story?"

She agreed. Perhaps it would be nice to get a break from her routine. And she was required back at J & J's only at five pm.

"Has Esther taught you how to counter an attack from behind?"

"No, not yet."

"That is pretty critical because assailants often try to attack from the rear via a choke, either with their hands or their arms.

Here, let me demonstrate with you grabbing my neck from behind with your extended arm," he suggested.

"Good. Now, see what I do. First – I tuck my chin in as close to my neck as possible, over your grasping fingers or arm. This gives me a little room to breathe. By looking down it allows me to see where your feet are which is very important for my counter attack. Then, I curl my hands into hooks, and with all five fingers compressed tight together, I bring them up, elbows facing out and up, and hook them into your arms or fists – whichever is holding my neck from behind. Then I pull down sharply, from my waist, while moving to the side and using one arm to either elbow you in the solar plexus or my hand to smash into your groin. This will in most cases free you of the assailant's grip. Got it?" he asked.

"I think so. Though it seems complicated."

"With a little practise, you should be able to master the moves. Okay. Let's now try it with me as the assailant."

They did it over and over again till Ed was confident Smita had the basic moves down to a smooth flow. The hour was up.

"Time for a quick coffee before I head back to my boring job."

He was keenly interested in her background, how she found herself in Australia and then here at a gym in Banana Alley. As she shared her story, he gradually understood the roots of her simmering anger and intensity, so obvious to those who knew her well.

"So what's happened to Pravin. Is he still in your life?" he asked.

"No. His attack in the gym was recorded on CCTV. This provided adequate evidence for a police case against him, a restraining order by the court on him, as well as grounds for our divorce. I am back to my maiden name, which is a huge relief."

"And that is?" Ed asked.

"Devi. Smita Devi. I can't express what a relief this is. It's been a horrible journey. And all because I did not have the heart to stand up to my dad's dying wishes. If he only knew what he condemned me to."

"But then, you'd never have come to Australia, and you'd not have met me. So that should more than adequately make up for all that angst, right?"

"Ed, you joke about it, but you'll never know how wrenching and dehumanising it was to essentially become a slave, to lose your individuality and dignity, and be utterly dependant on someone like him."

"I'm sorry, Smita. That was pretty insensitive. I can feel the pain; but you're right, I will never really know how much you must have gone through."

She began querying him about his life. Apparently, Ed found out just a few years ago about his aboriginal origins. His mother had been taken into custody in the early 1960s; he had been born while she was in custody, presumably to a white father. He was adopted by a white Australian family. He loved his adoptive family, but was still on a quest to find his original parents.

Smita was intrigued, having little knowledge of Aboriginal history in Australia.

"How did you feel about suddenly realizing you were partly of aboriginal ancestry?" she asked.

"Shocked," he said, simply, shaking his head. "It took me quite a while to digest that and even accept it. The prejudice against aboriginals in Australian society still persists. Initially, I was not sure I wanted to be known that I was of this ancestry."

"Have you now accepted it?"

"Absolutely. Fully. I'm proud of it. It took a lot of learning and emotional hard work. But I'm now really proud to belong to a lineage that dates back thousands of years in this country."

"Are you bitter about now knowing that your mother was a stolen child, and that you were given up for adoption; and not knowing who she really is?"

He shook his head thoughtfully. "I came to realise, over time, Smita, that being bitter does not help anyone – neither me nor my community. Instead, I work hard on how I can best contribute. So, while I work as a finance professional in a corporate job, besides

Krav, my preoccupation is how I can help and contribute to uplifting the education and economic wellbeing of my community. One day, I must take you to the club which I help run for aboriginal young people. It's like a second family to me. It's a place where the kids can feel at home, use a library to study, a technical section where volunteers come to teach them different trade skills, an arts room where they can learn and experiment with painting, dancing or whatever artistic enterprise they wish. It also has a gymnasium."

"That sounds impressive." Smita was genuinely impressed.

"We receive generous support from the government and the corporate sector. And we have some strong leaders within the community. This makes a big difference."

* * *

The following Thursday they had taken a break from practise and were rehydrating themselves. Ed asked, offhandedly, "Hey Smiley, I've been thinking about these night muggers that we keep hearing about. I'm sure you've read about them. Oddly, these guys don't seem to rob their victims. And it's always men who seem to be assaulted. Not women. Pretty strange, right?" he concluded.

"Yes," she grunted, and ignored the comment.

Ed did not let it go. "I was wondering if I went out late at night in the CBD, just for the heck of it, whether these guys would try assaulting me?"

"Ed, curiosity killed the cat. Be happy with where you are. Now let's get on with practice, rather than pointless speculation."

He did not respond, but got to his feet again, ready to go on with the session.

As he was leaving for his office, he asked, "Hey Smiley. How about a coffee or a meal together tonight or tomorrow night? Tomorrow is Friday, a great night to be out."

"Ed, you know I work late at Jill's gym. Too late to have a dinner out. And with my job hours at J & J's and my practice sessions here on Krav, there is hardly any time for a break."

"Come on, Smiley. At least for a coffee?"

"Okay. We'll make it sometime next week, on condition you stop calling me 'Smiley'?"

"Deal if you smile for me now?"

Grudgingly, she did smile, tentatively at first, and then more broadly. He spontaneously came over, gave her a close hug, like it was the most natural thing in the world, and went to collect his things.

At the door, he called —"I hate to give up that nickname, but I'm hoping that I will get a smile again tomorrow. Bye." And he was off.

CHAPTER 17

It was six months since Detective Inspector Mal Simpson had last visited for a meeting with Senior Constable Emma Dickson and Constable Andrew Cream at the Spencer Street City West Police Complex. He requested another meeting.

They met in the same meeting room.

Simpson arrived noticeably out of breath despite his short walk from his nearby office. His large frame, a result of fondness for beer and meat pies, seemed to strain his chair as it creaked under his weight.

"Hi guys. Good to see you again. Seems the case of the mysterious muggings grows ever more mysterious. I've been asked to help with the investigation; at your request I understand."

"We're glad you're on board, Mal. Yes. We asked for your help because the case appears to be snowballing. Your continuity from six months when we first met on similar cases, is important."

"Can we review the highlights of the case for my benefit and bring me up to date with the current status".

Emma began. "Starting with those incidents under the rail bridge from across Crown Casino more than six months ago, every week or so we've had a case of a man, typically young, beaten up badly in what probably has been hand-to-hand combat. No weapons of attack ever crop up in any of the cases. And unlike that second case which involved three young men, the rest have been usually individuals though once there were two victims. We've had at least 15 cases reported since that first one."

Emma continued, consulting her notes, "The most interesting factor is the consistencies. In every case, the location has been the Melbourne CBD or the immediate suburbs like Brunswick, Fitzroy, Richmond and the Docklands. In none of the cases has the victim ever tried to call us for help. The call has come from passersby who find the victim in trouble. This suggests there could be, and probably are, more unreported cases."

Andrew then added. "In every case, when we've asked for a driver's licence from the victim for identification, he's been unable to produce it. Also, none of the victims have been forthcoming about the details of the attack on them. It's always the same kind of vague story about being assaulted by a group of men, or they simply choose not to say anything at all."

Simpson inquired, "Have there been other cases of assaults within the CBD during the last few months that do not match this pattern?"

"Yes," replied Emma. "There have been seven other incidents over the last six months. These are more typical - an attempted robbery, retail shop break-ins or some drunks getting it out of their system after a night out drinking. None of these other cases show the typical features of the assaults on young men that I have just described."

"So, any conclusions or suggestions from your investigation?" asked Mal.

"You mean speculation? To be truthful, we're at a dead end. We don't even know whether we have cases which we can justly pursue. The so-called victims refuse to register a complaint or a case. They refuse to give evidence. It's as if they've either bumped into a street pole injuring themselves, and are embarrassed to say so, or have encountered a gang of thugs who've threatened them with hell and brimstone if they breathe a word about the attack. And in every one of these cases – there's been no robbery. Just severe physical hurt, usually to the face, neck and groin, and strangely, the loss of the driver's licence," Emma explained.

"It almost sounds like the work of a martial artist, perhaps practising? Though the loss of the driver's licences baffles me," ventured Mal.

Both Emma and Andrew chuckled. "Interesting you say so. We've both considered the martial arts angle. But it seems pretty weird and cruel to so consistently practise your art on unsuspecting people."

"Has the press caught up with this?" asked Mal.

"This is what worries us," replied Emma. "And that's why we asked for help. I think the press smells a rat. The crime reporters keep a close eye on the crime stats and are noticing a pattern. They're starting to ask questions. When they don't get clear answers from us, they think we're hiding something."

Mal thought a bit, and then volunteered. "Perhaps one course of action is for us to investigate all the martial art gyms in the city and surrounds. I'm not sure how many they are?" He looked inquiringly at Emma.

She laughed. "We did think of that option. If you selected just the Muay Thai Kickboxing gyms in the city and surrounds, there would be over 20. In addition, we have numerous regular gyms that also offer martial arts and boxing classes. So it's going to be a daunting task. But I agree. We have to start somewhere."

"Should we bring in a case profiler before we go off checking out the gyms?" asked Emma. "Andrew and I've been trying our amateur skills at it. But perhaps a professional may be able to give us a clearer picture?"

Mal agreed to arrange for a profiler. They also agreed to divide the city into three areas and each took on the task of investigating the martial arts gyms in their assigned area.

* * *

Smita was alone in the gym. It was past 11 pm. Jill had left her early as was usual these days.

She drank thirstily from her water bottle, recovering from her warm up routine before the night's work which awaited her. She was satisfied with her fitness, her strength, her Krav skills. Taking down Pravin, and meting out those severe punishments to the three rapists and murderers was testimony enough. Then the other ventures had followed as she took her vendetta to other predatory men.

She heard the incidents had been puzzling the police. Recently, her social media accounts informed her that the press was also catching on. Good. She hoped this would send a clear message to potential predators.

As she recovered her breath, she looked around the gym, her sanctuary. She felt at home here; more than in the house she shared. She spent most of her day here. Now she would dress for her night's mission and leave for the city streets, seeking out those who preyed on women.

She had been at this task for well over six months. She had taken down between fifteen and twenty assailants, potential rapists. They deserved what they got. Her secret drawer at her home was filling with the driver's licenses she'd forced them to surrender after she'd beaten them up. She hoped the surrender of these identity cards would ensure they behaved and treated women with more respect.

However, she was beginning to feel the strain. Not physically. The demands on her body and skills were more than manageable.

It was her spirit. She was beginning to feel drained. She had become irritable at times in the gym, something that never occurred before. Ed kept telling her she was too intense. She needed to lighten up. Every time he invited her out for a coffee or a meal, she declined. She knew she remained a mystery to him. She was also aware he was attracted to her; and she to him. But could she afford to relax now?

The regular assaults on women weighed on her mind. She admitted, she'd never resolve this issue single-handedly. That was unrealistic. But she struggled with the idea of stopping. She wondered whether there was another way to address the issue. In the meantime, her relationships were suffering; her plans for a career were on hold. It would be a shame if Ed moved on.

She finally closed the gym for the night. It was a Friday night. She had made it a practice to seek out sexual predators on the last three days of the week. They were typically on the hunt these nights, preying on single women who were returning from a night out. The dark lonely streets of the city and surrounding suburbs were the ideal playground for them.

She walked along Market Street, not far from Banana Alley. She decided she'd make her way to King Street, the night club area. While that street was busy enough to discourage open sexual assaults, the little lanes off the main street were ideal for predators to hide and wait.

As was her practice, she collected herself mentally and physically for the challenge ahead. Awareness was critical. She walked up Market Street, on her way to her destination. Suddenly and unexpectedly she found herself grasped violently by an arm around her neck, the assailant behind her. This was an early one, she thought, as one arm held her neck firmly while the other came around groping her body. This was also a first. She had never been attacked from behind before. Keep cool, she advised herself. She recalled the defence and counterstrike movements she had practised with Ed for such an attack.

Her arms came up in front of her, elbows facing up. Her hands hooked into the arm gripping her. She bent her neck to give her breathing relief, and pulled down hard on the arm while trying to move to her side. To no avail. The attacker was strong, and huge. He towered behind her, almost looking down over her. His arms were enormous.

In the meantime, the grip around her neck tightened, making it hard to breathe. Smita realised she might be in over her head finally. This possibility had always been a known risk. But she had not planned adequately for the eventuality.

The assailant had now almost torn off her blouse completely with his other groping hand, and was grasping at her breasts. The arm round her neck remained in the iron-like grip. Try as she might, she could not release herself. She looked down and tried to stamp hard on his feet. He had boots. Her foot had little impact.

She was now desperate. He appeared to be getting more sexually aroused with the struggle. In a last frantic move, she brought her arms up again but this time her hands grabbed a large tuft of hair on his head, one in each hand. She was grateful he wasn't bald. She gripped the hair as firmly as she could and pulled with all her might, crunching forward at the same time. Her reward was two large tufts of hair, bunched in each hand, flying down in front of her.

"Awww!" he screamed. "Bitch. I'll fuck you to death," he yelled as he let her neck go and stepped back, clutching his head in pain with both hands then bringing them down to check, expecting to see them bathed in blood. When he looked up again, she saw his eyes ablaze with anger. His sexual arousal was now forgotten. He wanted revenge. He expected her to run. He was ready to pursue.

Smita faced a critical decision – run or confront. Reason suggested she flee. He was too big to handle. But the thought occurred - the bastard would have raped her if she hadn't set herself free. He'd find another helpless woman and she couldn't let that happen. She must remain focused on her mission.

Much to his surprise, she stood her ground. She breathed deeply trying to recover as quickly as she could from the neck assault. Now it was to be a frontal assault. She was more comfortable with this; but he was big. She wondered how she was going to cope with his size and strength.

Instinctively, she rose to her toes to match his height. She did not wait for him to attack. She launched herself into a flying kick, as powerful as she could muster, and aimed at his windpipe. He did not expect it. It landed as targeted, and he collapsed like a deflated balloon. It was a potentially lethal move. This was the first time she had tried this move with this force on a real person. Ed had warned her it was dangerous, possibly life threatening. Fractures of the cartilage structures of the larynx or trachea could cause air to escape into the neck and chest, leading to significant respiratory compromise.

But she felt she had little option, given the man's strength, aggressiveness, and determination. It was possibly her life against his.

He lay on the ground, writhing, struggling to breathe. No time to pursue the usual driver's license routine, she decided. She needed to get help for him as soon as possible. There was no phone booth close by to call for emergency help. She would not use her own phone which could be traced. She did the next best thing that came to mind - she let off an almighty scream and repeated it again for good measure. She was sure it would be heard somewhere; this was the city, and it was a Friday night. She then scooted, torn blouse and all, into the nearest lane she could find and made her way unobtrusively towards Banana Alley. It wasn't long before she heard the sirens. She hoped the guy was still alive by the time help arrived.

She was shaken by the encounter. It had finally happened – a situation which had spiralled out of her control. And possibly, resulting in a death. She hoped the man survived despite his violent aggression.

Back in the gym, she got herself a new blouse, then made her way home by a tram. She reached her house nervous, unsettled, and drained. That was a close shave, she thought ruefully. She had come close to losing her life, and possibly taking another's. She had left him writhing on the ground, holding his throat, and struggling to breathe. The image would stay with her for a while.

She examined herself in the mirror and saw a large dark welt around her neck indicating the strength of the assailant's chokehold. This was going to need some pretty nifty explanations the next day at work. Her neck was throbbing; it was painful to even turn her head.

She applied ice to the injury, as she lay on the bed trying to regain her balance.

She was deeply unhappy with herself. She acknowledged she had somehow lost her way in pursuit of her vendetta. In seeking power and domination over predatory men, she had in fact become a pale imitation of the predators she so despised.

Where had the happy, cheerful, friendly and warm Smita gone? She had become bitter, vengeful, angry and power hungry.

There was no purpose to now despising herself. She needed to reclaim who she really was. She had to go back to the Smita that Jill loved and befriended; the Smita that Ed found so engaging and who he teased so unceasingly, in the hope of bringing forth the smiles and spontaneity he knew lay within.

She was missing out on life with this vendetta thing. It was time to leave it all behind. How many more predatory men was she going to teach a lesson to? There seemed to be an insatiable supply.

There must be a more constructive way of achieving her goal without sacrificing her own internal wellbeing and spontaneity.

The cause remained – empowering women to overcome adversity; to cope with predatory men; to assist women assert their rights, particularly in abusive relationships. But it was women themselves who could and would do it. Her role should be to somehow find useful ways of supporting them in this endeavour.

Jill and Ed would help her find new ways, she decided.

CHAPTER 18

The next day she arrived for work, a scarf wrapped tightly around her neck. Her face looked drawn and tired. She had barely slept that night, reeling from her close encounter with death, but relieved to be alive. She shuddered as she recollected how close he had come to throttling her. She had no idea where she had found the strength to fight back. It had been sheer instinct - tearing his hair out, forcing him to release his stranglehold. It was the same instinct that had made his windpipe her target, bringing him down in one strike. But there was no sense of triumph. Her soul felt empty. Her body drained. She had almost taken his life, if the news media was to be believed. He was, apparently, in a serious condition in hospital and unable to even speak to the police.

As she skimmed the news outlets on her phone, her hands began to shake; she broke into a sweat; her heart beat faster as she read the numerous reports of the 'weekend mugger', apparently at work again. Demands for urgent police action seemed to be mounting.

Doubts assailed her, piling on unceasingly as she tried to concentrate on her work and welcome clients as they entered the gym. Saturday mornings were typically busy, a popular time at the gym.

Jill finally arrived. As soon as she saw Smita, she sensed something was amiss. She was most solicitous, wanting to know what was wrong. Why the scarf? Shouldn't Smita take the day off if she was unwell? Smita brushed off her concerns, insisting she was fine, just a little under the weather. But she could tell that Jill's suspicions were growing.

As the morning progressed, gym-goers chatted about the morning news headlines and last night's mugging incident on the close by Market Street. The men in particular ribbed each other about how they now needed to be more careful than the women, on their night out. Perhaps it was time to start avoiding Friday nights altogether.

Smita kept away from Jill as much as she could that morning, busying herself around the gym. But she could see Jill glancing at her regularly, questions written all over her face. As the morning wore on, focusing on her work became increasingly difficult. Her body was sore. Her neck throbbed constantly. Her head ached.

By lunch time, the pain in her neck was unbearable. She reluctantly approached Jill.

"Jill, I'm sorry, but do you mind I take the afternoon off? I do feel under the weather."

Jill looked at her with concern. She put her arm around Smita. Smita winced with pain. Her whole body felt like pins and needles. She had not realised how much the incident had affected her body.

Jill noticed the wince and moved away. "Of course, my dear. Please do. Is there anything I can do? You really do look unwell."

"I'll be fine, Jill. Really. Thank you. I just need to sleep it off, I think."

Then, before Jill could ask any more questions, she fled the gym.

* * *

Jill's suspicions grew as the day wore on. Normally, nothing ever seemed to get Smita down as far as Jill could remember. Ever since she had met a nervous Smita who had walked into her office seeking a job nearly three years ago, she had come to know this woman as indomitable, driven.

They had become close friends over this period. Jill had been touched by how Smita always looked out for her. Besides becoming a key contributor to the business, and helping Jill grow it substantially, she also had a hand in bringing Jill and William together. The romance was now blooming and had made a significant difference to Jill's personal life. While Smita owed Jill for giving her a job and then lodging her when she was injured, Smita had paid back in spades. She had become a close and dear friend.

"Hi Ed. You looking for Smita?"

Ed had sauntered into the gym. These days he visited the gym on weekends too, hoping to spend time with Smita.

"Yea. Where is she hiding?"

"Gone home, Ed," Jill replied.

"Gone home? That's unusual. Is she ill or something?" he queried, his concern evident.

"I'm worried, Ed. Sit. I need to talk about something," Jill said in a serious tone.

Ed sat, looking uncertain about the nature of this conversation.

"I'm not sure where to begin or even that I should be discussing this with you, Ed. But there's no one else I can talk with about this. And I hope I'm right in thinking that you care for Smita as much as I do."

Ed's attention perked. "Now you have me worried too, Jill. What happened to Smita? Is she okay?"

"She came in this morning with a big scarf around her neck. I think it was to conceal an injury on her neck which she could only have got overnight. Her face was drawn and she looked exhausted; like she had not slept last night. She refused to talk about it, saying she was just a bit under the weather. But she obviously could not cope with work; she asked if she could go home since she needed to sleep it off."

"Jeez. Doesn't sound like Smita," Ed remarked.

"Exactly, Ed. Have you read the latest media reports this morning?"

"I'm not a newsfeed person, Jill. Does it have something to do with Smita?"

"It's about the latest escapades of the 'weekend mugger' as the press call this person. I suppose you've heard about the muggings taking place over the last few months in the city on weekend nights?"

"Yes," he replied, wondering if Jill was thinking along the same lines as he did.

"There's a guy in hospital with a severe neck injury from a mugging last night. Again, a guy. All the muggings being reported are of young guys. I don't hear of muggings of women anymore in the city. Have you?"

"Come to think of it, no."

"Look at it like this, Ed. Smita spends most of her time either here in J&J's or in the next door Krav gym, working or practising. She seems to have no other interest beyond helping with the gym and continually improving her fitness and Krav skills. There must be a reason for such dedication, right?"

"I suppose so. She's certainly come a long way in a very short time in her martial arts skills. I don't recollect knowing anyone else in the martial arts community, and I know quite a few practitioners, who've become so skilled so quickly. But I assumed it was a hobby."

"Ed, has she told you about her life's journey over the last few years?"

Ed hesitated before answering. "Only some bits and pieces."

Jill elaborated. "She's had a tough time with men, starting with her father, though his intentions were good despite being selfish. Pravin was a nightmare. Then she was almost raped and her best friend Meg was killed by would-be rapists. There might be more she hasn't shared. I wouldn't blame her if she thinks she wants to put all men in their rightful place."

"I've had similar thoughts, Jill" admitted Ed. "But it's hard to believe Smita would choose such an extreme way to deal with it."

"Ed, sometimes circumstances push us in certain directions. I'm discussing this with you because I think we both care deeply for her. We need to help her get out of this situation if she is really involved."

"You're convinced she is indeed the mugger?"

"Look, these are the facts the media is reporting. Last night's case was exactly similar to the spate of muggings happening virtually every weekend. They are not gang related, and there is never any associated robbery. The victims always refuse to be interviewed by the press or say anything about their attacker. As I said, all the muggings were of young men. In fact, the numbers of assaults and attempted rapes on women in the last six months is substantially down."

"Wouldn't the CCTVs on the city streets have caught anything of these incidents on their cameras?"

"That's what worries me, Ed. If they have, then Smita is in real trouble."

"So what do you suggest we do about this?"

"We have to get Smita to talk about it herself. Accusations will simply make her more defensive, and withdraw into her shell. As far as I can see, we are her only two friends. We have a responsibility to gradually help her get out of this. I'm sure she can. At heart she is kind and gentle. Anger has seeped down and taken over. She needs to gradually let it go."

Ed sighed. "Okay. Deal. I'll certainly give it my best shot."

* * *

Assistant Superintendent Julian Mason, responsible for law and order in Melbourne City and immediate suburbs, was well informed about the local situation. He read the newspapers and monitored social media for public opinion daily. Mason valued these sources for providing a broader perspective as his daily internal police briefings could sometimes be biased.

At 10 am that morning, Detective Inspector Simpson, Senior Constable Emma Dickson, and Constable Andrew Cream arrived for a meeting with him. Mason invited them to sit down. He wanted to discuss the ongoing investigation.

"Good morning and thank you for coming. I don't usually delve into day-to-day cases. But when a pattern emerges, it always concerns me. I wouldn't be surprised if it concerned our politicians as well. And when it does, they'll be on the phone to me. So, I need your first-hand brief on these muggings, not just the sanitised bullshit that comes to my table each morning."

Detective Inspector Simpson began to respond but Mason interrupted him. "If you don't mind, Simpson, I'd prefer you first,

Senior Constable Dickson. You are after all the person on the ground dealing with this."

"Thank you, sir," said Dickson. "In summary, as you've observed, there is an intriguing trend here. The victims are always young individual males; never females. In fact, the record of female muggings in the city and surrounds has decreased over the last six months, almost proportionate to the increase in the number of male muggings. We're not sure these two trends are related. Secondly, we do have males regularly involved in fights in the city particularly at nights; but those incidents are usually related to groups or gangs coming into conflict after a night out drinking. None of these cases exhibit indications of this. A few of the cases have been captured on CCTV.

The images we have are fuzzy due to poor night lighting. But in all the cases where we do have camera images, the incidents are between two individuals, where one attacks the other; the attacked person then turns tables on the attacker and brings him down."

Dickson continued, "The would-be attacker is then subjected to a severe beating, but with no sign of weapons such as knives, batons or guns. So we are forced to assume that the perpetrator is possibly a martial arts specialist."

"Interesting," remarked the Assistant Superintendent. "So we appear to have a roving individual, who specialises in martial arts and practises his skills on ordinary citizens. It seems odd that such a character would suddenly emerge over the last six months, that is, if it is indeed the same person in all these incidents."

The Assistant Superintendent continued, "And by the way, are you telling me the CCTV footage we have so far has been unable to identify the person who metes out the beatings?"

"Yes, sir. The images are too hazy for identification. The only definite issue we have found is that the individual who is initially attacked but then counters the attack is always slightly built."

"What do you mean slightly built?"

"Well, more like a female. But we are reluctant to definitely confirm this given the haziness of the images."

Mason queried, "Anything remarkable about the victims besides the fact that they are young and male?"

"Yes, sir. All the victims have lost their driver's licences, which they can't account for. Except for the case two days ago. This man was seriously injured, in his windpipe, and is still in hospital in critical condition. Chances are that he may not recover. He has also lost two large tufts of hair with scalp, presumably ripped off during the incident. It would have been very painful to have that amount of hair pulled out at one time.

The act of pulling hair, sir," she continued, "is typically a defence used by someone at a physical disadvantage. Given that the injured man is quite big and robust, it's possible he was the aggressor, and the other person, likely smaller, resorted to pulling his hair in self-defence, before kicking his windpipe. This scenario fits particularly if the larger man grabbed the smaller individual from behind."

"Understood. Continue with your investigation. But I'm more interested in what proactive steps we're taking to curb these incidents. Detective Inspector you have a go now."

The Detective Inspector responded. "We've initiated an investigation of all the martial arts gyms in the city. There are well over 40 of them with hundreds of practitioners. So it's going to be a mammoth task. Also, we've asked for increased night patrols through the city streets, particularly for the window of Friday to Sunday."

The Superintendent interrupted. "Have you considered using a profiler to stitch together a picture of the assailant or assailants?"

"Yes sir, we have. In summary, the profiler suggests the obvious - the assailant is probably an individual rather than a gang. He or she is a loner, possibly between the ages of 20 to 30 years. The assailant is motivated by a personal vendetta against young men stemming from past violence or sexual assault. The assailant could be a young woman or gay man who has acquired martial arts skills."

He continued, "It's probable that the victims have initiated the attack or assault on the assailant in the first place. This begs the question whether the assailant is deliberating provoking the victims to assault him or her. The locale of the attacks is the city and its immediate suburbs. This suggests the assailant is possibly a resident of these areas. The consistent loss of driver's licences among the victims implies the assailant wants to maintain some control or a threat over the victims to prevent further sexual assaults by them."

"Good work. Keep me updated on the investigation's progress. We can't let this situation escalate."

CHAPTER 19

It was the Monday after the Friday mugging incident on Market Street. In St. Vincent's Hospital in Fitzroy, Big Jake lay in his bed, in a ward of with three other patients. His throat was bandaged heavily; he was struggling to breathe. A drip feed was connected to his right hand. Emotionally, he was still in shock at what had happened on Friday night on Market Street. Talk about the unexpected. How the fuck did that little skimp of a woman get him down so effectively? It was unbelievable.

Here he was, the leader of a gang, all fucked up, lying in a bloody hospital room, surrounded by the sick and the smell of antiseptics. Pathetic. Jake felt both fury and embarrassment.

He knew the police were eager to interview him as soon as the docs permitted. Though he could whisper, a significant improvement from the previous day, he still relied on the drip feed since swallowing was too painful and medically inadvisable.

There were murmurings at the door of the ward and in walked his younger brother Chad with Jaz, his best friend. Both were huge, imposing young men, heavily tattooed, blond haired and piercing eyes. They strutted into the room rather than walked, surveying the other three patients with domineering looks.

"What the fuck happened?" asked Chad, as he both approached Big Jake's bed and leaned down to talk.

Big Jake, exhausted and humiliated, was in no mood to talk. All he wanted was to lie quietly and hope that, as the docs had indicated, he'd recover fully, though slowly. Besides, the truth was embarrassing. He dared not allow even the slightest rumour of it emerge.

He looked up and nodded in recognition. Chad held his hand and squeezed. Big Jake squeezed back and tried to shrug indicating in sign language he couldn't talk.

"No need to talk, bro." They'd been advised by the nurse, before entering, not to encourage Big Jake to speak. "No worries. We'll find this bastard and take care of him. Was it one guy or more? Just show us with your fingers."

Big Jake held up three fingers. Three would probably be an excuse enough for becoming a cropper.

"Must have been those Asian ninja fuckers, right?" Chad speculated.

Big Jake nodded, eager to end the conversation.

"No worries, mate. We will take them on, Big Jake. We'll show them motherfuckers who's the boss in town."

Chad and Jaz sat a while at his bedside, planning next steps while Big Jake hoped the whole bloody thing would just blow away. He wanted no more questions. No more probing. The fucking humiliation was too much to bear. Just the image of her totally unexpected flying kick approaching him, and then the stinging, shooting pain in his throat was too much to cope with just now. But one day, yes one day, he would eventually find her. And then, there would be hell to pay.

* * *

On the other side of town, in North Melbourne, Duc Nguyen, head of the Association of Martial Arts Clubs of Melbourne, was on the phone with his friend Somsak in Richmond.

"Hey Somsak. How you going? Seen the news about the Melbourne Night-Mugger incident on Friday night?" Duc inquired.

"Yup, I have. Who the fuck is it? Do you know? Not getting us any good press, is it?" Somsak replied.

"The press and police as usual seem to be ganging up on the martial arts community, calling us thugs and out of control. I don't know who this guy or guys are, but they're giving us a bloody bad name, and we can't just sit back and take it."

Somsak ran a martial arts club in Richmond. He was close to Duc. They were about the same age, in their late thirties. They had linked and chequered careers since their youth. Firebrands in their heyday, they were often in trouble with the police. But with age, they had matured. They were now respectable martial arts gym owners and savvy businessmen. They had capitalised successfully on the growing fitness trend and had encouraged colleagues and friends to also start up martial arts classes or clubs. Duc was now the head of the Association of Martial Arts Clubs in Victoria, and Somsak was his deputy. They now faced a reputational crisis due to the recent incidents.

"Yup Duc. I've been following the news. Bloody concerning. The media have a habit of whipping up issues. But these attacks are becoming a trend and giving our industry a bad name. I think the executive committee should meet soon to decide on some proactive response."

They agreed to convene the meeting on Wednesday at Duc's gym in North Melbourne.

* * *

Ed was worried for Smita. It did not take a genius to work out that she harboured a deep need for justice and vengeance against sexual predators. Her experiences probably justified her feelings.

He had closely followed her behaviour patterns ever since growing close to her. She never socialized after dark. She worked seven days a week, and trained intensively at her martial arts skills, though she was almost as good as him. The increasing reports that a martial arts specialist was taking down young men, while the assaults on women had decreased, could not but lead to the conclusion that the person responsible was none other than his dear friend. A troubling conclusion.

Fighting was a risky business, and especially so when it was a female versus a male, however skilled the female was. His worry increased.

He walked into J & J's after his afternoon Krav session on Monday. Smita had not turned up for her sparring session with him. She was at the reception desk, a scarf around her neck, looking pale and drawn.

"Hey Smiley. What's with the scarf? Skipping practice today?"

She brushed it off. "Just not feeling well. Anyway, good to take a break sometime, right?" she replied with a forced smile.

He changed the subject.

"Hey, why don't you come with me this Thursday evening to visit my Aboriginal Club in Fitzroy? You've always said you'd be interested. I'm there every Thursday evening to give martial arts classes and have a chat with the kids. Can you make it? Later we can have a quick meal."

He could see her ambivalence. Then, a surprise.

"Sure. I'll come. But I'll have to arrange with Jill for an early release from the gym. She may have a date on Thursday night."

"Leave that to me." Ed promptly walked over to Jill who was with a client, and asked for a moment of her time when she was free.

"Sure. Let's do it now if it doesn't take long. My client can manage on her own for a bit."

They moved away.

"I want to take Smita to visit my Aboriginal Club in Fitzroy on Thursday evening. She's agreed but she's on duty; can you release her?"

"Ed," Jill said in a whisper, "I'd be really grateful if you could take her out. Not sure how you managed to persuade her. I can now easily afford casuals, and have been in any case thinking of taking on a new staff. So yes, please do take her out."

Ed smiled. "Actually, I did not have to try too hard. It's a good sign. Perhaps she's realising she needs to change course. And, if I can get her into the habit of taking time off, maybe we can all have a double date with you and William?"

His eyes twinkled.

Jill laughed. "She's been naughty, telling on me. That sounds wonderful. How about next week?"

"Great. I'll take you up on that." He winked at Jill, left her, and sauntered back to Smita.

"Hey Smiley."

She interrupted him. "You promised you would not use that name, right?"

He grinned sheepishly. "Sorry. I was in a good mood. Okay, Smits, the boss has said yes. In fact she insists. Thursday night is a date. I'll see you at 6 pm."

He gave her thumbs up and left to go back to his work.

* * *

The executive committee of the Association of Martial Arts Clubs of Melbourne convened on Wednesday evening at Duc's North Melbourne gym.

The sole agenda item was addressing the recent string of martial arts-related attacks in the city and suburbs, and the negative publicity this was giving their businesses. The attendees had made queries from all their associated clubs before arriving. No one seemed to know who this person was or the motivation for this sudden spurt of attacks.

They unanimously agreed it was in their interest to take a proactive stance. They'd issue a statement to both the police and the media, dissociating their member clubs from the attacks and offering cooperation with the police in the investigations.

Then Charlie Hu, the owner of a club in Collingwood, piped up.

"I've been thinking of an additional option. Why don't we get a group of guys, on a rotating basis, to walk the streets of the city for a few hours each night? We can't let this bastard keep giving us a bad name?"

"Hold on now, Charlie," said Duc. "I don't want to make this situation worse. What if we do find him, what then? We pick a fight? And then the police come in and say – see, we knew it was you guys all along?"

Charlie was not to be dissuaded. He wanted some action. "No, Duc. We can't just sit back. Okay. Let's at least agree we make the rounds each night, to message this guy he can't go on like this. No violence. We'll not start a fight. Okay?"

Duc was not convinced. But he saw he could not turn Charlie.

They left the meeting with Duc and Somsak convinced Charlie was going to exacerbate the situation. But a majority thought it would be a good idea to at least try Charlie's suggestion for a while.

Duc's and Somsak's worry would prove to be prescient.

* * *

On the other side of town, in the precinct of Collingwood, Chad and Jaz called for a meeting of the White Boys Fight Club at their favourite local pub.

"Chad, I heard Big Jake got beaten a few nights ago in the city and is now in hospital. What the fuck happened?" asked Boxer Jones as he entered.

"The bastard's been fucked. He can only whisper. Kicked in the throat. The docs say he won't be able to speak clearly for a while. He's in shit street."

"Did he say who did this to him? We can't let the motherfucker get away with it."

"Big Jake can't talk. I asked him how many attackers. He indicated three. I told him we'll get revenge for him."

The White Boys Fight Club was an informal club, almost secret, with no set headquarters, and only informal membership of young, white males who were disenchanted with the recent influx of immigrants to Australia.

The young men claimed they represented the view of many white Aussies that the old way of life and culture of white Australia was fast losing ground, giving way to Asian, South Asian, Middle Eastern and African immigrants. Group members claimed they were preparing for what they believed would be an upcoming race conflict in Australia.

The group had "cells" in multiple states across Australia, and were also in communication with white supremacy groups in the United States and Europe.

They wanted to "cleanse" Australia and referred to ethnic and religious minority groups as 'unters', a reference to the Nazi Germany word 'Untermensch', meaning sub-human.

Boxer Jones was one of the leaders of the group in the city area. He lived in Collingwood and hated seeing how the Asian population was quietly taking over the city.

Boxer peered into his beer. "I need to have a think on this. We just can't let it go" he kept saying, shaking his head.

"What if it is one of these Asian fuckers? Next thing we know they'll be trumpeting it on the fucking billboards and we'll look like shit. Can't let it happen."

"By the way," said Chad, "my Facebook newsfeed says this is happening every weekend. One of our young guys is copping it every week. Can you believe that? This is a fucking invasion. We can't just lie down and take it."

Boxer Jones agreed.

"I'll get some bros together. We'll take this front on. It's a fucking challenge. I'll call around. Some of us need to do some roving around town this weekend. I want to find and put these bastards down. But only those who are up for a fucking fight should come. If we get into a fight, I want to come out on top. We meet Friday night here."

CHAPTER 20

I t was Wednesday morning when Senior Constable Emma Dickson walked into J&J's Gym. Jill, who was at the desk, looked up inquiringly, surprised to see the senior police officer again.

"Hello Jill. I wonder if I can have a few moments of yours and Smita's?" Dickson asked.

"Sure, Officer. I'll get Smita. She is around in the gym somewhere."

Jill returned with Smita, who was still wearing her scarf.

Emma noted this with interest.

"Hi. Thanks for your time. Can we sit if you don't mind?"

Jill invited Dickson to a corner in the front office where there was a little table and some chairs.

"You've probably heard there have been muggings regularly in the city and surrounding suburbs over the last six months. It's become a concerning trend. We're taking it seriously. We're now investigating all the gyms who teach martial arts to ask whether the owners and staff have seen anything suspicious."

Both Jill and Smita looked at each other. Jill wanted to see Smita's reaction. They both shrugged.

Jill answered "Yes, Officer. We've heard of the muggings. I've been worried and I've warned Smita to be cautious when we close each night and on her way home. But no, nothing out of the ordinary here."

"I know both of you are martial arts experts," said Dickson.

"Are we?" challenged Jill. "I am not sure about the 'expert' part, Officer. But nevertheless, are you saying we, too, are suspects? I believe its young men who've been mugged. You don't realistically think either of us could do that?"

"Come on, Jill. I've seen how you took down that guy in the robbery assault in this gym, and how Smita took down her husband. But no, you guys are not suspects - as yet. However, I do need to know your whereabouts on the last weekend starting last week Friday night. "

Jill appeared slightly offended by the question. Smita remained silent, though her heart beat faster. This was coming too close for her comfort.

"You're serious, right, Officer?"

"As I said, Jill, we've taken on the task of monitoring all the martial arts practitioners in the city's gyms and are spot checking their whereabouts at certain times. So, no offence. But I do need to know."

"That's a pretty big task," suggested Jill. "This gym itself probably has ten to fifteen practitioners; the Krav gym next door has some 30 at least. There must be hundreds across the city. This seems to be becoming a major operation."

"Yes. It's a huge task. But the muggings have become a trend, Jill, and we have to now take them seriously in the interest of public safety."

Suddenly, Smita reached for her phone, scrolled down and handed it to Dickson. "Could you please take a look at this report and tell me what you think?" Smita asked.

Jill was puzzled at Smita's unexpected move. Dickson, equally surprised, took the phone and read. It was an ABC report of a week ago. It that said violent attacks on women across Melbourne and its suburbs had risen fifteen percent over the last year. Approximately one woman a week was being assaulted, either in a domestic violence situation or attacked by a stranger. The stats for Australia as a whole were even worse.

"May I ask," queried Smita, "would you also call this a trend or perhaps an epidemic? And are the police doing anything about it?"

Dickson read again; then stayed silent for a while.

Finally, she looked at Smita. "We're taking the issue of domestic violence also very seriously, believe me."

"Is that so?" asked Smita, plucking up her courage. "Then perhaps you may wish to give me a minute more of your time and read this."

She took back the phone, scrolled again and gave it back to Dickson. It was a short article, again from ABC, describing a recent incident where police landed up at a city apartment after a 000 call, could not understand the language the woman was blabbering in, obviously distressed. Her smooth-talking English-speaking husband explained that she was mentally unstable and was becoming violent. The officers took his statement and promptly arrested the woman. It turned out, after later investigations, that he was the violent abuser. Mounting evidence suggested misidentification is alarmingly common and is derailing the lives of potentially thousands of women around the country every year.

"What are you trying to say, Smita? That we should not be doing this investigation? That we should not be interviewing women like you and Jill?" demanded Emma.

Smita shrugged. She finally said, quietly, "I wish you guys would take the violence against women as seriously as you do other crimes. That's all I am asking."

Dickson grew more empathetic. "I see your point, Smita. I do agree that violence against women is becoming a major issue. I promise you the police are trying to do better. Okay? But just now, we have to address these muggings. Let's talk about those martial arts practitioners in your gym, as well as your whereabouts last Friday evening."

Smita gave her a cynical smile. Dickson was not pleased to be put in a tough spot.

* * *

Senior Constable Dickson left the interview at J & J's in a reflective mood. She found the two women intriguing. She could not shake the feeling there might be a link between them and the muggings, though it seemed, at first sight, rather a stretch. She had encountered both women in the aftermath of violent situations with men, and both had come out on top. She remembered Smita from hospital when she interviewed her about the attempted rape and the murder of her friend, Meg. It was evident Smita, in particular, was frustrated by the aggression of men and their violence against women. She resolved to keep her suspicions to herself, for now. But she planned to keep a close eye on their activities.

*　*　*

The interview with Senior Constable Dickson left both Jill and Smita thoughtful. Smita immediately moved away and busied herself in the gym, clearly trying to avoid any further discussion about the interview.

Jill was now more than ever, convinced that Smita was the mysterious night mugger. She empathised with Smita's reasons. The woman had been through hell the last couple of years, largely at the hands of exploitative and predatory men. Jill resolved to gently steer Smita from her dangerous path and obsession. She was grateful for Ed's support in this endeavour.

Smita however, was grappling with deep guilt. The interview had inadvertently implicated her closest friend and benefactor. She was deeply indebted to Jill for both her job and the opportunity to master Krav Maga. The thought of implicating Jill in her troubles weighed heavily on her. She could not afford to drag Jill further into the mess that seemed to be overtaking her.

She decided that if there was the slightest indication that the police were going to take their suspicions about her and Jill any further, she would immediately offer Jill her resignation. Though this brought on a deep sense of sadness. Jill had become her pillar. Her friendship lit up Smita's life. Also, her life had now been built around physical fitness and providing training to others. She loved her work and her job. It had also brought her in contact with Ed. It would be wrenching to leave.

151

CHAPTER 21

It was Thursday evening. Ed arrived at the gym at 6 pm as planned. The stubborn welt around Smita's neck had slowly faded though not as quickly as she'd have liked. Marks were still visible if one looked closely. She had stopped wearing the scarf but chose a high neck jumper to help conceal the remaining marks.

"Hi Smits. Your date has arrived," he announced.

"This is not a date, Mr. Ed Houghton, just so you know. I've only agreed to visit your Aboriginal Youth Club. But I won't argue. Not a good way to start the evening. Let's go."

It was a pleasant experience, walking the streets of Melbourne with Ed. She was growing fonder of him by the week. She was concerned, though. Was it wise to encourage this relationship? After all, she still had a mission. But then the question arose – when would the mission end? There seemed to be a never ending stream of young, violent men, always on the look out to harass women. But in truth, she was growing tired. It was not a normal life. She longed for the ordinariness of a regular life.

Then there was last Friday night's encounter. It highlighted the risks she was taking. The police were also now on guard, closely monitoring the situation. Things were getting perilously dangerous.

"So, how's the neck?" he asked suddenly.

She was startled. She had forgotten. Her hand unconsciously moved to her neck. She wasn't wearing a scarf today, but she was relieved she had on a high-neck jumper, hiding the remnants of the welt.

She quickly, almost guiltily, lowered her hand. He had noticed her spontaneous reaction.

"What do you mean - the neck?" she asked. "There's no problem with my neck, thank you," she replied sharply.

"Still feeling a bit under the weather?" he persisted.

"Ed, can we not talk about my health. I appreciate your concern. But now I'm more interested in learning about your Aboriginal Youth Club."

He took the hint and moved on to explain how the Club had started, it's funding sources, and who was involved. As she listened, her interest grew. She also realized this was the first time in the last two years or so, that she was involving herself in something other than work, Krav and her mission.

The Club was housed in a repurposed two-storey pub on the corner of two streets in Collingwood. The local Council, in collaboration with the State Government, had converted it into a centre for aboriginal youth. Beyond the front door entrance, was a longish corridor. On one side was a study room with rows of desks and computers, where some kids were studying. On the opposite side was a well-stocked library. Upstairs was a large room converted into a technical centre where kids learned trade skills from volunteers. Downstairs, at the end of the corridor, was another large room turned into a gym. In one corner a small group of youngsters practised martial arts; the other corner had boxing bags hanging from the ceiling. A third corner housed gym equipment including rowing machines, treadmills and dumbbells. Behind the building was a long garage, now a dormitory for boys and girls from remote communities in Victoria where no local schools were available.

The kids gave Ed a rousing welcome as they entered the facility. In the gym, the kids practising martial arts swarmed around him, playfully trying to take him down. Smita watched as Ed skilfully engaged with them, demonstrating not only the kids' skill, most aged between twelve and fifteen, but also his caring approach. He treated them with care and respect.

Eventually, Ed called time out and introduced Smita, telling them she too was an expert at martial arts. The five girls of the group were thrilled. They pulled her aside and asked her to spar with them. She was surprised by their skills. She asked where they had learned these. Apparently, Ed was their sole instructor. He visited once a week and sometimes on weekends, focussing on fitness and martial arts. She realized this was serious commitment on his part. Her respect for him deepened.

Before Smita realised it, it was well past 8 pm. The Club was nearing its closing time. Some seniors were now moving around reminding everyone that only 15 minutes remained.

The youngsters, the girls in particular, were now clinging to Smita. To them she was a revelation. The same colour, yet not aboriginal. Female and yet as skilled at Krav as Ed. She had become their hero in just one evening. They made her promise to return with Ed again.

As parents and guardians began arriving to take some kids home. Smita inquired where they came from. As far as she could estimate, there must have been at least 30 kids at the Centre that evening, involved in various activities. Just 12 lived in the dorm.

"Neighbouring suburbs, generally," answered Ed. "We have big public housing units in Carlton, Richmond and North Melbourne. Many come from there. The Centre is easily accessible by public transport from these suburbs. Though not all are here each evening. Some come especially for the fitness and martial arts classes. Others for tutoring in maths and science."

* * *

Later, over dinner in a restaurant on Victoria Street in Richmond, they ate Vietnamese, a favourite cuisine for both. They chatted about the Centre, as Smita learned details about each kid. She was amazed that Ed knew the back story of every kid. Some stories were heartbreakingly tragic. She was moved at how emotional and teary he became when recounting some.

"But now, let's talk about you, Smita."

She became wary; on guard again.

"I realize I hardly know you, Smita. Behind your superwoman mask of steeliness, competence and focus there's more. I'm trying to understand better. Can you help me?"

She laughed. "You make me sound like an ogre."

He leaned forward, took her hand, looked into her eyes. "Smita, every person needs to confide in someone; to let their guard down. I want to be that friend for you. I know you've had a hard life. I can only guess how difficult it must have been living with your ex. I have heard about the attempted rape and hospitalization from Jill. Look. I don't want to pry. Only to be helpful. Please trust me."

Smita's eyes welled with tears, touched by his earnestness and sincerity.

"So, what do you want to know?" she asked, deciding to open up to him.

He looked at her for a while. Then said, cautiously, "Please don't be upset by what I am to say. I only have your best interests at heart. But can you please reconsider these vendetta nights? They don't help you or your cause, Smita."

She was startled. She sat back in stunned silence. She knew he had suspicions, but his directness caught her off guard.

"What do you know about me or my mission, Ed?"

"I know you're bitter, Smita. But bitterness doesn't help anyone, especially not you. You deserve a better life. Give yourself a chance please. It seems like you're taking on the burdens of all women. This isn't going to resolve anything. The issue with predatory men usually starts in their youth - violent backgrounds, broken families, poor parenting, and the kind of values instilled in their malleable years. If you want to resolve their aggressiveness, you need to work with them when young. That's why I work with the Club."

She stayed silent. He was still holding her hand. She did not withdraw it. His candour and concern touched her. And his advice was sound, she realised.

Then, her shoulders sagged. "I'm tired, Ed," she confessed. "This mission has been exhausting. I've often questioned whether it's the appropriate strategy. I keep asking myself the question - when are men going to learn to respect and treat women better? It seems no one cares - not the police; not the government; not even the parents of these boys."

"Yes, Smita. The issue seems almost insurmountable. But if women gain enough momentum in this endeavour, there may be hope. It took centuries for women to get the vote. Women still struggle for free childcare and equal pay. I'm with you on helping women fight for their rights, and getting men to respect them more. Can we put our heads together and brainstorm strategies rather than you risking your life each weekend night?"

She was surprised by her relief at his words. His empathy for her cause moved her. She felt she had found someone who truly seemed to understand.

After a while, she sighed.

"Think about it, Smita. We don't need to discuss it further tonight. Let it be with you. Then, over the next week or so, let's get together and explore alternative approaches."

* * *

After dinner, they headed towards Brunswick where Smita lived. Ed insisted on accompanying her to her shared house. Hand in hand they walked, marking a pivotal moment for Smita. Ed had somehow broken though her defences, her barriers. Or was it the kids? Probably both. She seemed happy. The happiest he'd seen her since he first met her in Banana Alley.

They were at the end of Victoria Street, leaving the Vietnamese district, when they heard yelling and shouting from a side street. Both looked. In a flash, before Ed could understand what was going on, Smita dashed towards the commotion. It appeared four young Vietnamese youths had encircled a large, hairy man, shoddily dressed, and looking like a homeless person. Two of the youths were aggressively attacking him, with kicks and blows, martial arts style, while the other two stood by, taunting. The big man fought back gamely, but he was no match for the youths' strength and skills.

Smita yelled as she charged at the group, "Bernie, no worries. I'm here. You guys lay off." She launched, shoulder-first, into the two youths who were attacking the man she called Bernie.

Smita's attack took them by surprise. She managed to floor both with her momentum. But they were up in an instance, obviously experienced martial arts practitioners. They now spread out, flanking her and Bernie on four sides, taking up fighting stances, ready for combat.

"Hold it. Just hold it, everyone," Ed commanded, coming up behind Smita. She was surprised at the authority of his voice.

The Vietnamese combatants swivelled to address this new entrant.

"Hold it, I said," Ed repeated firmly, for the third time. "Can we talk? It's important to talk. We don't want a fight. Why were you guys attacking this big guy?" he demanded.

Ed's calm and commanding demeanour had a noticeable impact. Everyone involved stopped, mid action, and waited.

Ed continued. "Guys, there are four of you attacking this single guy. And he is older. That's not fair, especially in marital arts. We always play fair. You know that."

One of the four then spoke up. "We're monitoring the streets. Too many muggings. This is our territory. This guy coming into our territory. We don't allow."

"Your territory?" asked Ed. "Mate. I'm Aboriginal. Talking of territory, this is my territory. And you guys, as well as this guy here, have invaded my territory. So let's not talk about territory. Now what's the problem with him here," he said, pointing to Bernie, "walking through this area?"

"We no like homeless people. And too many muggings. We're now checking all."

"Look mate," continued Ed. "This area belongs to everybody. Not just you guys. This is a free country. Now if you want a fight, I too will join in and we'll give you guys a fight. But this Bernie guy, who I've just met, seems to be simply going about his business. He appears homeless, but it's no skin off your nose, mate, as long as he does not harm your property. And I can't see him doing any of that. So will you guys just back off and let us go peacefully?"

The four looked at each other. The leader then nodded to the others, signalling they back down and let Smita, Bernie and Ed go their way.

As the four moved to one side, Smita, Bernie and Ed cautiously backed off into the other. They then made their way towards Hoddle Street. Smita was holding Bernie's hand. Bernie himself seemed rather amused by the whole incident. He kept shaking his head and giggling.

"What you giggling about, Bernie?" demanded Smita.

"Love, where and when in the heavens did you become a martial arts expert?" he asked in wonder.

"Her fairy godmother," Ed quipped, drily.

"What fairy godmother?" Smita glowered at him.

"Yeah. Her fairy godmother visited recently, touched her butt with her wand while she was asleep, and she awoke a martial arts expert. For which you should be grateful, Bernie."

Bernie giggled again, and hugged Smita.

"But never mind this chatter," continued Ed. "How the hell do you two know each other? I'm getting jealous."

"I'll tell you in a moment, Ed. But Bernie, please tell me, are you okay? Did those guys harm you? I'd hate for you to be hurt."

Bernie teared up. Ed was amused. But Smita remained earnest.

"I'm okay, love. I was heading back from the Salvation Army centre in Collingwood. I was on my way to Flinders when those guys waylaid me. I've no idea why. Everyone now seems to be in a fighting mood these days. And you too, Smita. But I'm grateful for your help. And yours as well, mate. By the way, what's your name?"

"Ed. And yours I gather is Bernie. Come on Bernie. Let's grab a coffee in this joint here, and you tell me your story. Anyone who Smita likes so much is my friend as well."

Over coffee they exchanged their stories.

"Collingwood is rather far from your usual haunts at the train stations." Ed remarked.

"I was in the area, to see a friend, Uncle Jim. And then decided to visit the Salvation Army centre."

"You mean Uncle Jim of the Aboriginal Youth Club?" asked Ed.

"The same. Yes, he lives at the back of the Aboriginal Youth Club which is close by here. He manages the dormitory for homeless kids. He and I go back many years. We're both Aboriginal."

"Yea. I know him. Now isn't that a coincidence? Smita and I were at the Club this evening. I'm there every week. I know Uncle Jim. Now I can tell him I've met up with the bad company he keeps, right? But tell me how did you and Uncle Jim meet?"

Bernie laughed. "It's a long story. Both he and I are from the stolen generation; we were both taken as babies. We grew up in the same boarding house in Geelong and were abused by the same Christian brothers. A lot in common, right?" Bernie giggled.

"By the time we were twelve, we had had enough. We jumped the fence and have not looked back since. Good old Jim eventually got a stable job. I remain the wanderer," he giggled again.

"Really sorry to hear your story, Bernie," said Ed. "You know, I could find you a job too, if you wish," he volunteered.

"Thank you, my boy. But Uncle Bernie is now too old to change his ways. Like I told Smita once, I'm content with my life. My joy would be to see you both again from time to time."

"Why not, Bernie. Smita too will now be working at the Aboriginal Club on Thursdays, right, Smita?"

Ed did not wait for her agreement. "Come and say a hello to us as well as Uncle Jim when you visit. As for Uncle Jim, I promise I'll be asking him all the shenanigans you guys were up to as teenagers."

* * *

That night, as Smita lay in bed, she reflected on all the lovely people she had met since her arrival in Australia – Melody, the Melbourne Volunteers staff, Bernie, Meg and John, Jill and now Ed and his youngsters at the Club.

CHAPTER 22

I t was late Friday night as Smita closed the gym at the usual time of 10 pm. Her thoughts drifted to the previous Friday – an eventful night she would rather forget. As she made her way up Queen Street on a cold and windy night, she felt relief at skipping her usual Friday and weekend night patrols in the city. The confrontation and narrow escape last Friday had brought her weariness to the fore. And underscored the futility of her campaign. She was still sore from that encounter.

She'd been on her vendetta for over two years if she counted the time she'd spent on training. Her weekend patrols and confrontations in the city streets had once been a thrilling challenge, providing an adrenaline rush and a sense of vindication. But now, she questioned the value and the effectiveness of her strategy in addressing the core problem.

Ed's recent advice had further muddied the waters and added to her internal conflict. The evening out at the Aboriginal Youth Club the day before had left her with a lot to think about.

As Smita approached Bourke Street on her way home to Brunswick, she heard shouts and screams coming from the west of the city grid, in the direction of King Street. Pedestrians scurried away from the area of commotion while some youths were sprinting towards the noise, phones glued to their ears. It looked like a call to arms. The police sirens soon followed. She was relieved to be an observer rather than a participant of whatever melee was happening.

As she boarded the tram at La Trobe Street, she received a message. She sat in her seat and checked. It was Ed. The message was short –

"I hope you are not near the junction of Lonsdale and King. Huge fight and riot ongoing. PLEASE tell me you are not on your Friday night rounds and involved?"

She smiled at his concern. She replied to assure him she was on a tram on the way home. But the riot concerned her. She wondered what had triggered it.

* * *

Constables Jim Dory and Kevin Roman were patrolling the city, street by street. At 10.30 pm it was still early for a typical Friday night. The city was unusually quiet. They were both grumpy and unhappy. The weather was cold and windy. By all rights, they should have been safely ensconced in the warmth of their patrol car, driving around the city and enjoying a hot cup of coffee from their cup holders. But that bloody Superintendent Julian Boy Mason had issued instructions a week ago – "Out of your cars, please; on the street, on foot. I want visible police presence". Fucking idiot. The guys at the top had forgotten what the beat was like on the ground in cold, windy Melbourne.

They were on Bourke Street, making their way west towards Spencer Street. They were chatting about the footy game which had just finished at the MCG. The Bombers had bombed again, this time against St Kilda. It had been a terrible season so far, thought Dory, an ardent Bombers' supporter. He still held out hope; it was only mid-season. Roman couldn't care less. He kept up with the table, but he was more a rugby fan than Aussie rules.

At the junction of Bourke and Queen a call came in - an incident on King Street near the Lonsdale junction. They sprinted towards the location. It wasn't far from where they were.

They arrived at a trot but were brought to a sudden stop, aghast. The scene ahead of them on King Street was literal mayhem. There were around thirty young men, all engaged in close combat, some in pairs, some in small groups. A few combatants wielded broken beer bottles as weapons. Others relied on brute force, charging into each other, arms and fists swinging. Someone threw a projectile towards one of the shop windows, shattering it and sending shards across the footpath. Onlookers scattered for cover; while new arrivals gathered to cheer different parties. Traffic had halted, while the fight continued.

There were two recognisable groups among the combatants, each on a different side of the street. On one side were the Asians, small made, lithe and fit, fighting in their typical combat style of acrobatic kicks and body sleights. On the other side were the whites; generally larger, mostly skinheads and bearded, working out a sweat even in the cold night, swinging arms and fists, and kicking out at random.

Constable Dory pulled out his whistle and readied his pepper spray can in the other hand. Constable Roman made an urgent call for reinforcements. Both blew their whistles for all they were worth. Neither attempted to enter the fray. It was simply too disorganized and chaotic for just two officers to make any useful impact.

The scene resembled a war zone, with flailing arms, shouts, screams, and angry abuse. Mixed in the mayhem were women's screams, though these appeared to be coming from among the onlookers. Several bodies lay prone on the street, prompting Constable Roman to urgently call for ambulances.

Police reinforcements soon arrived, the police sirens and screeching tires announcing their arrival. Police officers emerged from their cars, equipped with pepper spray guns and batons. The ambulances followed soon thereafter, adding to the noise and confusion. The crowd started to disperse on cue. The incoming officers, with Dory and Roman, now formed an attack line and charged the remaining combatants shouting instructions to back off or get sprayed. They were backed by a second line of officers.

With the arrival of the police, the rival groups disbanded and scattered quickly. Some diehards though continued the fight. There were about three small groups still engaging when police attacked with aggression, separating the combatants. Arrests were made and things finally began quietening down.

The paramedics got to work, bringing out the stretchers, picking up the bodies, administering to each hoping there were no life threatening injuries.

An hour later, the situation was under control. The senior officer in charge called out instructions to the officers still on the scene, directing them to fan out on all sides to ensure the rioters had indeed dispersed and were not just standing by to resume.

CHAPTER 23

Saturday was Smita's day off, thanks to a new arrangement with Jill. They now alternated weekends at the gym. Jill had recruited more staff to help manage the gym.

As she savoured her morning coffee, Smita browsed the latest news on her phone. She sat back stunned at reading the headlines –

"Brawl Between Rival Martial Arts Gangs Results in Serious Injuries"

"Law and Order Break Down Triggered by Weekend Muggings of Last Six Months"

"Police Have Lost Control"

Apparently, eight young men had been hospitalised following the gang fight last night on King Street. Well over thirty individuals had been involved. Nearby retail shops had suffered badly with shop windows broken. Fortunately, no bystanders were hurt. All the hospitalised were members of either the White Boys Club or the Asian Martial Arts Association.

"What have I done," thought Smita, as she held her head in her hands and poured over the details.

It had all started with the best of intentions – teaching young men to respect women better. Instead, it had led to this; what the press were describing as a breakdown of law and order in the city. And then connecting the law breakdown with the weekend night muggings. The whole issue had just got out of hand. The police would now be on the warpath, she was sure.

* * *

Ed was still in bed when his phone rang. It was Errol, an Indonesian martial arts trainer who taught Pencak Silat, the Indonesian martial arts style, at the Krav Maga gym at Banana Alley. Ed had taken lessons from him and regularly exchanged fighting tips. They had become close over the years

"Hi mate, were you involved in the martial arts fracas last night on King Street?" Errol asked, concern in his voice.

"No worries mate. I've been in bed all night. I heard there was a riot out there. But I didn't know it involved martial arts guys. Where did you hear this?"

"One of my Indonesian friends is in hospital. His elder brother called me this morning. He was mad at me and the whole martial arts community. He claimed our martial arts classes have resulted in young men becoming violent and poisoning his younger brother's mind. I got a lot of shit. Just heard him out. Allowed him to let off steam. But Ed, this situation is getting out of control. I was hoping you weren't involved."

"Thanks, Errol. But I'm good. Not involved."

"I heard Big Jake, the leader of the White Boys is in hospital due to a mugging the previous Friday night. His guys were out last night, looking for blood. They bumped into some Asian guys and now it's all a fucking mess. Giving us all a bad name, mate. Not good."

Ed commiserated, but his mind had moved to Smita. He called her after Errol had called off.

"Hi Smits, you okay?"

"Yup. Why the early morning call, Ed?"

"Did you read the media headlines this morning?" he asked.

There was a silence from Smita. He waited.

Finally, she sighed and said, "Look Ed. I've made mistakes. I had good intentions, but the issue has got out of control. The riot last night and those hospitalisations are probably due to my actions. I feel terrible. I don't know how I can repair all of this. Will going to the police and fessing up help, do you think?"

"No, Smits. Leave it alone. While your actions might have been an initial trigger, this fracas was brought on by the White Boys and the Asians. It will sort itself out. But, as I said last Thursday, it's probably better you stop your weekend vendettas."

"Yes, Ed. I've already decided to stop. Thanks for your support. I don't know what I would have done without you and Jill."

"No worries, Smits. You want to meet today and talk more about it?"

She eagerly agreed to meet for lunch.

*   *   *

That morning the Spencer Street police headquarters was unusually abuzz with activity. Assistant Superintendent Mason had convened an urgent meeting. He wanted a complete brief of the events of the previous night. The morning news had criticised the police for losing control of the muggings and street violence in the city. Last night's 'riots' as they termed it, portrayed the culmination of growing lawlessness in the city.

Photographs blazoned the front pages of the newspapers and social media, with headlines indicating that the riots appeared to be racial in nature. Commentators were questioning if race conflict had again reared its ugly head and was this a restart of the racial riots Melbourne had experienced a few years ago?

Constables Dory and Roman, though exhausted, were present at the meeting. The Assistant Superintendent wanted their version of events. Also present were Detective Mal Simpson and Senior Constable Emma Dickson, who were leading the ongoing investigation into the weekend muggings, though they had not been present at the previous night's riot scene.

The Assistant Superintendent was agitated and fuming. This was not a good look for him, he knew. The pollies would soon be on the phone wanting explanations, as the press began laying the blame at their door. He wanted details – how many were involved in last night's fracas? Were there any arrests? Was there any information of what triggered the conflict? Was it all related to the recent spate of night muggings on the weekends? The fusillade of questions continued.

Dory, Roman, Dickson, Simpson and the officers who were on the scene the night before struggled to keep up with his questions. The conclusion emerging was that the riot on King Street last night was indeed connected with the night muggings. Interviews of some offenders who had been arrested indicated that there were two rival groups, one representing the White Boys and the other the Asian Martial Arts Association. Each group had mounted preventative night patrols because they each suspected the opposing side was responsible for the muggings and were taking over the city streets.

"This is a right royal mess," Mason commented, dryly. "To top it all, from all you've told me, we still don't know who exactly has been responsible for these muggings? Correct?"

No one around the table dared provide the obvious answer.

"So? What are we going to do differently to get to the bottom of this? Obviously your current approaches are not working, right? We now have two issues to deal with. First, those muggings. I want us to get to the bottom of them as soon as possible. The second is this gang warfare which the muggings apparently triggered. We simply cannot have this escalate. It needs to be stopped immediately."

Sergeant Higgins, who had overseen the police response to the riot scene the night before, volunteered his view. "Sir, my officers are already interviewing some of those being treated in hospital with injuries. I also have officers trying to trace down members of both gangs. The Asian Martial Arts group are easier since they generally belong to the fight clubs around the city. We will get to them today, and warn them off any more confrontations. The other group is more difficult. I understand they go by the name of the White Boys Club. They're an amorphous group. No specific location. We've identified their leader. He is the brother of the man still in hospital from the mugging the previous Friday. He is under temporary detention, and we intend to round up the others involved."

"Okay. Seems like some progress there. But what about the muggings which triggered it all? We can't afford to have any more of these. I want the night foot patrols to increase even further. But we need to find those muggers. The bastards seem to be a systematic and focused bunch."

Senior Constable Emma Dickson coughed and spoke up. "Sir, if I may. There is only one theory as far as I can see, that might fit the facts. May I explain?"

"Yes, yes, go ahead," Mason said impatiently.

"Sir, we all know that every mugging in the city and surrounds over the last six to eight months has targeted young men. No women, interestingly, have reported any muggings or attacks during these months. The city seems to have become, suddenly, a safe haven for women."

"Interesting," Mason murmured. "Any comments from the rest of you on this observation?"

No comments were offered around the table. Some nodded in assent.

"Okay Dickson, continue."

"The other curious features of these muggings, Sir, if I may summarise again though we are all aware of them, is that the victims are never the ones to report the attack. It's always passersby; the victims never volunteer clear information on the assailants; and in every case the victims have lost their driver's licences; nothing else. This suggests the motive isn't robbery; it's more to do about holding leverage over the victims, possibly to prevent the victims doing something that the assailant does not want them to do."

"Finally, with the exception of the most recent case, where the victim is still in St Vincent's, the injuries have been severe, but never serious enough for hospitalisation. No open wounds either."

"Okay, Officer. So what's your theory please?" the Assistant Superintendent demanded impatiently.

"I suggest, Sir, that the assailants are females who are on a vendetta against young predatory men. They wait to be assaulted, and then turn tables on their offenders. It's the only theory that fits the facts."

"Christ! Are you saying we now have a battle of the sexes? Any comment," he demanded as he looked around the table.

Detective Simpson, feeling sidelined, expressed his scepticism. This was after all his case. "I find it hard to believe, Sir, that the injuries caused could have been by females. A case in point is the last mugging where the victim is still in hospital. He is huge in size; has had cases of assault registered against him in the past, and is known to be violent. I find it difficult to believe females could have injured him so badly."

Mason looked around the table. There was a heavy silence.

"These muggings have been happening for some months now. I understand some of them were caught on CCTV cameras. I'm still waiting for a detailed analysis of those images. Perhaps that can shed light on whether Officer Dickson's theory has some validity," Mason pointed out.

Detective Simpson replied, "Sir, we have staff reviewing the footage and trying to analyse them. The images are vague at best. But we will get a separate report on this to you soon."

"Simpson, I want that analysis by Monday. Is that clear? Now, what does that last victim himself have to say about his attackers?" asked Mason.

"We're still waiting to interview him, sir. His larynx has been severely injured and the doctors aren't allowing him to talk till it heals. In any case, he seems reluctant to speak to any of us. We will await more information from him."

"Look, I want no more muggings or riots in the city. Is that clear?" Mason demanded. "I want the night foot patrols in the city to be doubled. I want to hear what you find out from this latest victim as soon as he is allowed to speak. And I want, by the end of today, a report on my table telling me what your next steps are. Detective Simpson, you are now the head of the operation. And if it is indeed women martial arts practitioners who are responsible for these muggings, I want as many of them interviewed and checked as soon as possible. Thank you. That will be all."

The Assistant Superintendent stood up and left the conference room, fuming and muttering. He seemed frustrated with the little progress made on the case. The officers around the table looked at each other, some rolling their eyes. It was always difficult when a case hit a wall, like in this one, and the seats up the ladder started banging the table for results.

"Okay, folks, any ideas to offer for our report?" Detective Simpson asked. "We have to provide the Super something to make him happy."

"Why don't you tell him in more detail the inquiries we've started with the martial arts gyms in the city? We're half way through. That should keep him happy for a while. It may also give us some leads," suggested Officer Andrew.

"Okay. I'll email you guys a draft of my report by 3 pm this afternoon. If you have any comments, get back to me by 4 pm to allow me meet the boss' deadline."

CHAPTER 24

Smita met Ed at a brunch restaurant on Fitzroy Street, a weekend yuppie favourite. It was close to where both lived. Eleven in the morning and the restaurant was already bustling with the Saturday brunch crowd.

Ed seemed to have got there early to reserve a table. She saw him as she entered, nursing a coffee at a corner table, scanning his phone. He rose and gave her a comforting hug. It seemed to say - relax, I'm here; don't worry. She gave him a grateful look and sat down. But her shoulders sagged. She had never felt so helpless since her early days with Pravin. She could not think straight, her mind in turmoil.

Overnight she'd decided it was best she confess to the police and take the consequences. She shuddered at the thought of prison. But she had been brought up to take responsibility. Ever since she left Pravin, she'd never given in to helplessness or apathy. She was not going to do so now. She'd take her medicine.

Ed reached out and held her hand. He seemed to realise how conflicted and worried she was.

"It's over, Ed. I've decided to turn myself in," she announced as she sat.

"Take it easy. Let's order then talk."

After they placed their orders, he invited her to talk. "Okay. Tell me all now. What's this about handing yourself in? Why? I'm going to listen and then we can discuss. Okay?"

She poured her heart out. She explained her motivations behind the vendetta. It was no more just about Pravin and the men who assaulted her and killed Meg. It was anger against and frustration with men in general and their rapacious behaviour. How they considered all women as fair game, for their pleasure, without any thought of the consequences for the female. When would they grow out of their teenage testosterone driven urges? They needed to be taught a lesson, a harsh one so they remembered. They needed to know women could be their equals, even physically.

She talked about upbringing in the South Asian culture. The preferential treatment boys were given, while the girls were systematically diminished. The concept of arranged marriages and the dowry system and the idea that the man was always master of the woman; she was there to be of service to him and his extended family.

She stopped abruptly, realising she had got carried away. Her food lay in front of her, untouched. And so was Ed's. How thoughtless of her. But it was a relief to share her burden with Ed. As she talked she realised how important he'd become to her. She reached across and held his hand tight, her eyes telling him how grateful she was.

"I'm sorry, Ed. Let's eat. It was good to get all that out. But it's not the point of our meeting this morning. We need to talk if I'm going to take the first step to getting into prison, right?" She managed a small smile.

He smiled, and they both began eating. They talked while they ate.

"So, you think you need to now fess up to the police, is it?"

"Yes," she replied. "What other option do I have? I started this mess, and now with the riots, I'm afraid it will get further out of hand. I also think they have suspicions about my role in the muggings."

She shared about the visit by Senior Constable Dickson and the discussion the officer had had with Jill and her. "What worries me is that I may be dragging Jill into this as well."

"Well," said Ed. "If you stop your weekend adventures, then the muggings will stop, right?"

"I assume so. Though I hope the rival gangs do not continue their clashes."

"Even if you handed yourself in, I doubt that would have any effect on these potential clashes. That's a boat that's already sailed. The best both we and the police can hope for is that the temperature within this crowd dies down, and probably will if the muggings stop and the police step up their patrols?"

He continued. "If you've agreed to stop the muggings, what is the point in turning yourself in? Those guys you've defended yourself against during this vendetta, do not seem to have made any complaint. In fact, as far as I know from the press reports, they have not told the truth to the police or anyone else. And if the police have CCTV of the muggings, they would have seen that every case was one of self-defence. Further, if they had identified you, we wouldn't be sitting here having lunch."

She thought about it. What Ed said made sense.

"So what's your advice then?" she asked, feeling her relief rising.

"Look Smits. I see clearly that the issue of violence and ill treatment of women affects you deeply and you want to do something about it. Let's put our heads together and see what we can do, realistically. I agree it's a huge problem. The rates of domestic violence which I read about in the media are extraordinary. You and I are not going to solve this problem by ourselves. It's too huge, too widespread. But there are ways we can contribute. So – we have a joint project on our hands, dear."

She wanted to give him a hug, but just squeezed his hand in appreciation.

* * *

On Sunday morning, Detective Simpson and Senior Constable Dickson sat opposite Mark Jameson, the data analyst who'd been assigned to analyse the CCTV footage of the last month's muggings. None of them was happy to work on a Sunday. But the Super was expecting results by Monday.

"It's taken a while, Sir. CCTV cameras are placed usually at street junctions as well as interspersed on particularly busy streets in the city. There are about sixty surveillance cameras distributed across the Melbourne CBD and surrounds. You will appreciate it's impossible for our cameras to have complete coverage of all the streets. So they are not always in a position to capture every criminal incident," Jameson explained.

"For instance, there is no surveillance camera on Market Street since this is neither a main street nor a busy one. So, unfortunately we have no footage of the previous Friday night's incident. We've analysed in depth the images of reported incidents over the last thirty days, where we have coverage. There have been five."

"In every case, a man is seen to attack a woman walking alone. She fends off the attacker with the skill of a martial arts specialist, and beats the man into submission. She then appears to force the man to kneel and give her a credit card or an ID. The pattern is the same across all captured incidents. It's weird," Jameson reported.

"I need you to clarify," Dickson suggested. "In every incident it's the man who attacks first? And the woman is walking alone?"

"Yes, Officer," Jameson confirmed, adding that this might explain why the victims weren't the ones reporting the incidents.

"Now," asked Detective Simpson, "is it the same woman in the incidents captured by your cameras?"

"The footage is too fuzzy to make definitive identifications. Variables such as the distance of the incident from the camera or poor lighting, or both contribute to the fuzziness. But the profile of the woman appears similar in each case. The features though are indistinguishable."

Simpson sighed with frustration. "Looks like we're going to have to interview all the victims of these muggings once again to convince them we need an identification."

"We can certainly try," said Dickson. "But I doubt they're going to be any more forthcoming than they were in the first instance."

"Even if we confront those of whom we have CCTV coverage of?" Simpson asked.

"All the more so, Mal. The CCTV shows that in every case, the victim was the initial assailant. Do you really think that when confronted with that footage the victims will be more willing to talk? Even less so, I think, when they see themselves being overpowered by a woman."

Mal Simpson smiled.

"Perhaps we should at the very least interview the case of the previous Friday who is still in hospital."

"Agreed. Let's do that."

* * *

Big Jake lay in his hospital bed, looking out of the window, wondering how much longer he'd have to stay in this shitty hospital. The nurses were nice enough, some pretty. And it was great to be waited on twenty four hours. But they never allowed him a full night's rest. They were in and out, checking his temperature, taking his pulse, feeling his throat, making sure he was comfortable, and administering to his companions in the ward. What a fucked-up place this was.

To make matters worse, he could still hardly speak. It all came out in a whisper. These arse-hole doctors were now saying he'd have to go through voice therapy, bulk injections (whatever that fucking meant – he did not like the sound of it), surgery or a combination of treatments. And all this would take at least six months before he got his voice back. What a fucked-up situation, and all because of that wimp of a woman.

It was a shitty mess, no doubt. He'd now been told that his brother Chad was under custody after a fight with the Asians last Friday night. He hoped he was alright. He was not bothered about the arrest. The White Boys Club had a lawyer, Jess, and he'd get Chad out pretty quick. But he was hoping Chad had not been injured.

He was still cursing his luck when in walked two police officers. He recognised them from their first visit a week ago. The woman looked cute.

The beefy guy spoke first.

"Hello. We're from the police. I am Detective Simpson. This is Senior Constable Dickson. We tried to talk to you a week ago, but the doctors did not allow us due to your health condition."

Big Jake indicated, with sign language at which he had become rather adept, that he still could not speak. The last thing he wanted to do was answer their fucking questions.

"Yes, I understand," said the guy named Simpson. "The nurse indicated we should not push you to speak since your vocal cords are still healing. But, if possible, through sign language, can you confirm that if we showed you CCTV footage, you'd be able to identify your attacker?"

Big Jake panicked. God almighty. The bastards had CCTV footage of his attack and her taking him down. How much more humiliation could he bear? Then he remembered the Club lawyer's advice - always deny or say nothing.

He still could not shake his head easily due to his injury. So he indicated with his fingers and a shrug that his answer was negative.

"How many attackers were there?" asked the detective.

Ha. They were trying to trick him. He decided he'd be adamant and stick with his story.

He put up three fingers.

The detective shook his head and said, "But the CCTV says it was one person, not three." Simpson knew there was no CCTV footage of the incident, but he wanted to see Big Jake's reaction.

Big Jake remained unmoved. He put up three fingers again.

"But the CCTV footage says differently, sir," insisted the detective.

Big Jake tried to indicate, with his fingers and shrugs, that the coverage was probably not of him.

Simpson gave Dickson a frustrated glance, inviting her to try.

She piped in. "Sir, was a woman part of the three who attacked you?"

Ha. They were trying to trick him again. Silly fuckers. He indicated negative.

The police were getting nowhere, and Big Jake realised how useful his lawyer's instructions were. Just stand your ground and deny. Terrific strategy. He must remember to compliment him on it.

The officers finally left and Big Jake heaved a sigh of relief. He had thought for a moment they'd pull out a phone and show him video of his confrontation with that fucking woman. He'd hate to see that again; to see his humiliation in front of this policewoman.

* * *

Back at office, Simpson and Dickson discussed their next steps.

"So, what now?" asked Simpson. "Big Jake insists it was three men who attacked him. The victims of previous muggings give vague stories of multiple assailants. Yet the CCTV, though inconclusive on identification, indicates this is a lone woman at work."

"I've always thought this is the work of a lone woman," responded Dickson.

"So any ideas who? You've been doing a lot of interviewing the last week."

"I have an inkling. I intend to follow it up."

"You okay to share it with me?" Simpson interest had perked up.

"Let it be with me just now. I'm in any case still conducting interviews, as is Andrew, of martial arts practitioners from the city gyms. We will be done early in the coming week."

"We don't have a week, Emma. The Super will hit the ceiling if we have an attack next weekend again."

"I don't think you need to worry, Mal."

"You seem rather confident. You better be right. I wish I knew why you're unwilling to share with me your so called 'inkling'."

"Let's call it a hunch, at this stage, Mal. As you well know, hunches are hunches. They mean nothing till one follows through and actually gets an opening. So don't worry. I'll be in touch."

CHAPTER 25

On the Monday following the riotous weekend. Jill was at the gym's reception desk when Senior Constable Dickson walked in with a stern expression on her face, lips compressed.

Dickson's visit last week had left both her and Smita feeling uneasy, in part because it had left a lot unsaid. The visit had raised Jill's suspicions about Smita, but she had decided not to pursue them with her. Though she wondered why Dickson had not made any attempt to confront Smita if she really had evidence. Jill kept hoping she had read the situation wrong, and Smita was indeed completely innocent of these muggings.

Now here was Dickson once again.

"Hi. I'd like to speak with both you and Smita, together." It was more a demand than a request.

What was it this time? Jill wondered. She sighed and called out to Smita to join them. They sat at the small table at the back of the reception.

"Thank you for your time. We've been interviewing various gyms and marital arts practitioners as part of our ongoing inquiries related to the Friday and weekend muggings. This is a follow up visit on the same matter, if you don't mind," Dickson began.

Jill observed Smita cautiously, sensing her unease.

"The last time both of you admitted you are martial arts practitioners. Where and when did you guys learn your skills?" queried Dickson.

"Is that really important, Officer," asked Jill, impatient with the irrelevance of the question. "Both Smita and I have openly admitted we're practitioners. What difference would it make where we learned our skills?"

"Let's leave that to us, if you don't mind. May I ask again, where and when?"

Dickson turned to Smita, looking for an answer from her first. Smita looked cornered.

Jill came to her rescue. "Officer, I learned my skills from the next door gym some four years ago. After that attempted robbery incident in our gym about two years ago, Smita asked me where she could learn. I directed her next door also."

Smita finally spoke up. "Officer, as you know we close the gym late every evening. After the case of attempted robbery, I decided that I too should learn marital arts, for my own safety. I'm hoping I did not do anything against the law here," she asked.

"Who was your trainer?"

"Esther, in the next door gym."

"Thank you. You know, I do keep worrying about these muggings and about the safety of women like you. But fortunately, over the last six to eight months, no woman has been mugged. Now isn't that interesting?"

She paused.

"Aren't you happy with that, Officer?" asked Smita.

"As a police officer, I'd prefer that no one, repeat no one – male or female, is assaulted on our city's streets. Now, do either of you have any inkling of who the person or persons are who are doing these muggings?"

Both Jill and Smita looked at each other and shrugged.

"Well, I'm hoping that after that almighty riot that took place on Friday night, triggered by these muggings, the person or persons responsible will realize it's time they stopped. There are better ways of addressing some issues than through violence. Violence only begets more violence, as some wise person once said.

And by the way," she continued, almost as an aside, "we've recovered relevant footage from our CCTV cameras now. They show rather interesting findings."

Jill heard Smita take in a sharp breath, her anxiety palpable. She decided being defensive was not helping. "Are you here to share with us your findings, Officer?"

Dickson smiled. Jill realized she too had noticed Smita's reaction. There seemed to be a hint of strategic play on Dickson's part.

"No Jill. That time will come. One thing is for sure. The person responsible is a skilled martial arts expert. I'm visiting to warn you that protecting any such person is akin to aiding a criminal," Dickson warned.

"I hope you will now be able to arrest the person concerned," responded Jill, looking Dickson in the eye. "We too are worried. We'd love this business to come to an end. It's giving our martial arts community a bad name."

Dickson left them looking rather nonplussed. Jill wondered what the purpose of that visit was. Dickson did not appear to have elicited any substantive new information from them. Or was it just to give Smita a message?

* * *

Smita sat down with a sigh after Dickson had departed.

"Can I have a moment of yours, Jill?" she asked quietly.

Jill nodded and sat beside her. She knew what was coming.

"Jill I'm truly sorry for having dragged you into this mess. I hate that this is the way I've repaid your kindness. I'm willing to resign immediately. That's the least I can do. It's just not right what I've done."

Smita left unsaid the obvious. Jill did not push her to clarify. They both intuitively understood where each stood.

Jill reached out, held Smita's hand and gave it a little squeeze. "I understand, Smita. I really do. I possibly would have done exactly what you have if I was in your shoes. Look, I think you've decided to leave all that behind. If that's so, it's wise. I think Senior Constable

Dickson has also guessed the truth. She is giving you a way out. Please accept it and let's all move on. Okay?"

Smita was now in tears. For the first time, since the beatings she received from Pravin, she was crying again. It all spilt out. The tension she'd been harbouring within her poured out. Jill sat next to her, holding her, saying nothing.

Suddenly a client appeared at the door. Both looked up. Smita collected herself. The client looked startled seeing tears on Smita's face. They reassured her all was well.

"We'll talk later, Jill." Smita gathered herself and got back to work.

* * *

That afternoon, Detective Mal Simpson received a call from the Assistant Superintendent.

"What's the status of the investigation into the muggings, Mal?"

Simpson was miffed that Dickson had refused to share with him the suspected mugger's identity.

"Sir, I think Senior Constable Dickson may have uncovered the identity of the mugger. The CCTV footage is fuzzy. Too blurry for a positive identification. But I think she knows. She's been visiting the gyms in the area and has probably identified a suspect. However, she refuses to divulge the name to me."

"That's unforgivable, Mal. I want you and Dickson in my office first thing tomorrow morning. I have an hour at that time. I want to get to the bottom of this immediately."

Simpson smiled to himself. "Yes, Sir. We will be there."

* * *

That evening, Jill and Smita left the gym in the charge of other staff and wandered down Little Collins Street to a quiet bar. Over drinks, Smita shared details of her journey since she began learning Krav, much of which Jill had already guessed. She also shared her conversation with Ed over the weekend.

"I'm ashamed where all this has led," concluded Smita. "Fortunately, no one has been killed. But that poor guy from the week before, and others from the last Friday riots, are still in hospital."

"I've no sympathy for him, Smita. Neither should you. He got what he deserves. I think he will recover and I hope he learns his lesson. As for the rioters, they also got what they deserved."

She continued. "The more important issue is – where to from here. Smita? I'm hoping you will stay with me at the gym. You've become a critical part of my business."

"That choice may soon be taken from me, Jill. If Dickson decides to arrest me."

"I think I agree with Ed's assessment of the situation, Smita. If Dickson did indeed have definitive evidence, she would have arrested you already. She would have been forced to. Her visit today was to warn you off your vendetta. I suspect she even has some empathy for you. She knows of the assault on you and the attempted rape. About Pravin's attack. She's seen a lot more in her kind of business. She'll be happy to hear you have sworn off your crusade."

"I would love to stay on at the gym, Jill, if you will still have me. It's where I found a refuge from my tattered life in Melbourne. The gym and you have become my anchors. I would hate to leave it."

Jill nodded. "Good. I'm happy to hear that. I have big plans for the gym. As a start, I intend to take on more staff so that you and I can have a more sensible life balance. And you can think of becoming a licensed trainer yourself. "

"I've always wanted to become a professional in whatever field it was going to be," replied Smita. "It looks like physical fitness chose me. Yes. I think I will now become a personal trainer, and possibly," she smiled, "a trainer in the martial arts as well."

"Here's another idea, Smita. I know the issue of helping women cope with predatory men is a major issue for you. It's been your single-minded mission this last year. So how about you get your licence in the next few months. Then you and I begin a free martial arts school at our gym for women in self-defence. I will also ask Esther if she wants to volunteer. How does that sound?"

Smita's eyes teared up. "Jill, you're a jewel. You know I've been struggling these last couple of months at what to make of my life; how I can help women without being on this senseless vendetta that I embarked on. Thank you. You've given me a way out. A great way forward."

"Okay. Let's drink to that and our future joint enterprise. I rarely drink but tonight's a celebration to the future."

CHAPTER 26

The next day, Smita was at her desk at the gym when a call came in.

"Hi, Smita, this is Melody here."

Smita's heart warmed to hear Melody's voice. She felt guilty for losing touch amidst her own chaotic life.

"Hi, Melody, how have you been? I'm sorry I should be calling oftener. How are the little ones?"

"All good, Smita. But just now, there's an Indian lady here who says she heard you worked here at Melbourne Volunteers. She's come here wanting to talk to you. Her name is Nirmala. We told her you don't work here anymore; she's now asking for your telephone number. I'm reluctant to give it without your permission. Are you okay if I give it to her? She does seem a bit distressed."

Smita wondered what this was about. She did not know anyone by the name of Nirmala. She had had virtually no contact with the Indian community since leaving Glen Waverley. Her past experiences had left her with a deep aversion to the insular attitudes prevalent in some parts of the Indian community, especially the patriarchal norms and practices like dowry.

She was cautious about this request. But if she could help another Indian woman, why not?

"Did she say what she wanted to talk to me about?"

"No, Smita. But she seems agitated."

"Okay, Melody. You can give my number to her. If I can help, I will."

Melody continued, "I hope you're doing well, Smita. We've been hearing about the muggings and riots taking place in Melbourne city. I hope you're keeping safe."

Smita smiled. "Yes, Melody. All's good, thanks. And how's everyone at Melbourne Volunteers?"

"We're all doing fine. We often think of you and your resourcefulness, Smita. We miss you and all wish you well. Take care."

She hung up.

* * *

The expected call came sooner than Smita had anticipated.

"Hello, Smita. You don't know me. My name is Nirmala. I'm Pravin's new wife."

Smita was speechless. She'd never expected Pravin to re-enter her life. She had hoped she was done with him for good. Here he was, raising his menacing presence again via a new wife. She was tempted to end the call immediately.

Hearing only silence at the other end of the line, Nirmala continued, "Smita, I promise I'm not calling to create any trouble for you. Pravin does not know that I'm contacting you. Can we please talk?"

Smita reluctantly agreed. Nirmala did seem to be in distress.

"Thank you for giving me your number, Smita. I learned about you from the wives of Pravin's friends. They told me you had worked with Melbourne Volunteers. So, I went to them to contact you. Smita, I think I am facing the same trouble you once did. I need your help."

Smita remained silent. She was deeply conflicted. On one hand, she wanted nothing to do with Pravin. He had been a huge disrupting experience in her life. Besides, she was once again in a difficult period due to the police investigations. The last thing she wanted was more complications. Yet, Nirmala sounded sincere and in desperate need of help.

"What can I do for you?" she asked.

"Smita, Pravin and I got married four months ago. Since the time I have arrived in Australia it's been a nightmare. He physically abuses me every day. He does not allow me to leave the house except with him. He gives me very little money. I have to cater to his every need. He keeps complaining that the dowry my parents gave him and his family was inadequate though my family has spent the equivalent of over $100,000 on my dowry and the wedding. I have no life of my own anymore. I now understand why you divorced him."

Smita sighed. It was the same old story.

"You have my deepest sympathies, Nirmala. But I'm not sure I can help you."

"Smita, you managed to break free from his control. I want to know how? I can't just walk out of the house because I have no money. I don't know Melbourne or Australia. I've never been out of Glen Waverley. The only people I know are Pravin's friends. Can you please help me? Please."

Nirmala was now sobbing uncontrollably.

As much as she hated being drawn back into Pravin's life again, Smita knew in her heart she should help this desperate woman.

"Do you really want to leave him?"

"Yes, yes. Please. I can't live with him. He's a monster."

"Do you want to go back to India?" Smita asked. "I can provide you with money for your plane ticket."

"My parents will not accept me back, Smita," she sobbed. "I know. They will say they've paid a huge dowry to Pravin and his family and now I need to somehow make it work. They will insist I should be grateful to be in such a great country with lots of opportunities. They will simply not be able to understand."

Smita recalled her own situation from over three years ago. This was an eerie replica.

But how could she help? The last thing she wanted in her current situation was yet another complication. It was even possible that in the next week or so, she could be in prison, despite all that Ed and Jill had said. However, she realised she had to help this lady.

"Okay, Nirmala. First, do not tell Pravin that you've spoken with me under any circumstances. Is that clear?"

"Yes, yes. I promise," she said between sobs.

"Next, I need to clarify; do you have a permanent visa?"

"I am not sure," she said. "He's taken my passport."

The bastard, thought Smita. He's learned from his experience of me leaving him.

"This is difficult, Nirmala. If you leave him without your passport, and you have a dependant visa, he can ask for you to be deported. And the authorities will probably do so. I was planning to get you here to Melbourne city and see if we could get an NGO to help you. But without your passport and visa, even they'd find it impossible."

Nirmala was silent, obviously deeply disappointed.

"But you managed to get away from him, Smita. How did you manage to get your passport from him?"

"I had always refused to surrender it to him, Nirmala."

"I could not help it, Smita. The moment I landed in Melbourne, he took it, and it's still with him."

"Nirmala, it is essential that you somehow get possession of it, before you attempt to leave. Then we'll try to get the authorities to convert that visa into a regular permanent visa on the grounds of domestic abuse. Unfortunately, this is a long process. But don't give up hope. Plan your next steps carefully. But first, get that passport and call me."

"Thanks, Smita. You've at least given me hope of a way out. But I really don't know how I'm going to get my passport."

"When he's at work, search every nook and corner. I don't think he'd be taking it to work each day. When you have your passport, ring me, and I'll have a plan ready for you. Okay?"

She hung up but was obviously still in distress.

* * *

Smita sat back, her mind in turmoil. Here we go, all over again. That horrible man was now inserting himself into her life once more. Then she realised that it was Nirmala who was in a whole heap of trouble, much more than she was.

"What's on your mind, Smita?" asked Jill, coming to the reception from inside the gym.

"The nightmare rises again, Jill."

"Why? Is Dickson still bothering you?" she asked.

"No, it's Pravin. His new wife."

"What?" exclaimed Jill in shock. "Pravin has a new wife? Has she contacted you?"

Smita shared with Jill the phone call she'd just received, Pravin's abuse over the supposedly insufficient dowry, and Nirmala wanting to flee.

"That damn dowry issue all over again." Jill exclaimed, shaking her head in exasperation.

"Jill, you won't believe it, but the dowry system began with the best of intentions. It was meant for parents to give the bride what would be her inheritance in advance, as she was leaving her family and joining another. The money was intended primarily for her benefit, considering the very real possibility of ill-treatment by her husband and his family. Unfortunately, it has now become a tool in the hands of men and their families to exploit the wife.

It's a classic example, Jill, of culture subverting tradition to favour men and enslave women. The pity is that the community, generally, still adheres to what we would call a medieval practice in this day and age. It is, in fact, unlawful now in India."

"I wonder how many Indian women suffer like you and Nirmala have?" remarked Jill.

"Unfortunately, too many. Even here in Australia. I have firsthand knowledge of it. Thanks to you, I've survived."

"You don't give yourself the credit you deserve, Smita."

"But I owe it to my Indian sisters here in Australia, to now work for their cause."

CHAPTER 27

It was the Tuesday following the Friday riot. Detective Simpson called Senior Constable Dickson at 9 am,

"Hi, Emma. The Assistant Super's in a frisky mood. He wants to meet us in his office pronto. It's about the mugger and the riots. Can you come over to my office and we'll go in together?"

Dickson wondered what was going on as she walked the short distance from the Melbourne West Police Station to the Victoria Police Headquarters next door on Spencer Street. It had been obvious Mason was worried about the media attention, his own reputation, even about the politicians potentially getting involved. But they had already met on Saturday morning after the riot. What was so urgent now? A nagging feeling told her to be careful.

Simpson was waiting.

"What's the big deal?" she demanded on entering his office. "I thought you'd given him a detailed enough report over the weekend."

"Let's see," he said, in a flat toned, non-committal manner. He avoided her eyes as he rose to accompany her to Mason's office on the next floor. The nagging feeling now turned into a distinct suspicion. She wondered what game Simpson was playing.

"Come in," the Assistant Super called impatiently as they waited at the door.

He got straight to the point, in his typical style, a deep frown etched in his brows. "Look, Dickson, I understand you have some idea who this mugger is. I want to know why we're pussyfooting around. When are we going to initiate arrest proceedings?"

Dickson gave Simpson a piercing look. He had obviously told on her. She gathered herself.

"Sir, I do have an idea who this person is, but the CCTV footage we have is fuzzy, and a definitive identification will be difficult, if not impossible. A lawyer will drive a truck through it if that's our only evidence. Also..."

"Can we leave that to the prosecutor?" interrupted the Assistant Super, his frown growing deeper, the lips pressed tightly and his posture stiffer.

Dickson stared back at him. She hated men interrupting her. She continued, determined to make her points. "Second, Sir, in every case where we have footage, the so-called victim is actually the initiator of the assault. The woman is simply defending herself, albeit aggressively. Now, that will be more difficult for our prosecutor to circumvent," she added, somewhat pointedly.

The Assistant Superintendent grunted, clearly not happy.

"Third, this lone woman who consistently appears in the footage, seems to have done us police a favour. In the last six months, there hasn't been a single case of an assault on a woman in the CBD."

She paused. There was silence around the table, as Mason and Simpson processed this information. She looked at Simpson, challenging him to respond. He shifted uncomfortably in his chair.

"Interesting," remarked Mason, appearing somewhat mollified, as he digested this new information.

Then, a moment later, he added, "So are you suggesting we just let this woman continue with her crusade and sit back to enjoy the show?"

Detective Simpson sniggered.

The Assistant Superintendent looked at him sternly, then back at Dickson. "Yes?" he invited Dickson.

"Sir, I intend to call her in and talk it over."

"For God's sake, Dickson, she is a mugger," huffed the Assistant Superintendent, a look of exasperation on his face. "Now you want to counsel her?"

"Sir, with due respect, she is not a mugger. In every instance, she is defending herself."

"Then why the hell is she out and about every Friday and weekend night, as seems to be the case? Surely not just for fresh air."

"Sir, with respect, this is a free country, and whoever wants to walk the streets at whatever time, is free to do so."

Another grunt. He was getting unhappier.

"Sir, my guess is she's been severely abused by men in the past. She's now embarked on a crusade, as you term it, on behalf of all women. She wants to show that women are not, after all, that vulnerable. I intend to ask her, in fact, I will insist, that she stops, or we will indeed initiate proceedings against her. I do not intend to tell her our evidence is actually weak. Let her infer that we have clear footage of her encounters. The result, I suggest, is that the muggings will stop. But I don't think it's a bad idea to encourage women in general to take up self-defence skills, given that men will not change easily."

Mason sat silent, looking intently at Dickson. Then a slight smile played at the corner of his lips. He seemed to have understood the point.

"Ok. You both can go. But if I hear there are any further muggings by this female, I will hold you personally accountable, Officer Dickson."

"Yes, sir. And if there are muggings by male assailants against women?"

"You are now being facetious, Officer. Thank you for your time, both of you."

As they left, Dickson turned to Simpson.

"Hope you enjoyed that meeting, Mal. See you at the next mugging, which, I assure you, will be committed by a male." She walked back to her office without waiting for Simpson's response.

* * *

The same day, Smita got a call from Senior Constable Dickson.

"Hello Smita. Senior Constable Dickson here. We met recently in connection with the ongoing muggings and riots."

191

Smita's heart skipped a beat. She closed her eyes, fearing the worst had arrived. Is this it, she wondered? Maybe they had finally found definitive evidence.

"Can you come in to the West Melbourne Police Station on Spencer Street, at 11am this morning? Please ask for me at the front desk."

Jill was not in the gym that morning. However, another staff member, Amy, was on duty. Smita informed Amy that she'd been called to the police station and would be leaving. She asked Amy to tell Jill where she was when Jill arrived.

Amy looked worried.

"Don't worry, dear. It's just the ongoing issue of the martial arts gang riot of last week. The police are following up inquiries with all the gyms."

Instead of heading straight to the police station which was a fifteen minute walk from the gym, Smita went towards the river, and found a bench along its north bank. She remembered Bernie's advice – "Sit by the river, watch its water flow gently by, and let your spirit be calmed by its ripples."

She sat there, feeling anxious and tense, wondering what the next hour held in store. If it was prison, so be it. She wouldn't fight the inevitable. She had no regrets about the path she had chosen. While Jill and Ed were right that there were indeed more constructive ways of assisting the cause of women, she didn't regret the punishments she had meted out to the predatory men she had encountered.

Gradually, the peace and quiet of the river calmed her. She reflected on the last time she had sat here and watched the water flow by. That was three years ago. A lot had happened since then. The bottom line was she was happy with where she was now, unless they were going to throw her in prison. If so, she wondered what would become of poor Nirmala with no one available to help her. At least she had two great friends who would stand by her whatever the outcome of this encounter with the police. She kept her fingers crossed and began her walk to the police station.

* * *

At the reception desk in the police station, she asked for Senior Constable Dickson. She was led into a small meeting room with a desk and chairs on each side. She was shown the visitors chair and told to wait. She sat, fidgeting nervously.

Dickson entered shortly thereafter. Smita rose from her seat.

"Hi Smita. Glad you could make it. Please sit"

That did not sound like the prelude to an arrest. Should she feel relieved? She acknowledged Dickson's greeting and took her seat again.

Dickson sat opposite her, notebook on the desk, pen in hand, and looked directly into her eyes.

"Okay, Smita. We need to clarify a few things and then talk about a couple of related issues. I'd like to confirm again, if I may, your activities after you left the gym on the Friday of the week prior to the riots. It was a little after10 pm? Correct?"

Smita confirmed, although the truth was that she had left much later. Each weekend night, after locking up the gym, she went through the routine of preparing herself both mentally and physically for the assault she expected once she left to walk the streets. So she left typically well past 10.30 pm.

"And did you go straight home?" Dickson asked.

"Yes," replied Smita, somewhat tentatively.

"You know we have CCTV on the city streets, right?" Dickson suggested.

Smita shrugged. It appeared the police were going through the motions, even though they likely knew everything. She reconciled that her time was up and she was prepared to face the consequences. It was surprising how calm she'd become. She waited for Dickson to present the video evidence of her on Market Street that Friday night after 10.30 pm.

But Dickson didn't do that. Instead, she continued, "The CCTV images we have of these muggings consistently show a woman as the mugger in every encounter."

"Are you suggesting that woman is me?" asked Smita, now certain the arrest was imminent.

Dickson did not answer immediately. She seemed to be considering her choice of words carefully.

"I'll be frank with you, Smita. The CCTV footage is fuzzy. But the woman in it does resemble you."

Smita felt a wave of relief internally. Ed had been right. They did not have definitive evidence.

"But you insist I am the so-called mugger even though you can't clearly identify the woman?" she asked.

Dickson ignored her question and continued.

"What if I tell you that if we were to search your house, we would find a secret drawer containing a number of driver's licences that you have no business possessing?"

Smita sat in shocked silence. Heaviness descended upon her. Time seemed to slow. How did Dickson know about the driver's licenses? Had they extracted that information from the victims when they had asked for identification? And did they really intend to search her house?

She remained silent for a while. Finally, she shrugged and countered, "Please tell me, Officer, what you want from me?"

"I am not sure what I want from you, Smita. But I do want the muggings to stop. Immediately. Perhaps you have a connection to them and perhaps you don't. There are factors that strongly point to you. However, I've called you in today to tell you the attacks are serving no purpose. Let me be upfront with you. We know this is the work of a lone woman. This woman is obviously very skilled at marital arts and can defend herself against men, or at least against most of them. What I need to know is what motivates such a woman?"

Smita was silent again, debating how to respond. Finally, she said, "Officer, the first time you visited the gym to interview Jill and me, perhaps two weeks ago, we had a conversation about the rate of assaults on women in Melbourne, and in Australia in general. Do you remember?"

"Yes, Smita, I do."

"Isn't it time that women started to stand up to men? And that the police assist women in doing so?"

"Yes, I agree, Smita. But there are different ways of 'standing up' to men, as you term it. Are you suggesting that we women become as physically aggressive as some men are? That we resort to violence in the process? Can you imagine the kind of world we would deteriorate into? It is women who are holding society together – be it as mothers, negotiators, peacemakers, teachers. And we do it quietly, usually without recognition for our contributions."

Smita was again silent.

"For instance, in my job in the police force, I've encountered a lot of aggression and misbehaviour over the years. I've learned to stand up in my own way. Now, men in the work force have learned to respect my limits. The battle, however, continues. It's not easy.

There are ways of addressing aggression without counter aggression. Please think about it. I think you are a very courageous woman. I've seen and heard the details of how you have escaped a very difficult domestic violence situation. I think you are now a woman with a cause – to help other women. Please find productive ways of doing so."

With that, she was dismissed, though there was no definite indication that she was completely off the hook.

* * *

Smita didn't know whether to laugh or cry as she left the police station. There was no elation, just an overwhelming sense of relief. She found a seat on a bench on the street and took in the air, the noise, the atmosphere around her. She realised she had come dangerously close to losing her freedom. It was just fortunate Senior Constable Dickson was a woman who understood Smita's perspective. She had been given a second chance and couldn't afford to squander it. The cause remained same. The issue was the strategy.

She sat on the bench, watching the world go by, savouring the freedom she had come so close to losing. She glanced across at the police station thinking – "I could have been there, locked in a cell, on my way to who knows which women's prison. I'm lucky to have escaped."

So now, where to from here? She resolved she had new challenges ahead of her. She was serious about the idea that Jill had presented of starting a free self-defence school for women at the gym. But the more interesting proposition was working with Ed at the Aboriginal Club. There was something deeply appealing about it. Perhaps it was the innocence and spontaneity of young teenagers, and the opportunity to share with them her own life's learnings. And of course, she needed to help Nirmala. She had a responsibility to give her a chance at a new life path in Melbourne.

CHAPTER 28

It was Thursday and Smita was at the gym, looking forward to an evening at the Aboriginal Club and dinner with Ed. Amy at the front desk called out to inform her that Officer Dickson was on the line.

Smita had hoped she was done with the police. As she picked up the phone, a horrifying thought crossed her mind: what if Dickson had uncovered more evidence?

Taking a deep breath she answered the call. "Good afternoon. Smita speaking."

"Hi Smita, this is Senior Constable Dickson."

"Yes, Senior Constable, what can I do for you?"

"I have two officers from the Eastern Suburbs Police Area Command at Mount Waverley here at the West Melbourne Police Station. They want to interview you. They are willing to come to the gym or you can come here. Your choice."

Mount Waverley? Was this about Pravin? Why would they want to talk to her? It didn't sound like they were giving her a choice, despite what Dickson said. Trying to keep the tension out of her voice, she agreed to come immediately and hung up. She was growing weary of this cat and mouse game. What could it be now? She grabbed her bag and made her way to the West Melbourne police station on Spencer Street.

* * *

At the police station, Dickson led her to a larger meeting room than the one they had used the time before. Two men were already seated, with coffee cups on the table in front of them. One was in civilian clothes, tall and thin with a weathered face. He nodded when she entered. The other was a young and handsome male officer in police uniform.

"Hello. I am Detective John Winston," the craggy-faced man announced, "and this here is Constable Tony Simons. We are from the Eastern Suburbs Police Area Command at Mount Waverley. We're looking for a Smita Devi. I assume you are her?"

Smita nodded and took a seat at the invitation of Dickson who also joined the meeting.

Smita's heart was racing. New players in the situation raised questions. Did that mean there was fresh evidence? And if so, what was it and where did it come from? And why all the way from Mount Waverley, near Glen Waverley, where Pravin lived? Questions kept piling in her mind.

"What can I do for you?" she asked.

Detective Winston began. "Did you happen to know Nirmala Pandey?"

Smita was taken aback. Given the surname, she assumed they were referring to Nirmala, Pravin's wife.

"Well, she did give me a call a few days ago," admitted Smita, cautious now about what was unfolding.

"What was the call about?" asked Winston.

Smita was irritated by his abruptness. He made no attempt to be civil. Her irritation probably showed.

"I don't think Nirmala would appreciate me sharing that," she answered curtly. "If I have her permission, I will certainly tell you about the conversation."

Winston sighed and glanced at his fellow police officers as if debating his next move. Then with an effort, he said, "I'm afraid Nirmala is now deceased. She died yesterday evening, probably by suicide. Her phone shows a number we have traced back to you. We're here to find out more about that conversation and whether it has any relevance to her death. Her death is under investigation."

Smita sat back in shock, closed her eyes and tried to process the information. She attempted to visualize the Nirmala she had never seen, but whom she had vaguely pictured as she sobbed over a phone conversation just a few days ago. Silence hung in the room.

"Smita we need your help," Wilson continued. "Her husband claims he knows nothing that would have triggered her actions. We understand you and he were once married, and there were instances of domestic abuse. We now find that Nirmala had been in contact with you. In this context, that conversation is crucial for our investigation."

Smita remained silent, wishing she had Ed or Jill to guide her. What should she do?

Detective Winston's patience seemed to be wearing thin. "Look Smita, I can understand this is difficult for you. But it's essential we have the details of that conversation."

Oh how she hated that man, Pravin. The bastard was either responsible for driving Nirmala to her death or, worse, directly involved. And he was now, once again, dragging her into his miserable life. She bit her lip as she debated her response.

Finally, she decided to share the information they sought, but not without conditions. "How did she die? If you tell me, I will share with you the details of my conversation with her."

Winston leaned forward and said, quietly, "She burned herself to death."

Smita buried her face in her hands and wept. She felt a deep anguish and sorrow for Nirmala. What a horrific way to die. This wasn't the Nirmala she had spoken to, the Nirmala who wanted out from her marriage, and to find a way of making something of her life. This was the tragic fate that so many Indian families subjected their lovely young women to. Her sobbing intensified. Officer Dickson leaned over and placed a comforting hand on Smita's back, trying to calm her.

This time the officers waited patiently.

She finally looked up, gave Dickson a grateful look, then wiped her tears and shared with them the details of the conversation. They meticulously reviewed the specifics, ensuring they captured all the nuances. They also sought confirmation that this was indeed the first and only conversation she had had with Nirmala. Smita confirmed.

Officer Dickson observed Smita in silence, listening to her account.

Detective Winston then inquired, "Was the issue of dowry one of contention between you and Pravin during your marriage?"

"Very much so. Pravin is a greedy, selfish man. His family, particularly his mother, is even worse. They constantly demanded more money be sent to them from Australia. Despite my parents having spent about $80,000 on our wedding and in dowry cash, they and he were never satisfied. In Nirmala's case, it was more than $100,000."

Anger against Pravin now welled within her. She was convinced he had somehow been responsible for Nirmala's death.

She looked Winston in the eye, intense and fierce, and said firmly, "I don't know the true cause of her death. But it certainly wasn't suicide. Nirmala was unhappy when she spoke to me. But she was definitely not suicidal. She was young, hopeful and seeking a second chance in life."

"Are you suggesting that her husband, Pravin, has had something to do with her death?"

"I am suggesting nothing except to say, she did not sound like someone contemplating suicide when she spoke with me. I am certain of that."

* * *

Smita returned to the gym from the police station, deeply depressed by Nirmala's suicide. While she appeared to have escaped arrest for her vendettas, this news weighed her down with guilt for not having been able to do more to assist Nirmala. In reality though, there was little she could do without Nirmala getting possession of her passport.

She reflected on the typical plight of young Indian women who came to Australia as newlywed brides. She thought about the process of her own arranged marriage back in India some four years ago. She increasingly believed it was a scam. In India, most marriages were arranged by the parents of the couple. Young Indian men were presented by their parents in India to the parents of young women as a desirable marriage prospect. The fact that the man had permanent residency in Australia, and presumably a good job, allowed his parents to extract attractive dowries, and demand that the bride's family cover most if not all of the wedding expenses.

The idea of young women being treated as commodities, ownership of whom is transferred from the fathers of their families to the new husbands, infuriated her. This had been exactly her experience, and now it had been Nirmala's. Her determination to fight for the rights of women, specifically newlywed Indian brides in Australia, grew stronger.

She decided to investigate how frequently this was happening in Australia. Sitting at her desk at the gym's reception, she typed into Google – "dowries and domestic violence in Australia". Several search results appeared. Some were news articles discussing the rise in cases of domestic violence related to dowries. However, one item attracted her attention – a recently published book titled, *"Daughters of Durga…Dowries, Gender Violence and Family in Australia,* by Manjula Datta O'Conner. Reading further, she learned that Dr. O'Conner was a clinical psychiatrist and Chair of the Royal Australian and New Zealand College of Psychiatrists Family Violence Psychiatry Network. Despite the lengthy title, her Indian-sounding first and middle names implied she had Indian heritage, and her position indicated expertise in researching this issue. Intrigued, Smita immediately placed an online order for the book.

* * *

That evening, she set aside her worries as Ed arrived punctually at 6 pm to pick her up. After saying goodbye to Jill, she left with Ed for the Aboriginal Youth Club.

It was Thursday, just a week since her first visit to the Club. She looked forward to catching up with the kids again and perhaps even meeting Bernie. On the way, Ed wanted to know if there were any more follow ups by the police. Smita shared the latest information.

"A lot has happened since we last met, Ed." She recounted her conversation with Dickson, that Dickson knew she was the weekend night mugger, about the driver's licences she'd been confiscating from attackers, and Dickson's counsel to her.

Ed stopped mid stride. "Hold on. Let's just sit here on this bench. I need to hear this all again and digest it. Do you mean she actually told you she knows you are the mugger and yet did not arrest you?"

"Yup. As you guessed, Ed, I don't think they have definitive enough evidence. The CCTV images are fuzzy."

"And the licences?"

"She knows they are missing from her interviews of the victims. The rest, I think, is guesswork. Though she's spot on."

"This is incredible news, Smits. It seems you're in the clear. That's a huge relief. I also think Dickson has a lot behind her severe exterior. She knows where you're coming from and wants to help. I hope you're going to take her advice."

"Come on, Ed. You already know I've sworn off from the crusade business. But I'm not worried anymore about myself. It's poor Nirmala I can't stop thinking of."

"Who?

"Oh, sorry. I haven't as yet told you about Nirmala. A lot has happened in the last few days."

She proceeded to tell him about the call she received on Monday, first from Melody and then from Nirmala; her advice to Nirmala; and then yesterday the news about her alleged suicide.

"Jeez. That is so sad and depressing. How you coping with all of this?"

"I feel terrible, Ed. I'm convinced Nirmala did not commit suicide."

"Are you implying what I think you are?" he inquired.

"Yes. Except that I have no evidence. I hope the police find some. But I can't just let it go. I can't let Pravin off the hook. I need to find out more details."

"Are you serious?" questioned Ed. "Don't you already have enough on your plate? You've barely escaped arrest thanks to a sympathetic Dickson? Now you want to entangle yourself in another crusade?"

"Ed, can't you see the sheer injustice, the cruelty of it all. Pravin first receives a dowry windfall from my parents. Then, once I leave him and get a divorce, he promptly marries again and gets another windfall. And this gives him an idea, right? This arranged marriage business appears to be a sure fire way of getting easy money, though I suspect he will be more careful with how he handles his next wife to avoid raising suspicions from the police."

"That's pretty extreme, Smits. You're painting him as a cold-blooded murderer, without any evidence."

"All I know, Ed, is that the Nirmala I spoke with was in no way suicidal. She was like me. She wanted to just get away and somehow make something of her life. I am determined not to allow Pravin to repeat the disaster he has somehow brought upon poor Nirmala."

They resumed their journey to the Cub again. Smita's heart lightened when she saw the young girls again. She forgot about her troubles, for a time at least.

CHAPTER 29

It was Friday morning, and Senior Constable Dickson called again. Smita felt a rush of nerves. She was not entirely convinced she was off the hook. On the other hand, she'd been thinking hard about Nirmala and her alleged suicide. She could not let it go. She needed the police to investigate her death further. Dickson might just be a receptive collaborator in this project.

"Hey Smita. I have a favour to ask," Dickson began.

The unexpected request took Smita by surprise. "Sure," she responded cautiously. "What can I do for you?"

"I am the head of an informal group within the police which is looking at new ways to address domestic violence. I'm aware of your own story of domestic violence. Would you be willing to come and share your experience with our group of officers and answer their questions? I believe your perspective would be invaluable."

Smita was dumbstruck, unsure how to respond. Then she saw the opportunity. If she agreed to help, perhaps there could be a quid pro quo arranged with Dickson. She was eager to pursue Nirmala's case further and had limited options open outside of working with Dickson.

"What exactly are you expecting of me, Officer, when you say that I 'share my experience'?"

"I mean just that, Smita. Share as much as you are comfortable with about your experiences with domestic violence. How did it start? What were the triggers? Did you report it to the police? If not, why not? When you finally did, what more could the police have done to help you cope better? And then take questions from our officers."

Dickson continued. "Look, this may or may not come to you as a surprise. But the police are trying hard to better understand how to respond to domestic violence situations. To be truthful, not all officers think it's their job. Some doubt they are equipped for what they often think is the job of a counsellor. However, there are things they can probably do within their capacity. The group is searching for options."

Smita found this intriguing. "I've never spoken in public, Officer. But I can try. Yes, I will come and share my experiences to the best of my ability. I genuinely want to help the police gain a better understanding of these situations. When and where would you like me to come?"

* * *

Smita followed Senior Constable Dickson into the room, nervous butterflies fluttering in her stomach. They were at the Police Headquarters on Spencer Street. She had agreed to share her experience as an abused woman with the police group. She had never spoken to a gathering before, much less to a group of police officers. She was acutely aware that until recently, she was often in violation of the law, even if it was supposedly in the name of a good cause.

However, she felt she owed Dickson. This was also an opportunity to leave her violent strategies behind, and start making a contribution in a more positive way. She remained deeply committed to the cause.

There were about forty officers in the room, seated in rows of about eight each. As she entered, behind Dickson, she distinctly heard a male officer in the front row near the door make the comment – "hot chocolate!". It jarred; almost stopping her in her tracks. But in that moment, all her nervousness gave way to anger. She struggled to keep her emotions in check, reminding herself of her Krav training: focus on the objective and don't let emotions get in the way. She was now eager to get on with the presentation.

Dickson introduced Smita to the officers as a survivor who had successfully emerged from an abusive marriage. The purpose of the meeting was for Smita to share her experiences, and provide the officers an opportunity to ask her questions, trying to understand the situation from the perspective of a domestic violence victim.

She began by scanning the room, making eye contact with as many officers as she could. She smiled, thanked Dickson and acknowledged the opportunity to speak to the group. However, before delving into the substance of her story, she asked the group to bear with her while she clarified something.

Her gaze fixed on the officer who had made the "hot chocolate" comment. Looking him directly in the eye she said, "Officer, I understand you like hot chocolate?" She smiled engagingly, taking the edge off the question. "May I ask - is it the 'hot' part; or the 'chocolate' that you prefer?"

The officer in question was a large, heavyset man with bushy eyebrows, and a bright reddish face. At Smita's question, he turned even redder. The officers on each side of him, who'd heard his comment, rolled their eyes, and looked down at the floor. The other officers moved uncomfortably in their seats, wondering what this was about, as not everyone had heard the comment.

Seeing that no answer was forthcoming, Smita continued, "Have you ever tried a fat-free white vanilla, Officer? It's pretty tasteless."

Dickson was now growing uncomfortable, as were many in the room. To their relief, Smita moved on. She had made her point and she used it as a starting point for her presentation.

"What is abuse?" she asked. "It's not always violent. More often than not, it's psychological, where one party or partner uses language, mind games, and threats to harass, intimidate, and bully the other. It comes from a deep lack of respect and empathy for the other."

She continued, "The first issue is to recognise abuse for what it is. To the outside world, the offender is usually skilled at presenting a peaceful and collaborative demeanour. He is often persuasive, and it becomes difficult to believe he is actually an abuser. In my case,

Pravin was a respectable, hardworking man, who, on the surface, appeared harmless."

She then moved to discuss the specific strategies her husband had used to abuse her, from depriving her of opportunities to earn, to restricting her movements, checking her computer and phone for messages, demanding she be at his beck and call, especially when he returned from work, consistently belittling her both privately and in front of friends, and ultimately resorting to physical violence including beatings and forced rape.

She explained how she had filed her complaint with the local police in Glen Waverley. But apparently, without witnesses, it was her word against her husband's. This was usually the crux of the problem. Who do the police believe?

The listeners then began asking questions. They wanted to know about the arranged marriage and dowry system. They were shocked when she explained that while the statistic for the occurrence of domestic violence in Australia was one in four women, among the Indian community, it was one in three. She referred them to a recent book which she had discovered on the internet published in Melbourne - *Daughters of Durga: Dowries, Gender, Violence and Family in Australia*, which explained how the arranged marriage system and dowries often, though not always, led to domestic violence.

The simplest solution is to usually separate the parties and place restraining orders on both. However, you still have an abuser around. This behaviour is deep in their psyche. And they will likely offend again. This is the big challenge. She then explained how in her case, Pravin had married again, and had again allegedly abused his wife.

Smita admitted, at this point, she had no answers. She was not a psychologist. She could only share her experience.

An officer at the back suddenly spoke up. "Smita, just for your information, in my precinct, I've come across three suicides by young women of Indian origin over the last couple of years. It seemed too much of a coincidence that all of them were of Indian origin. So what you say makes a lot of sense."

There were many questions and she answered them as frankly and objectively as possible. The officer, who had made the snide comment on her entry, remained quiet all through, his demeanour subdued.

After over an hour, Dickson finally called a stop to the meeting. She invited Smita and the group to join for a coffee outside. As they left, the officer who had made the snide comment approached Smita.

"Hi. I'm Ken. I apologise for that comment. It was insensitive. I was trying to be funny, but it was completely uncalled for and hurtful. I'm sorry. I've learned something today."

Smita accepted his apology gracefully. "Thank you, Officer. I hope we will meet up again and under different circumstances where I can be of help."

When departing, Dickson thanked her profusely. Smita smiled and replied, "Emma, if I may call you by your first name, it is you who has done me a huge favour I will not forget. And anytime you need my help, please don't hesitate to reach out, especially if it's relating to abused women."

* * *

They walked back to Dickson's office in the building next door. Dickson was enthusiastic about the meeting and how useful it was for the police officers who attended.

Smita's mind however, was on another issue. As Dickson was about to leave her to enter her building, Smita asked, "Can I make a request?"

Dickson nodded.

"Can you help me meet with or talk to Detective Winston once again?" Smita explained her reasons for doubting Pravin's story about Nirmala's suicide.

"Is this about getting revenge on Pravin?" Dickson asked, trying to gauge Smita's intentions.

"Absolutely not, Emma. This is solely about justice for Nirmala. She did not deserve to die, especially in such a terrible way."

"You think the detective has overlooked something, is it?" Dickson queried.

"Not overlooked, but perhaps been misled by Pravin. He is the most devious man I have met. He is clever."

"Look, it will be completely up to Detective Winston if he wants to meet you or talk to you again. In any case, I doubt he will be willing to come all the way to our police station in West Melbourne. Perhaps he may agree to a telephone or zoom conversation."

Dickson agreed to try and set up contact in the next day or two.

CHAPTER 30

Smita had spent the next couple of days trying to immerse herself in work, attending to clients, working at the reception and cleaning up. Despite her efforts, she could not get her mind away from Nirmala and the tragic fate she had met in Melbourne.

She tried to imagine what Nirmala must have looked like. Probably in her early twenties, in the prime of life, pretty, slender, and petite. Nirmala must have arrived Melbourne excited to be a new migrant, to start a new life in a new country. A life filled with possibilities.

She wondered about Indian culture and its systematic suppression and exploitation of women. On the one hand, motherhood is deeply respected for its contribution to society. The Goddess Durga is upheld in Hinduism as Shakti or Devi, the protective mother of the universe. She symbolized protection of all that was good and harmonious in the world.

Yet, reflected Smita, in the ordinary lives of women, particularly young women, newly wed brides were viewed as chattel, the property of the fathers or of the new husbands, and if they asserted their individuality, they were often labelled as 'loose', or available as prey.

Smita wondered where this paradox came from. The law in India banned the system of dowry in 1961. Yet, sixty decades later, it still thrived and was exported to countries worldwide through the Indian diaspora.

She reflected on her own journey. Her father's last six months, before he died, were consumed with a desire to get her married. But why? Did he think she couldn't manage her own life and decisions? The reality was that he feared social sanction from their extended family and friends, if he did not fulfil his perceived 'duty'. The family's status in their society would have suffered long after he was gone.

It was a vicious, nasty cycle. The young bride was not just offered to the new husband and his family, but rather exchanged, for a price - the dowry, which paradoxically the bride's family had to pay. She then became captive to her husband and his family, often subjected to a life of servitude. When she in turn grew older and had her own children, she would prefer male children who would bring in dowry riches to the family, and be available to serve both her son and herself till she passed away.

Smita had managed to escape this vicious cycle. But Nirmala had not been as fortunate. She wondered how many others suffered similar fates. The previous night, as part of her ongoing research into the issue of dowry in Australia, she came across the Al Jazeera documentary in 2017, *Australia's Dowry Deaths*. She also read the 2015 submission of Ms Jatinder Kaur, director of JK Diversity Consultants and an accredited mental health social worker, to The Royal Commission into Family Violence of the Government of Victoria. Ms Kaur had listed the names of Indian victims of domestic violence, killed by their husbands or fathers in Melbourne and Sydney over the period 2010 to 2015. These were the known cases of homicides. There were many cases of suicides which were never investigated.

Her thoughts were interrupted by a call from Dickson. For someone who had avoided contact with the law till rather recently, Smita was surprised how connected she had become with them.

"Smita, we need your help immediately. There was a triple 000 call from an apartment in Southbank. It was passed on to me at the West Melbourne station. I could not understand the woman. She definitely had an Indian accent and was speaking in a foreign language, probably Hindi. The only English words she kept saying were – 'help, help' and the address. I have asked the Critical Incident Team to follow up immediately. They will need the help of a translator. They're on their way to the apartment. Can you help? They will be passing by your gym in a few minutes. Is it possible to join them as an interpreter?"

There goes my evening, thought Smita. But the incident raised suspicions. She said she'd be happy to help and would be on the footpath outside the gym waiting for the police car.

* * *

Not long after, the sirens approached and the car stopped for her to jump in. They headed over the river on Queensbridge Street to Southbank.

"Hi, I'm Clover, this is Noah and the guy driving is Dick. Thanks for being available to help. When we arrive at the apartment, you, Noah, and I will go up. The apartment is on the sixth floor. Dick will stay with the car. By the way, Emma speaks very highly of you."

Smita was surprised by the news but pleased to hear it. The car finally drew up at an apartment building on City Road. The three jumped out, entered the foyer, and keyed in the apartment number the lady had given.

A man came on the intercom. "Yes, who is it?" he asked in a rather rough voice with an Indian accent.

"This is the police. Please let us up via the elevator," Clover replied.

"We have no need for the police, please. This is a false alarm. Please excuse," the man responded, then shut down the intercom.

Clover and Noah exchanged glances, sensing the urgency of the situation. They seemed to know how to handle such situations. They made a beeline to the building manager's office located at the back of the foyer. An aggressive bang on the door brought out a mousey looking man in an untidy suit, taken aback by this unexpected visit.

"We're the police," Clover stated assertively. "We have an emergency call for Apartment 604. Can you please take us up?" After explaining the situation and displaying their IDs, the manager reluctantly agreed. Using his master key, he accompanied them up to the sixth floor.

At the door of the apartment, Clover knocked aggressively, and announced their arrival. "Police here. Open up."

A man's rough voice responded from within the apartment. "No problem here, I told you. No need of police. All good here. Please go away."

Clover moved closer to the door and issued a stern warning, "We've received a distress call from this apartment, sir. If you do not open the door immediately, we will force entry. And you will be charged with obstructing police in the course of their duties."

Then, a woman's shout emerged, muffled, from within the apartment. "Help police, help police."

Clover wasn't sure he'd heard correctly, but Noah and Smita both confirmed it was a distressed woman.

Now Clover addressed the apartment door more forcefully, "We're coming in even if we have to break down the door." Other apartment doors on the floor began opening, as curious neighbours stepped out to investigate the commotion.

Finally, the door opened, slowly, revealing a stocky, moustached Indian man, scowling at the visitors. Standing well behind him, within the living room, was an elderly couple, likely his parents. They both appeared upset and distressed at the police invasion of their home.

"What is it? There is no problem here. Why do you come to disturb people?" the man grumbled.

Clover surveyed the scene inside and hoped that their intervention had not inadvertently created a bigger problem than he had hoped to resolve.

Just then, a cry for help rang out from what seemed to be the powder room, adjacent to the living room. "Police, police, help me, please, police."

Both Clover and Noah both looked at Smita and gestured for her to follow them as they strode determinedly past the man who had opened the door, and despite his continuing protestations.

Smita approached the door of the powder room and spoke in Hindi, "Hello. My name is Smita. I am with the police. What is the problem?"

The Indian man abruptly stepped forward, between Smita and the door of the powder room door, and responded to Smita in Hindi. "There is no problem here. Please go. This is private property."

A high pitched female voice from within the powder room then spoke in Hindi, her distress evident. "Please help me. My husband and my in-laws have made me a slave. I called the police. Please call them. I need their help. I will end my life if I have to continue to stay in this place. Please help."

She was in obvious distress. Smita translated for Clover and Noah, and attempted to calm her. "Why don't you come out and talk to us?"

The Indian man again forcefully intervened, shouting, "Don't listen to her. She's gone mad. We need to take her to the hospital."

"Don't listen to him, please," screamed back the woman from the powder room, pleading in Hindi. "I told you, my husband hits me, makes me work day and night. My mother-in-law curses me, saying I don't deserve to live with them. Please call the police. I will not come out till they are here"

Clover and Noah looked nonplussed. Smita translated again.

Clover took charge. "Tell her we are the police. She can open the door to verify. We will protect her and hear her story. And you sir," he said addressing the Indian man, "please step aside, I insist."

Smita translated Clover's instructions. The door opened, cautiously. In the meantime, the husband began offering a torrent of explanations in English. "Lies. All lies. She is misbehaving all the time. Ever since she married. She does not treat my parents properly. She does not know how to be a good wife."

A young, dishevelled, teary woman emerged from the powder room, dressed in a saree, a haunted look in her eyes. When she saw Smita and the police uniforms, she almost collapsed, sobbing, into Smita's arms. Smita led her to a couch in the living room, where the man's elderly parents were now seated, looking on disapprovingly.

The woman shrank from them, sitting as far as possible. Then in Hindi she explained her situation once again, interrupted regularly by her abrasive husband. She pleaded for safe refuge. The mother-in-law joined her son in claiming the allegations were all false, and chastised Smita for siding with the white people.

Smita translated the heated exchange. There was a lull in the conversation. Clover nodded to Smita, indicating for her to stay with the woman, while he pulled Noah aside to discuss next steps. He then made a call.

All the while, the distraught woman, now somewhat calmed, clung to Smita, afraid to be left alone with her husband and his parents.

Finally, Clover came over and sat down, inviting the husband to sit as well. Noah remained standing.

"May I know your name sir?" he asked the husband.

"Arun," said the husband. "I protest. This is all nonsense. You can't just come in here, into my house, and listen to a mad woman's stories and believe her. She is getting out of her mind. This has been going on for some time now."

Clover raised his hand. "Please, sir. I do not want to pass judgement on your situation. That will be the job of an investigation and possibly a court."

"You mean you are blaming me for her terrible behaviour?" The husband was indignant.

"Sir, I am blaming no one. It is obvious that your wife does not want to live here anymore. She is in fear. We will take both your and her statements now; then we'll escort her to a safe place while an investigation proceeds."

"I protest. How can you just take my wife away? Her place is here."

"Sir, we are not taking her away." Clover replied calmly. "She seems to want to leave of her own accord. This is a free country, may I remind you. You have no right to detain her here if she wants to come with us."

The husband began protesting again. Clover raised his hand for silence. "Now can we get your statements, please?"

* * *

At the police station, Constables Clover and Noah debriefed their Sergeant and Senior Constable Dickson. Lakshmi, the distressed woman, was left in the care of another female officer with a cup of coffee in an adjacent room.

After hearing the officers' reports, the Sergeant turned to Smita. "What exactly is happening here, Smita? Lakshmi is obviously distressed and claims she is being abused and oppressed by both her husband and his parents. On the other hand, he claims she is making up stories and we should not believe anything she says."

Smita explained, "The situation seems rather typical, sir. Lakshmi, as a newly married woman, has essentially been 'gifted' by her father to her husband and his family, along with a dowry. She is expected to serve her husband and his family. Sometimes, the husband and his mother, in particular, are unhappy with the dowry, and vent their anger on the new wife."

"Christ. This is topsy-turvy human trafficking. You pay to offer a human gift?" the Sergeant remarked dryly.

Smita responded, "Sir, while this may appear exploitative to the Western eye, it is a customary practice among Indian families. It seems that Lakshmi has been over-exploited in this role, and she is now rebelling."

Curious, the Sergeant asked, "If young Indian women know this is their fate, why do they agree to these arranged marriages, Smita?"

"They often have little choice, sir. In my case, I had a promising career to look forward to and financial independence. But my father's dying wish was that he wanted me married. Call it emotional blackmail, perhaps, but I had to comply. In other cases, it's possible the woman may not have the means to be financially independent. Hence, a marriage becomes her financial security. Indian men with Australian residency are highly sought after because they are assumed to be well off and will provide the wife with an attractive life here in Australia. It often turns out to be a sour dream."

* * *

They brought Lakshmi back in. She seemed much calmer than when they had first picked her up. She thanked them profusely, in her broken English.

The Sergeant asked Smita to check with Lakshmi if she was certain she did not want to return to her husband. She confirmed. They inquired if she had her passport. They wanted to see her visa. She replied her husband always kept all her documents with him.

The Sergeant exchanged glances with Clover and remarked, "Well, that husband may not like another visit from us but we need to get both her passport as well as her personal belongings."

Smita agreed to provide shelter for Lakshmi for the night, while Senior Constable Dickson said she would try to arrange some temporary accommodation for her.

* * *

It was late that evening. It had been quite an eventful day, reflected Dickson. A call came in. She checked the number – Assistant Superintendent Mason. This was not unusual. Mason phoned in to his senior officers from time to time, when he had questions. But this time, she was worried. She answered with a degree of nervousness.

"Yes, sir?"

"Hello Dickson. I wanted to check in with you regarding this mugging case. Have you had a conversation with that suspected female mugger as you promised? I don't want disruptions this weekend. Personally, I believe we should have her behind bars. But I understand the evidence will not support it."

"Yes, sir. We've spoken at length. I can assure you she will not be on the streets this weekend. If there are any muggings, I can guarantee they will not be because of her."

"I hope she hasn't pulled the wool over your eyes. You seem pretty confident. Anyway, what's been keeping the West Melbourne police station busy? Anything I should be concerned about?"

"The domestic violence incidents seem to be on the rise, sir. Or perhaps, it's just women who are working up the courage to speak and resist the abuse."

217

She quickly debriefed him about the Southbank incident.

This interested him. The news of mounting domestic violence and the bad press that the police were receiving for not responding adequately was triggering constant queries and suggestions from politicians about how police responses could be improved.

"It may interest you to know, sir, that the person you refer to as the suspected female mugger, is herself a victim of domestic abuse. She could not endure it any longer and transformed herself from victim into an advocate for justice for women."

"Now isn't that interesting? Anyway, I hope you're right and she will be off the streets this weekend. And for good," he added as an afterthought.

CHAPTER 31

Dickson found a place for Lakshmi over the weekend, a refuge for migrant women. Lakshmi was reluctant to let Smita go. But Smita assured her she would be in touch, daily.

On Monday morning, Smita got the call she had been waiting for.

"Hi Smita. This is Officer Dickson. You wanted to speak to Detective Winston about Nirmala's suicide. I have him on the line. I'll connect you now."

Smita thanked Dickson. She had done her homework and was prepared for the call.

"Hi Smita, this is Detective Winston here," came the voice on the line.

"Thank you Detective, for the call. I really appreciate it."

"No problem, Smita. I'm not sure how I can assist, but Senior Constable Dickson suggests I should hear you out. What can I do to help?"

"Sir, I'm increasingly convinced Nirmala's death wasn't a suicide. She had no reason to do it. She had hope after contacting me and just needed her passport from Pravin to start afresh. I suspect a confrontation occurred between them over this."

"This is all conjecture, Smita. We don't have an iota of new evidence to further pursue this investigation."

"If I may ask, sir, what time did Nirmala supposedly commit suicide?"

"At about 10 pm at night."

"Was Pravin at home when she committed suicide?"

"Yes, he was."

"And what did he claim he was doing when it happened?"

"Watching TV."

"How did he know she had lit herself on fire?"

"He says he heard the screams."

"From where?"

"From the kitchen," he said.

"And what was she supposed to be doing in the kitchen?"

"Come on, Smita. Cleaning up after dinner, what else?"

"Have you asked him what show he was watching?"

"No. Why would I?"

"Do me a favour, please. Can you ask him and check if what he claims was indeed a program that was running that day?"

"What's your point?" Winston was getting impatient.

"I suspect Nirmala had an argument with Pravin after dinner that night and this led to a physical confrontation where he physically hurt her badly. Perhaps even made her unconscious. Then to hide the assault, he burnt her."

"Complete conjecture, Smita. You are clutching at straws. You read too many murder mysteries."

Smita ignored the jibe. "Sir, to my recollection, when I lived there, the cooking stove was electric. So, I keep wondering how a person can light herself on fire while using an electric stove. It's a hot plate, not an open fire."

"Well, you can get easily burnt with a hot plate."

"I agree. But not die, can you?"

"So, are you suggesting this was not a suicide but a possible murder?"

"Yes, I am. And I'm requesting for a more detailed questioning of Pravin and an autopsy."

"Well, the Coroner has administered a partial post-mortem already, for your information."

"What's a partial post-mortem, if I may ask?"

"It's an external examination of the body by a medical person, undertaken when there are no suspicious circumstances surrounding the death. She was declared dead due to body burns."

"Can I request for a full post-mortem, then? I am willing to pay for it."

"Only a close relative can request that. And Pravin, to my knowledge, has not."

"Naturally. Why would he."

"Look Smita," he said with growing impatience, "we have no evidence to suggest any foul play here, hence no reason to undertake a full post-mortem. However, I will leave my email address with you and if you remember anything of substance, you can always get in touch with me. But I advise against letting your imagination run wild with baseless theories not founded in fact. This appears to be a suicide and we intend to treat it as such."

He provided his email address and ended the call.

* * *

Smita was not going to give up so easily.

She called her brother Rohan in Mumbai. They had kept in touch sporadically, despite the fact that Smita was completely estranged from the rest of the family after her divorce from Pravin.

"Hi, Simmy," Rohan greeted her warmly.

She felt relieved he still behaved the same with her as he always had.

"Tell me Rohan, do you know who Pravin married after our divorce?"

"Are you telling me that bastard is still bothering you?"

"No, Rohan. But his second wife has now committed suicide here in Melbourne last week."

"Oh my. Thank God you left the bastard. But to answer your question, yes I do know them. Our caste is a pretty small community here in Mumbai."

"Can you get me the phone number of her father, please?"

"Why, Simmy? Why do you want to interfere in this now? You've got him out of your life. Let it be now."

"No, Rohan, I cannot. We women need to stand together. I need to talk to Nirmala's father, okay. That's all. Please."

"Okay. I'll check and text you back his number in an hour."

* * *

When she received the number, she did not hesitate. She called immediately.

"Hello. You probably do not know me, Mr. Modi. My name is Smita. I'm speaking from Melbourne."

"Is this the Smita who was married to Pravin in Melbourne?"

"Yes, it is. I'm calling first to say I am truly sorry about the recent loss of your daughter, Nirmala."

"We can't believe this has happened, Smita. We sent her to Melbourne with such great hopes. She is our only daughter. We spent most of our savings to finance her marriage and her dowry. And now, this. It is terrible. Both my wife and I are struggling with grief. We want to come to Melbourne for her last rites, but Pravin says because it's a suicide, the police still have possession of the body."

"Mr. Modi, I can't tell you how deeply sorry I too am. However, I'm calling to make a suggestion. A week before she died, Nirmala got in touch with me. She shared with me that Pravin had become very abusive, and she was determined to leave him. She was calling me to ask how I had managed to leave him and if I could help her. I said I would. Are you aware of this?"

There was silence on the line.

"Mr. Modi, are you still there?"

"Yes, yes, I am. But this is shocking. I never realised she was suffering so much. Why did she not call us?" he lamented.

"Daughters, once they leave their family via marriage, are reluctant to bother their parents. I asked her to consider returning to Mumbai. I would have paid for her ticket. But she felt she would be letting you and the family down after all that you've sacrificed to pay for her huge dowry. It's the story of many Indian newlywed brides when they come overseas."

"If only she had called, we would have helped," said Mr. Modi.

"I know, you would have," said Smita, though she doubted it. Once a family had married off their daughter, it was mission accomplished. They usually did not want to hear back from her. She was now a member of the new husband's extended family.

"I will come to the point of this call, Mr. Modi. I do not believe Nirmala committed suicide. When she spoke with me, she was keen to start a new life. Why then would she commit suicide less than a week later?"

"Are you suggesting there was some foul play here with regard to her death?" His voice indicated he found it hard to believe her.

"I'm only saying, Mr.Modi, that Nirmala did not in any way sound like she wanted to take her life when she spoke with me. And if this is so, then yes, it is possible she met her death through foul play."

"Oh my God. That would be terrible."

"Mr. Modi, I am not saying she was murdered. But I am saying I want to be absolutely certain she was not. I am assuming that you too would like the same assurance?"

"Yes, yes." He seemed to be struggling to come to grips with this new development. "Is there anything I can do to assist you in your inquires?"

"According to the law here, Mr. Modi, a coroner will undertake a full inquest of the death only on request of the immediate family. Since Pravin is her only family in Melbourne, he is the main point of contact. And he does not appear interested in a full autopsy. The police are not receptive to my requests since I am not a family member. If you want justice for Nirmala I think you should contact the authorities and inform them that you want a full inquest."

Mr. Modi thought about it for a while. "Do you think this will really help?"

"It won't help Nirmala, at this stage. But I would think that if there is even the slightest possibility that she was murdered, then you and your wife would want justice for her."

"Yes, yes."

"On the surface, it appears Nirmala burnt herself. I for one will never believe that. She wanted to live, to make a new life away from Pravin. And we discussed how she could. So why would she have resorted to such a painful death when she knew there was a way out of her unhappy marriage. I am suggesting that you ask for a full inquest which will examine the condition of the body beyond the surface burns that Nirmala sustained. We want to know if she has been subjected to any violence by another person prior to her burning."

"This is very painful for us to think about." He was now sobbing.

"I know it is, Mr. Modi. But if you want justice for Nirmala you need to do this. Please think about it. I will now give you the email address of the detective in charge of the investigation. It will be your decision to contact him on email and make this request. If you do want the inquest, you will need to act quickly, before the police surrender the body to Pravin. And if you do contact the police on this, please copy me and tell them I will be your local contact. I assume you will wish for me to pursue this for the sake of your daughter. But it is your decision."

Mr. Modi took down Winston's email address, as well as Smita's and promised to send the email immediately. Smita assured him she would keep him informed at every step of the process.

Smita was now wondering if she was biting off too much. But she was now committed.

* * *

Ed called to ask if she was up to lunch with him. She readily agreed. There was a lot to talk about.

Over lunch she briefed him on the developments of the last two days.

"Jesus. You've been a busy body," Ed remarked.

"Ed, don't be mean. You're making it look like I love poking my nose into other people's business."

"Of course, you do," he persisted, though his eyes were twinkling and a slight smile played on his lips.

"Look, this is serious, and I need your advice."

"You've come to the right place, Ma'am. This is premium counselling service, on demand."

"Can you stop joking, please?"

"Ok. Shoot."

"This issue of dowry-related abuse of women within my community is much larger than I had realised. I've been so self-absorbed over the last few years; I had never thought that if Pravin had treated me like he did, what might be the plight of other young women who come to Australia on their husband's visas. When I think back to those lunch and dinner parties which Pravin used to take me to with his friends, I realise those women were not a very happy lot. They always seemed to be on guard; perhaps, a little suppressed."

"I see Joan of Arc moving to a new issue. Am I right?"

"Call me what you want, Ed. But I need to help these women. As a start, I want justice for Nirmala."

"On that I do have some advice, my dear. I hope you see that you are setting up a new confrontation with Pravin. I doubt he has ever forgiven you for leaving him, and then bringing him down in public in the gym. If he gets a second chance, he will want his pound of flesh. And it looks to me that you are going to give him his second chance."

"I am not sure where you are going on this."

"Just think it through. If indeed you do get a full post-mortem conducted, and they find that Pravin was in some way instrumental in Nirmala's death, he will have yet another reason to seek vengeance on you. And this time, I suspect, he is going to be even more determined."

"I don't care, Ed. I will take him on, and all the Indian patriarchy who seem only interested in ensuring women remain submissive and enslaved to their hegemony. It's mind-boggling for how long they've used culture and tradition to subjugate women."

"Okay. If you want a fight, it seems like you're going to get it. But then you have to be prepared. You can count on me to help in any way I can. How can I not, enslaved as I am to the queen of the streets?"

"Ed," she smiled. "I do love you, you know."

"What? That's the first time you've used that word. Seriously?"

"Yes, seriously."

"I am ecstatic." He rose and gave her a deep kiss.

CHAPTER 32

The next day, Smita initiated a Facebook campaign and group titled – "Justice for the Dowry Abused". She invited South Asian newlyweds living in Australia, who felt they were being exploited by their husbands, be it due to dowry issues or for other reasons, to write in their stories or those of their friends and neighbours, under pseudonyms if necessary. To speak up for their rights. She also invited lawyers, social workers and those who felt for these women, to join in. Its aim was to provide support for those distressed, and to share stories of those who had successfully coped with and overcome their trauma.

The group went on stream the very next day. By the end of that day, three stories had already been posted, attracting numerous comments from viewers.

* * *

The next day, she received a call from Detective Winston.

"Smita? Hi. Have you by any chance given my email address to a Mr. Modi who is Nirmala's father in India?"

Smita wondered if he was upset. He shouldn't be. From her point of view, it was the duty of the police to get in touch with the family in India and brief them. They had been remiss in not doing so.

"Yes," she said. "Is it a problem?" she challenged.

"No. Not really. Anyway, you seem to have got your wish. The coroner has decided to authorise a full autopsy at the request of Mr.

Modi. Mr. Modi has requested that the autopsy be conducted as soon as possible. He has also authorised you to be his representative in Melbourne for this process until he arrives here. He has decided he may come down next week if the findings warrant it."

Smita raised her fist in silent celebration. They were finally taking the issue seriously.

"I hope you have not created a major issue here, Smita, when there may be none."

"We will see, Detective," she replied.

Three days later Smita received a copy of an email from Detective Winston to Mr Modi, informing him a full autopsy was scheduled the next day. A preliminary report would follow soon, though the full report would take longer.

She called Mr Modi to check if he had seen the email.

"Thank you, Smita. You've been very helpful. This is very distressing for us. If the autopsy results indicate that Pravin has somehow done something to lead to Nirmala's death, I will fly down to Melbourne. But my wife and I are still struggling with the fact that she died from burns, and further, that there is a possibility of foul play."

She commiserated and promised she would follow up the process on his behalf in Melbourne.

* * *

Three days later Smita received a copy of the preliminary autopsy report. She read it eagerly, then slammed her fist on the table in a mix of anger and vindication. Jill noticed and approached with concern.

The report revealed that Nirmala had sustained numerous fractures to her cheekbones, arms and ribs just before her death by burning. The Coroner recommended immediate police investigation into these injuries.

"I was right, Jill. I was right." She shared the news with Jill. They fist bumped in solidarity.

Then the realisation of Nirmala's suffering tempered their celebration. As the news sank in, both women sat in quiet shock, struggling to comprehend Nirmala's ordeal. Poor Nirmala must have suffered terribly before she died. Smita hoped she hadn't been conscious during the final, brutal act.

Later that day, Detective Winston called Smita. He was brief, conciliatory, though still sounded peeved. He asked if she had read the results of the autopsy.

He then informed her that Pravin had been arrested on suspicion of aggravated assault and culpable homicide. He went on to say that she would probably be called as a witness in the trial.

That same day she received a single line email from Pravin. "Bitch. I will not forget this."

Smita sat back and savoured the moment. Pravin had finally been brought to justice where he would face the consequences of his exploitation. She looked forward to being a witness.

She shared the news with Jill, then with Ed.

"I'm happy to hear, Smits. The bastard had this coming, though it would not have happened if it were not for your determined efforts. However, I'm afraid for you. He'll soon be on bail, undoubtedly. And in his state of mind, he will be unpredictable. What are you doing to protect yourself?"

"Look Ed, I've dealt with him in the past, and I can deal with him again. Please don't worry."

"But I do. And I think this time he will think through carefully how he attacks you. It will be done more cleverly than his last brash attempt."

"I will be prepared, Ed."

"Promise me one thing. If he attempts a physical attack, please text me immediately. You won't have much time. Just the word 'Pravin' and where you are. I will make a beeline to you."

She laughed off his concerns again. But he insisted. Finally, she promised she would do as he asked.

* * *

229

A week after the launching of the "Justice for the Dowry Abused" group, it had grown significantly, featuring fifteen stories of women who spoke of their experiences and how they were dealing with it. She suspected most were under pseudonyms. Both she and Jill shared the group with clients of the gym and friends. Word was spreading. The group now attracted over 1200 followers indicating growing frustration within the community.

There were numerous comments and suggestions, though some negative feedback as well, accusing the group of promoting racism and prejudice against the Indian culture. Not everyone was happy with the postings.

* * *

The same day she received a call from the representative of the Australian-Indian Association, based in Melbourne.

"Is this Smita Devi?"

"Yes."

"My name is Joshi. I represent the Australian-Indian Association in Melbourne. Our Executive Committee met yesterday and I've been asked to contact you. We're requesting you immediately take down this group you are promoting on Facebook, which denigrates our Indian culture."

"Hello Mr. Joshi. So nice to hear you keep up with Facebook and the travails of our young Indian sisters. What exactly are you and your men friends upset about?"

"Smita, this is not a joking matter. "

"Of course it isn't. Did you think I was joking? I am serious when I ask – what exactly are you and your male friends unhappy about in regard to the group?"

"The dowry abuse you claim as the focus of the group is not happening. These are made up stories of women who may be unhappy for other reasons. By making public these stories on Facebook, they and you are denigrating our community and encouraging racist comments and ideas. Please stop this group immediately. This is a demand from the highest level of our community in Australia."

"Mr. Joshi, did you get a dowry when you married your wife?"

He seemed taken aback by the question.

"That is no business of yours, Smita."

"Oh. So you did take a dowry, I see. And do you know that taking dowry is illegal in India as well as in Australia?"

"Will you stop these silly insinuations, please?"

"There is nothing silly about taking dowry, Mr. Joshi. It is illegal. You say the claims about dowry and related abuses are inaccurate. If they are, please join our group and provide a rejoinder to these claims which you say are unfounded."

"Look. I am calling to warn you that if you do not take down that group from Facebook, our Association will take legal action against you."

"Please go ahead, Mr. Joshi. In my view, I've done nothing wrong. I've simply provided a platform for those who've been exploited by this terrible practice. It's important for them to come forward and tell the community what has been happening behind closed doors. If you launch legal action, it will only give the issue more publicity. If that's what you want, go ahead," she challenged him.

"I have warned you." He abruptly ended the call.

In truth, Smita felt much less confident than she sounded. Legal action. It did not sound good. She was now really nervous. Was she getting out of her depth?

She called Ed immediately and recounted the call she received from Joshi. She was worried about his threatened legal action. She had no idea about the law here in Australia.

Ed reassured her that it was probably an empty threat. But he would ask a legal friend to check the Facebook group she had set up and get back to him if there appeared to be a strong enough basis for defamation.

She was relieved she had Jill and Ed to support her. Suddenly, the combat was not just physical anymore. It had become much more complex.

CHAPTER 33

Smita checked the Facebook group regularly at her break in the gym. A week had passed since the call from Mr. Joshi. She hadn't heard from him since, nor seen any response from the Association on the Facebook page. Despite this, she was aware that he and the Association would not give up easily.

Even more so, she reflected, as she reviewed the status of postings. The group was on fire. A virtual battle was ongoing between those who published their stories of exploitation and abuse, and those claiming it was all fiction, "stories of hysterical women". There were some thirty stories with numerous others recounting the experiences of friends. The group now boasted over 2000 followers.

Smita was pleased the group was fostering open discussion about an issue normally hidden behind closed doors. Both Jill and Ed actively contributed, sharing their perspectives on the new posts.

Around noon that day, a courier delivered an officious looking letter addressed to her and asked her to sign receipt. She opened the letter nervously. It was what she had been expecting. It was a letter from Nicholson and Partners, demanding the immediate removal of the Facebook group – "Justice for the Dowry Abused". The demand was made on behalf of their client, the Australian-Indian Association. Failure to comply within three days would result in a defamation suit.

Smita's hands trembled as she read the letter. Defamation? Could they really do that? Did they actually have a case? After all, what she had done was to simply provide a platform for people to upload their personal distress stories. It was their stories. She was not making them up. To her recollection, she herself had not posted any defamatory statement. She had just let people's stories tell the tale.

Overwhelmed and nervous, she called up the Facebook group page and reviewed each post, trying to figure out if any could be deemed defamatory. But, as she scrolled, her emotions and the complexity of the situation overcame her. The words began to blur. She began feeling completely out of depth.

Dealing with lawyers and the courts always made her nervous. She was wondering if, in her enthusiasm for her cause, she had bitten off more than she could cope with. Jill found her staring at the letter on her desk, her head resting within her hands, and the FB group page open.

"Something upset you, Smita?"

Smita handed the letter to Jill silently, inviting her to read.

The letter jolted Jill as well.

"The bastards. I'm not sure, Smita, whether this is simply bluster to frighten you off and persuade you to take down your group, or whether they really have a case and mean business. They've certainly made a definitive first step by hiring a solicitor firm. Shall I ask Joan to have a look or does Ed know anyone who can help? This may not be up Joan's alley."

Smita sighed in frustration. The progress she had been making was too good to be true.

"Yes, Jill. I've asked Ed to consult with a friend familiar with these cases. That was a few days ago, after the threats of Joshi on the phone. But now this letter. It raises the bar, makes the whole thing much more threatening. I simply do not have the resources to fight these people, and I think they know it. They may be just trying to frighten me away. Or they may be serious. I'll ask Ed to join us for lunch, if you're available, and we can talk."

Later at lunch, Ed reviewed the solicitor letter. He initially thought the defamation threat was a bluff. But he admitted it wasn't his area of expertise. He offered to have his friend review the letter.

"Can I take the letter? I'll get back to you by tomorrow."

"Sure. He is probably my last resort, Ed. Though even if he did suggest their case was weak, the issue still remains – should I continue with the FB group? I do not have the resources to fight the case. And this Association seems ready to spend."

She sighed again with frustration.

"It would be a pity to terminate the group now, Smita, after all the momentum you've gathered," suggested Jill. "It seems to be having an impact. I was hoping we'd get some journalist interested in writing about it in the media, referencing the FB group. This would compound coverage of the issue and give it even wider publicity."

Ed butted in. "Anyway, let me first consult my friend. I'll get back to you tomorrow and we can then meet again to decide where you go from here."

Then he brought up the issue of the post-mortem, and Pravin's arrest. It seemed to be of as much concern to him as the threatening letter.

"Have you heard anything after the post-mortem about the case against Pravin?"

"Detective Winston called to say he's been arrested, but then set free on bail, pending the trial. The scheduling of the trial will be up to the public prosecutor, and may take some weeks or even months as they consolidate their case."

Ed banged the table.

Smita and Jill both looked up in surprise.

"What's the issue, Ed?" asked Smita.

"Can't you see?" said Ed. "This means he's now free and will use the opportunity to seek out vengeance on you, Smita. Don't underestimate him. He is a bastard and will not forgive you easily."

Smita reflected "He'll be busy, though, getting his own lawyer and preparing his defence. I don't know where he's going to get money for defence. He always seemed to be in financial trouble. I also think he will be careful not to mess again with the law. After he assaulted me in the gym, he was arrested and had a case against him. I have no idea what happened to that case. But as I said, he'll be extra careful with the law now."

"I agree," replied Ed. "He'll have a lot on his plate. But I would not put it past him to find a way of getting back at you without allowing that to be traced back to him."

"Oh Smita. What have you done? You seem to have an art of collecting enemies," Jill chided.

Smita smiled and shrugged. "Just done what my conscience told me was right, Jill."

"Yes, dear. But in the process you're shaking up the citadels of misogyny and patriarchy in your community. Well done to have taken them on single-handedly."

"Not really. I've had you and Ed always at my back. And perhaps Officer Dickson. Don't know what I'd have done without you guys."

They left, with Ed promising to be in touch on the defamation letter issue.

* * *

Detective Winston called Smita to discuss Nirmala's case and Pravin. His attitude to Smita had shifted since the post-mortem results. She was now a key witness; and he was her main liaison with the prosecutor. He seemed to now view her as a collaborator rather than the irritating disrupter.

"Yes, Detective. I've received a letter from the prosecutor about preparing my testimony. Is that why you are calling?"

"Not exactly, Smita. This is more an unofficial call, than business. I've been dealing with Pravin prior to and consequent to his release on bail. I see the kind of man he really is. Thank you for your determination in seeking justice for Nirmala."

Ha, thought Smita. Quite a turnaround for this usually sour man. But she was gracious.

"Thank you, Detective, for your help in all of this."

235

"Anyway, the purpose of this call Smita is to warn you that I think Pravin will find some way of getting back at you. I have specifically warned him not to do anything vis-a-vis you since that would be illegal; it would be tampering with a witness. He knows this. But he may find a way via a third party and this is what worries me."

"Thank you for your concern. I agree. It's worrying. But then, I've asked for it. I must take my precautions."

"Yes. Please do. He will not give up easily."

CHAPTER 34

A few days later, Smita was walking home after work on a cold, wintry night. She walked the usual route, up Queen Street to Bourke or La Trobe, to get a tram there. It was dark, about 10.30pm. After nightfall, she maintained her practice of being hyper vigilant of the goings on around her. It had become second nature.

A sixth sense triggered. In the otherwise empty street she thought she spied a group of men in the distance behind her. They moved cautiously in the direction she was walking. At her street crossings, she turned to check and found they were gradually gaining on her, though they did not seem in a hurry. She thought they were Indian in appearance, given their colour and stature; but it was difficult to be sure in the dark. She found an excuse to stop and check her phone. On cue they did too.

Her instincts told her, this is it; the attack by Pravin she'd been expecting, except it was to be via proxies. Winston had suggested this would be his strategy. She prepared herself for the inevitable confrontation. Her heart raced. Her palms began perspiring though it was cold. She collected her mind and tried to bring her emotions under control

At the corner of Queen and Lonsdale streets, while she waited to cross, she got out her phone and sent Ed a text; one that they had agreed on - *Help. Pravin. Corner of Queen and La Trobe. ASAP please*. As she crossed Lonsdale, she slowed, hoping that by the time she reached the corner of La Trobe, Ed would have had time to catch up from wherever he was. She was hoping he was still somewhere in the CBD.

They probably guessed her strategy. They began closing in on her quicker. They were now some thirty metres away. She spied a couple of passersby on the other side of Queen and walking parallel to her and the thugs. But they'd probably ignore her call for help, as the would-be attackers were still some metres away.

She decided to initiate the confrontation rather than be taken by surprise.

At the Queen-La Trobe junction, she abruptly turned, dropped her bag and coat, and assumed a defensive stance. This caught them off guard. They stopped some fifteen metres away, further than they would have preferred when commencing the attack.

They fanned out, one facing her, the other two about a metre away on each side. They approached in formation. She steeled herself. She had not been in a physical confrontation for some months now. But the lessons and skills she had worked on in so disciplined a manner for over two years came to the fore. She still practised regularly with Ed at the Krav gym and on the dummies.

She had fought three men before, though admittedly, those were not as fit as these three appeared to be. She was sure Pravin had hired appropriate muscle and had duly briefed them. She wondered if he had confessed to them the humiliation she had subjected him to. Probably not. So they would not necessarily be that well prepared for what awaited them. On the other hand, she knew zilch about their skills and abilities.

The main strategy must be to hold them at bay till Ed's help or any other arrived.

They were now some five metres away. She had a good look at them.

The leader was dark skinned, bushy eyebrows, hair slickly combed back, leather jacket, runners. He was well built, slightly taller than her, and seemed to be putting on weight on his midriff. But he seemed fit, probably an experienced hood.

The other two were more non-descript, typical Indian men. Younger, slimmer and obviously hyper-aware of their looks. Dressed Bollywood style, tight pants, broad belts, colourful shirts under their jackets.

Time to taunt, distract, confuse, she decided.

"Three Indian morons, trying to assault a lone, unarmed woman. Have you guys no shame? Cowards! What did your Indian mothers teach you? Do you have no respect for Durga Devi and womanhood?"

She wondered if the mocking would have any effect.

Apparently not. Not an eye blinked; not a step faltered.

"So that chicken Pravin has hired you, is it? Three big muscled men, to take down one lone woman? You're all as spineless as your boss."

No reaction. The leader in the middle continued to stare at her, assessing her fighting stance, probably guessing at her skills. The other two, one on each side of him, kept glancing at him, looking for guidance on their first move.

The leader now advanced quicker. She saw their strategy. Try to snare her into a fight with the leader, while the other two then surrounded her to take her from the side or behind. She wondered whether the intention was to beat her up or to capture her for Pravin's personal attention.

She took a step back, then as the leader launched himself into her, expecting to bring her down with his bull rush, she stepped deftly aside to her left, kicked him hard in the groin with her right leg as he came forward, and in the same smooth movement, threw her right hand straight to the nose of the second attacker on her left who was moving into the fray.

The leader had not expected to be attacked. He doubled down in excruciating pain, holding his family jewels for dear life.

The one on his right was holding his nose, dazed, wondering what had hit him.

She swivelled to meet the attack of the third. He was fast. He came at her quick and lithe, forewarned and prepared. His right arm shot forward before she had completely recovered from attacking the first two. It caught her squarely on her jaw and she went down with the sheer force of the blow.

He followed with a kick towards her solar plexus. Despite her head spinning, she instinctively guessed what was coming. She rolled, as fast as she could, then leaped up nimbly. His kick grazed her side. No harm done; but her jaw ached. She had got her balance back and she was up and ready to go.

But so were the other two who had by now recovered from the initial onslaught. All back to square one, it appeared. But they were now more wary and prepared.

What now? Think, she told herself. Keep cool. The element of surprise is gone. It's now strategy, wits and skill.

This time the leader looked quickly at the sidekick on his left; a signal passed between them, and they moved to her in tandem, leaving the third guy behind as back up. It was obvious that while they had brute strength, they had limited marital arts skills. Though the leader appeared to be an experienced hoodlum; she'd have to be more careful.

She now backed, dancing from side to side, inviting the attacking two to follow. They inched forward but the leader seemed to be losing patience. This time he came at her like a boxer, arms leading, his stance ensuring his genitals were out of her reach. His colleague followed, by his side, both hoping to land hard punches.

She stopped backing, her right hand shot out, the speed of an arrow, palm open straight to the leader's throat, and through the gap between his boxer arms. It had to be a blow that counted. Its speed took him completely by surprise. A loud guttural sound emerged as he fell to the ground, clutching his throat.

But the other was following fast and shouldered her hard sending her staggering back. She maintained her balance, refusing to go down, and tried to collect herself. The leader was going to stay down for a while, she knew. That had been a harsh blow to his sensitive windpipe.

The two sidekicks now approached, one on each side. She looked each in the eye, then quickly turned to her left and made as if she was fleeing. They leaped into the chase only to find that within a few steps, she suddenly swivelled to meet them both frontal, aiming her trade-mark kick to the groin of the one on her left. She made sure it was a hard kick, one to keep him down for a while. He dropped to his knees, groaning in pain.

It was finally just the third. Where the hell was Ed, she wondered. But no time to think. She had to get this guy down.

The third assailant appeared to be gathering his wits, taking stock of his fallen comrades, and now ultra-cautious of Smita. She let him approach. Then she looked over his shoulder, waved with one hand and shouted, "Help", as if addressing someone behind him. He ventured a quick glance behind. In that moment, she rose on her toes, dancer-like, swivelled her body and flew into a flying kick aimed at the side of his head. It landed with the force of her flying momentum behind it. His head jerked back and he collapsed.

All three were now on the ground, in varying positions. The leader still lay prone, holding his throat and struggling to breathe. The second guy was on his knees, nursing his crotch, working through his agony. The third was now lying, still, on the ground. Smita hoped his injury was not life threatening. She stood and surveyed them with satisfaction. A hard night's work.

Suddenly, she felt an arm come around her throat, and grab her in a tight hold. This was a complete surprise. Where did this fourth person come from? A second arm came around the other side of her face, armed with a knife and held threatening to her face. Then she knew who, when he spoke.

"Bitch. You've had this coming for a long time. I want to now make you suffer."

It was Pravin. She was surprised that he'd risked joining his proxies. But then, she understood. He needed to be there to identify her. He must have then followed, in the shadows. He needed to do what he was going to now - to salve his need for revenge. He was going to disfigure her for life; in the despicable tradition of some jilted Indian men though they sometimes used acid to the woman's face.

He ripped her left cheek cleanly from ear to chin. A sharp pain shot through her. This is finally the end, she thought. It had been a good fight. He would now go for her neck, she was sure. Anger had blinded him to the consequences of his actions which would surely land heavily once he disposed of her.

The side of her face was stinging and bleeding profusely; she began feeling dizzy, perhaps with shock, perhaps due to the loss of blood.

"Now for the other side of your face, bitch," as he tried to move the knife to his other hand.

Suddenly, there was a roar from behind and Pravin dropped the knife as he was torn from her by some unseen force. She dropped to her knees, holding her wound as warm blood poured out.

In the same moment she heard a whistle. The police? Please, God, yes.

She was now bleeding profusely. She turned and saw Ed kneeling on a prone Pravin, hammering his face to pulp. Then he suddenly stopped when two police arrived.

He stepped back, pulled a handkerchief from his pocket and rushed to help stanch the blood flow from her face.

The police took charge. But faces were now swimming. She had lost a lot of blood; it had taken its toll. A few moments later the world turned black and blissful.

*   *   *

Constables Jim Dory and Kevin Roman were doing their usual foot patrol through the city, street by street, as the Assistant Superintendent had demanded. No patrol cars. On foot. It was rather quiet for a Friday night. The recent riot and muggings had dampened night life. Then they saw a man running up La Trobe Street towards Queen like he was fleeing the devil. They checked. No one was following. He was obviously responding to a call in the west part of the city. Christ. They hoped it was not yet another riot. The last had been bad enough. They followed in hot pursuit, but he was fast. Obviously super fit.

As they rounded the corner at Queen Street, they came upon the scene of a fight that seemed to have been in progress for a while - two men were on the ground, one sprawled motionless, the other holding his throat and making strange sounds; a third was on his knees, holding his crotch. The final two were in hand-to-hand combat, one on top of the other. The guy on top was the one they were pursuing. He appeared to be face-pummelling the other who was on the ground.

A woman knelt nearby, her face covered in blood, head bent in pain, watching.

It all made little sense. But the woman was obviously in need of urgent medical attention. As per the understanding between them, Constable Dory pulled out his whistle and blew with all his might as he advanced on the two men fighting on the ground. Constable Roman made two quick calls – one for an ambulance and the other for back up, indicating their location. Then he came to Dory's support as they approached to pull apart the fighting men.

The moment the police arrived, the guy on top rose in one fluid moment, pulled a handkerchief from his pocket and ran to the woman to help stem the flow of blood from her face. As he did so, he shouted to the policemen to arrest the other four.

Dory and Roman allowed the guy to minister to the woman while they handcuffed the other four. There would be time for questions and deeper investigation. For now, the woman's situation was dire, and in any case, no one was going anywhere until they had satisfactory answers. The Assistant Super would be mad when he heard of yet another case of mugging in the city.

When the police reinforcements and the ambulance arrived, the paramedics took over helping the woman. She had now fainted. Their first job was to stanch the flow of blood from her face. Her clothes were bathed in red. The guy who was helping her looked on with concern, trying to help as well. The stretcher was wheeled out and she was carefully lifted into it, while one ambo held a pack of ice to her injured face. The guy they had pursued and who had been helping the woman begged to be allowed to accompany the medicos to the hospital. He claimed she was his fiancée. He pulled out his phone and showed Dory the SOS message he had received shortly before he had set out in a run to the scene. Dory took his details and phone number, then allowed him to accompany the woman in the ambulance. They arrested the other four.

In the ambulance, Ed sent texts to both Jill and Senior Constable Dickson informing them of Smita's situation.

CHAPTER 35

S mita's eyes fluttered open. It had been a blissful sleep. She couldn't remember when she had fallen asleep, but she felt rested. The light was dimmed. All she could see was white all around - the walls, the bedsheets, and the window curtains. Then she wondered where she was? Certainly not in her bed. How did she come to be here? But wherever it was, it seemed far from conflict, from pain, from confrontation. She closed her eyes again just wanting to be as far away from everything as possible.

Then it all came back in a rush. Her hand went instinctively to her face. Another hand restrained her gently.

"Take it easy, love."

Blessed relief. It was Ed. She was okay. He would look after everything. It struck her how protected she felt in his company. It was a pleasant thought.

"You're going to be okay."

She tried to turn her head to him, and a shooting pain drove through her face.

"Take it easy," he repeated, gently. The memory of the night's event returned in crystal-clear detail. She played out the horror of the attack and fight with Pravin and his stooges.

Now she was in hospital, Ed by her side, his soothing voice and touch a constant reassurance.

"You're now in safe hands, love. All is well. And that will definitely be the last of your heroic adventures, if left to me."

She thought, yes, please. Could she just leave all her battles behind and go off with Ed? But to where? It did not matter. Ed was the most important anchor for her.

But then she thought of Lakshmi, who must be wondering why Smita had not contacted her. And all the other Nirmalas, waiting for help from their exploitative partners. Much as she would love to just lie there, in the arms of Ed, there was still work to be done. The relief was that she now had partners in the fight – Ed, Jill, Officer Dickson and the police.

She tried to smile. It was then she remembered what Pravin had done to her face. Panic and dismay descended on her. Had he disfigured her for life? Would Ed still love her with her mutilated face? It seemed to be almost completely covered in bandages. She attempted to speak and found it difficult because a tight dressing went all around her jaw and then over her head.

"Don't try to move or speak now. I will tell you what happened."

Ed recounted what had happened. It was apparently now the afternoon of the following day. Pravin and his colleagues had been arrested. Ed had accompanied her to the hospital in the ambulance and had been by her side all night and day. Officer Dickson had also visited, providing a full briefing to the hospital staff and the investigating officers, of the back story to the whole incident.

Ed told her she would be in hospital for a while. But she worried that Pravin had done irreparable damage to her face.

Ed reassured her. "You're going to be even prettier than before he did his dirty work, love. And then you will have so many admirers you won't have time for me."

"Oh, Ed," she mumbled. "You and your humour are irrepressible. But seriously; tell me truthfully what has happened to my face. And by the way, thank you so much for coming just in time. I have no idea how I will ever repay you."

"I keep my debt collector's book updated. No worries, love." He smiled.

Then he told her. The doctors had done a quick surgery to seal the wound. Fortunately it was a clean cut from ear to chin. The wound was not deep, thankfully, though she had lost a lot of blood. Once the wound healed, they would do plastic surgery and had promised she'd be even prettier than before.

"See, it's not just me, but the docs who believe so. The young ones already have an eye on you."

"Will you shut up, Ed. Now tell me, if you've been here all night and today, you've not slept. That's terrible. You must go now, and get some rest."

"And leave you to the wolves, here?"

"Seriously, Ed. You must go and rest. Thank you for all you've done."

* * *

Later that evening, Jill and Officer Dickson arrived to take over from Ed. Jill insisted on staying the night, despite Smita's protests.

Dickson brought encouraging news. "Pravin will be charged with aggravated assault in addition to his pending murder charge for Nirmala's death. He's probably looking at a lengthy prison sentence. So you can rest pretty, Smita."

Smita was deeply relieved. Paradoxically, she was also sad for Pravin. What a tragic turn his life had taken, she thought. She wondered what in his upbringing had contributed to him becoming such a cruel person.

Jill had interesting developments to share with her.

"Your story has attracted considerable media attention, dear. You are the new hero of the press. The newspapers have depicted your story as a dramatic tale of revenge, bravery and rescue. A lone woman, who outdid her husband's machinations and stooges, against all odds; and Ed, the heroic boyfriend who arrived just in time. A story made for the movies."

Smita would have grimaced if she could. Instead, she slowly shook her head. She wasn't happy.

"Oh, Jill. I wish they wouldn't dramatize all of this."

"Do you realise, Smita, your story is indeed dramatic? It makes for spicy reading which tabloids love. But there is good part to this all, which you'll be happy to hear. The subject of domestic violence is also getting a share of attention in the media."

Jill went on to describe how the media had covered Smita's campaign for dowry abused victims. The attempted disfigurement of her face had elicited comments of how such mutilation was rather common in South Asia when men felt they had been jilted by the women their families had chosen as their partner in life.

Debate in the media then focused on the issue of arranged marriages, the system of dowry giving, the related exploitation of the women that followed if the dowry was deemed inadequate. There were calls for politicians to monitor and ban the practice of dowry in Australia.

When Jill visited the next day, she had further news to share. A reporter friend had interviewed her at the gym last evening. She shared the story of the Australian – Indian Association's defamation threats against Smita's Facebook group.

This made a great story the next day. The women who read it joined Smita's FB group to pressure the Association to desist with its defamatory action. Expert commentary indicated the defamation case, like most others, would be weak; almost definitely unsuccessful. The Association finally had to give in. It deduced more harm was being done to their reputation by just pursuing this case.

* * *

Four weeks later, Smita visited the Police HQ on Spencer Street. Senior Constable Dickson had informed her that the Assistant Superintendent would like to see her with Dickson, once she was out of hospital.

Dickson met her outside the Superintendent's office. Smita was nervous.

"Hi, Emma." Smita and Dickson were now on a first name basis. "Is this about that gang riot, Emma, which he thought was due to me?"

Dickson laughed. "No worries, Smita. He's forgotten about that. And I doubt he or anyone else among the police besides me has as yet gathered that it was you who was the so-called night mugger. So do not give him any hint in that regard."

They entered. It was the first time Smita had met the Assistant Superintendent. He was a big, imposing man. Black hair, high eyebrows, piercing eyes, but a gentle smile. She could see how he could be intimidating if he wished to be.

He rose from his chair to welcome Smita and Dickson, and shook Smita's hand'.

"Hello, Smita. You're certainly making a name for yourself. I'm glad to meet you. Just wanted to have a little chat. So, thank you for making the time"

He seemed gracious, rather than officious as she had expected.

"We have much to thank you for, Smita."

She was taken aback.

"I mean that sincerely. Not facetiously. You've brought to my attention and that of our police force how extensive the prevalence of dowry abuse and domestic violence is within the community. We often overlook the root causes."

"Sir, have you had a look at the stories posted on the FB group page 'Justice for the Dowry Abused'?

"Yes. Senior Constable Dickson has brought this to my attention. They're an eye opener. Thank you for this initiative.

Also, I'm really sorry for what you've gone through by way of this brutal attack by your ex-husband. I have personally followed up his case with the Eastern Suburbs police. They're taking the charges against him very seriously. I'm hoping he will bear the full consequences of his actions.

But I've asked for a meeting today on another though related issue. We'd like to benefit from you Smita, as a consultant to the police on issues of violence against women particularly in the migrant community. I think the police force is sometimes at a disadvantage in such cases since we do not have an adequate understanding of the cultural issues at play. I don't envisage it will take much of your time, but I suspect your contributions will be invaluable. Senior Constable Dickson speaks very highly of your help in a recent case."

Smita was speechless. The offer to help had come as a complete surprise.

She finally gathered herself and thanked the Superintendent. She said how much she appreciated the request to help and she would always be available.

The Assistant Superintendent suggested Officer Dickson would be her point of contact henceforth.

They emerged from the meeting with Smita wondering if what had just happened was real. It was, after all, a rather dramatic turnaround for her fortunes.

* * *

A week later, Smita was back with Ed at the Aboriginal Youth Club. Her face was healing well and the scar was almost invisible, as the doctor had promised.

At the Club, she was greeted as a hero, with the young teenagers gathered around, eager to hear her story. Some of the girls asked if they could gently touch her cheek. She smiled and allowed them to.

Ed regaled them with the story of how she'd taken on three thugs, single-handedly, using her martial arts skills. They wanted her to show them how she'd done it.

She chided Ed. "Stop it now, Ed. You know, kids, he is exaggerating."

But as she talked with them, and gradually got back to practising martial arts moves with them, she saw in their eyes and youth, the promise of life. She wanted them to live happy and productive lives. She wanted to help them cope with the inevitable adversity they would encounter. She felt here was an opportunity to really make a difference.

* * *

"Smita, it's time we started up our free self-defence martial arts school for women. Let's ask Esther if she, too, will join in. We'll host the classes three times a week, in the evening, at my gym. Are you game?" asked Jill.

"I've been waiting, Jill. I'll also advertise it on my FB group page."

The classes began and soon became popular. Social media made sure of that.

Jill and Smita also converted one of the back rooms of the gym into a safe place for women to meet, talk, share, and support each other. Coffee and biscuits were always available.

Smita reflected how the gym had once been her personal refuge. Now it had become a sanctuary for many others, symbolising safety, empowerment, and community.

ACKNOWLEDGEMENTS

My deepest thanks to my wife, Matilda, and my children and their spouses – Shefali, Evan, Gerson and Julie – for their constant encouragement, feedback and support all through the writing of this novel.

I also thank my brother Conrad, and my friends - Joseph, Divya, and Vina - who so kindly reviewed the early drafts of the novel and provided invaluable feedback.

Finally, my thanks to ASPG, particularly William, Lodie and Wency, for their patience and professionalism as they guided me through every step of this publication.